GW01112207

From Sarah to Sara

First published 1999
ISBN 1 876261 08 0

Published by:

V.D.L. Publications
P.O. Box 178
Sandy Bay TAS 7006
Phone: (03) 6223 5245

In association with:

Tasbook Publishers
P.O. Box 4
Woodbridge TAS 7162
Fax/Phone: (03) 6225 1850

Printed and bound by:
Regal Press, 24 Wellington Street, Launceston, TAS 7250
Phone: (03) 6331 4222

All characters in this publication are fictitious and any resemblance to real persons living or dead, is purely coincidental.

The lifestyle as portrayed in the Journal reflects, as closely as possible the actual social and physical conditions of the convict era circa 1805-1855.

All rights reserved. No part of this publication may be reproduced, stored in, or introduced into, a retrieval system, or transmitted in any form or by any means, (electronic, mechanical, photocopying, recording or other), without the prior permission of the publishers and the copyright owner.

This book is sold subject to the condition that it shall not, by way of trade or otherwise, be lent, resold, hired out or otherwise circulated, without prior consent, in any form or binding or cover other than that in which it is published and without a similar condition being imposed on the subsequent purchaser.

© Tasbook Publishers

July 1999

Image Inside Cover courtesy Port Arthur Historic Collection

From Sarah to Sara

*For
With my love and good wishes
Eleanor Graeme-Evans*

A Novel by
ELEANOR GRAEME-EVANS

DEDICATION

To my husband

Squadron Leader F. Graeme-Evans R.A.F.

Per ardua ad astra

Through adversity to the stars

ACKNOWLEDGMENTS

Two great Tasmanian institutions and a number of people made it possible for me to write this novel, which was commenced in the mid 1960s.

The first was the Tasmanian Archives Office, since I needed a realistic approach to a subject I then knew little about - the lives of the convicts and settlers in the convict era 1804-1855. Archival staff helped me in every way possible and made the whole effort a joy and a most rewarding experience.

The second was the Hydro Electric Commission. I needed the contrast of the two periods and again their staff also gave me all the information and help I could possibly have needed. They provided me with transport, wet-weather clothing, and guided tours of the construction work then being done on the Gordon River road. Thus, I saw the wet rainforest in its pristine state and the conditions under which the Hydro employees worked in the field.

Close to twenty years later, in 1983, the finished manuscript was to win the coveted Alan Marshall award. For want of a publisher it was then put away and almost forgotten until by chance, last year at Redwood Village, Kingston, a neighbour, another writer Tony Kearney, asked me in conversation to show him something I had written.

To my astonishment his publisher Jim Moore then contacted me, asking permission to publish. Their combined enthusiasm, understanding and encouragement then became instrumental in bringing the manuscript to the printer's table.

Particular acknowledgment is due to Penelope Moore Amaral for typing and acting as a model for the front cover, and Stephen Edgar for proofreading.

Last but not least heartfelt thanks also to my son Alexander and Tasbook Publishers for their expert efforts in bringing the book forward through the printing and design stage, and to a most satisfactory launch.

Eleanor Graeme-Evans
Redwood Village
Kingston, July 1999

CHAPTER ONE

Thinking about it afterwards, Sara decided the shock was similar to that of being told that your next-door neighbour, who had talked to you over the fence a few hours previously, had just been picked up dead!

She had opened the front door and stood in the old porch watching John come walking towards her over the common. It had become a routine on summer evenings. It was a moment of anticipation—completion; he was home again. That night had been no different in as much as she saw him coming towards her, perhaps a little faster than usual; but his first remark was to change her life: 'I've got some real news for you tonight. We're going to emigrate!'

He was about two feet away when he said it, and the words were so unreal they didn't register. What did register was his thin, excited face, the eager way he put his arm around her, dispatch case and all, and literally whirled her through the door. She knew then.

Once inside the house all feeling died in her. The pictures of things she knew instinctively were going to become personal losses passed in front of her eyes. Emigrating meant going. This house would go. Max, their cocker spaniel who came bounding up to John, would go.

'I felt like getting out and pushing that bloody train. I nearly rang you, but there wasn't time,' he said.

His job, his safe secure job, would go. Suppose he didn't make good!

'Where are we going?' she asked him.

'Tasmania.'

'That's an island off Australia, isn't it?'

He laughed. 'One up to you. I didn't think your geography would rise to it. Let's sit down, I've got stacks of things to show you: brochures, pamphlets, pictures of the place—it's a sort of sunny England, I gather.'

He began pulling out little glossy folders. They spilled on the polished floor. Max pounced on some of them, and somewhere in Sara's mind a small voice said: 'Why didn't he tell me about all this before? He must have been thinking about it for a long time.' But aloud she said: 'You have given up your job.'

'Resigning in a couple of days. That will shake the old die-hards!'

'But—'

'There aren't any "buts". I'm practically sure I've got another. I'll know for certain tomorrow; nearly double the pay too.'

Would nearly double the pay be enough to wipe out what they had achieved here? She remembered the past. Everyone had said they were too young to marry. She had only just turned nineteen, he was twenty-two, with two more years ahead of him at the university. But they'd worked hard. She had got a job doing commercial designing; he had his scholarship, and had finished his degree. They had done well in the last six years; bought this cottage; restored it together. Some of the feeling began to return to her; pain when she remembered the fun they had had, the sense of achievement together. She knew too that the memory wouldn't mean a thing to him now.

Then came the doubts, which till then she had suppressed. She was so happy with him. She had thought marriage was a sharing of everything, a life companionship—but did he think so? There were so many things he seemed to keep to himself. It was almost as if he still lived in his own life and she was just an added pleasure—in bed and out of it. And he was the boss. He decided and took it for granted she would accept his decisions. This emigration for instance; he had never mentioned it, but it would change both of their lives—he must have been thinking of it for months but she had never been consulted. Just: 'We're going to emigrate.' She had no say one way or another.

Mentally she tried to shrug it off and realised that this is what she always did; had always done, whether it was with her father or with John. It was her way of dealing with problems. She wondered briefly if this was why she had married him—and then dismissed the thought. She caught up with his talk.

'They only sent for me in the middle of the afternoon. I had to invent a forgotten dental appointment.'

'They?'

'Tasmania House. I had an interview for the Hydro-Electric Commission in Tasmania.'

'What would the job be?'

'Second engineer; promotion if I make the grade. They'll take us out, provide us with a house.' He paused, his eyes looking round the cosy little panelled hall of the eighteenth-century cottage. 'It won't be like this of course.' A picture of the modern bungalow he'd been shown splashed in front of him. Sara wasn't going to like that, but he wouldn't show it to her yet; let her get used to the whole idea first. After all, he had rushed her a bit. She was taking it better than he had expected. There was another thing in that photograph too—sunlight, glorious, strong clear sunlight.

He looked down at her dark, soft hair and creamy skin. He was aware of what was going on in her mind. It was one of the reasons he had not told her about the idea of emigrating until things were almost settled. She'd get over it, he'd see to that. It was only a matter of prising her out of her rut. No man could have a better wife.

He said slowly: 'We'll make it ours, in our own way, as we did this.'

So he did remember! She forgave him much for that. Perhaps there would be compensations in this new life. The thought of a new life made her quail. She had never been the slightest bit adventurous. When John had left the university and become established in his job, he had made her give up hers. That was when they had started to restore the cottage. It had been a slow, difficult absorbing job. He would prepare the way for her over the weekend; she would carry on through the week, when she wasn't doing things in the village. She supposed it was a selfish life, but it wouldn't have been if they had had children. God knew she longed for them. She had even gone to specialists, whose instructions she had followed implicitly. She had tried to make John go too, but he had laughed and said he hadn't time; anyway, there was nothing wrong with him.

'You're not listening to what I'm saying,' he broke into her thoughts. 'I know, let's celebrate. Put on something and we'll go down to the pub.'

'But I've got the meal all ready.'

'Who cares about food? This is a night to remember. Just think, six months and we'll be in another world.'

She seized on that. Anything could happen in six months. 'Does it take as long as that?'

'Could do. Depends on how quickly they need me for the job. I'd think they will fly us out.'

She felt he was glad they had no ties or responsibilities. It was the one flaw in their otherwise marvellous marriage, that he never seemed to share her need for a child. She sighed. Perhaps they were not meant to have this last perfect thing. They were lucky in their marriage compared with so many of their friends. Perhaps no one was meant to attain perfection. Perhaps they were meant to go to this new life and she was being stupid. If only she had John's assurance, or second sight to see what was going to happen to them.

So she went to the pub with him and drank more gin and tonics than she could ever remember drinking before, which meant John had to take her home in a taxi and put her to bed.

Soon she discovered she was alone in her fears. Everyone applauded John. Even her own people approved the plan; her father particularly when he knew the job was a government one; her mother when she heard it was to be in Tasmania.

'Well,' she said, looking at her daughter with wide open eyes. 'What an extraordinary thing!'

'Why?' Sara asked.

'Because, my dear, a part of our family did the same thing more than a century ago—the forebears of your grandfather, who I'm sure you knew was a Tasmanian—although I know very little about him as he died before I was born.'

'You never told me—I mean, about our family having emigrated to Tasmania.'

'Somehow it never had anything to do with my life, certainly not with yours.'

'Are there any relations still out there that you know of?'

For a moment the void of the unknown seemed to shrink a little.

'There could be. Granny used to talk of an Emily who never missed the Christmas mail, and I believe there was a younger sister.'

'Who is Emily?'

'Emily Roland. She married a scientist and they went out around 1900, but the first lot of Rolands went out in the 1800s, or somewhere about that time. There was an old scandal too, I remember. Anyway, if Emily is alive she must be really old. Even the younger sister must be in her seventies or eighties. I must give your Aunt Marion a ring. She's always the one who keeps the family correspondence going.'

'Don't you know anything more than that, Mother? After all, they were "family".'

'Not really, dear. I gather things in England, financially, were getting difficult about that time—Industrial Revolution or something, wasn't it? Anyway, from all accounts the Rolands were not people to live a pinched existence. They'd rather face danger than poverty, and large grants of land were being offered to free settlers in the last century.'

'I suppose he had a large family. It couldn't have been fun moving with children in those days.'

'Oh yes, he did, but everybody did then.'

At last Sara said slowly: 'Did any of them come back, and—what was the scandal?'

'I believe some did, your great-great-uncle, for one. Much to everyone's surprise he made a distinguished career for himself in the importing business—from Australian wool, mainly. As for the scandal, I've never heard it discussed; it was just accepted. But the name of the girl it concerned was strangely enough, Sarah, spelt with an "h".'

So Aunt Marion had been duly rung and immediately supplied the information that the younger Roland sister was indeed alive, though old. An air letter was dispatched and another returned promptly, written in an old-fashioned hand in old-fashioned phraseology, but excitedly welcoming a young kinswoman to Tasmania.

Sara was quite happy with old people, and particularly so to think that at least there was someone of her own family in her new life. John was not so sure and could foresee uncomfortable and obligatory meetings in future. He was, however, grateful for anyone who would occupy Sara during what he guessed would be an exceedingly busy first few months for them both.

The few months seemed to fly by. There was so much to do, some good, some bad. It was difficult to break ties with old friends, discard beloved possessions and part company with old toys which had been childhood companions, but she steeled herself. She was going to a new country, almost a rebirth, so it was time to put away childish things. On the other hand, it was marvellous to—in good conscience—get rid of much rubbish like old clothes and furnishings she hadn't dared to do before.

As the plane took off from Heathrow, Sara looked out of the window and wondered if this would be her last sight of England. Australia was on the other side of the world, so far, far away. It was her first flight and she'd been a little apprehensive. She looked at John beside her, but he was engrossed in a book he'd bought for the flight. She returned to looking out the window at the land below and smiled at what she saw: fields and hedges like a neat patchwork quilt, cut from materials of various shades of green. Soon, clouds were racing past the window cutting off her last look at England; she felt hemmed in as if in a fog, but in less than a minute the plane emerged through the clouds into the clearest blue sky she had ever seen. They were flying above the clouds, and all she could see, for what seemed like endless miles, were white fluffy clouds, with no sign of the earth below them. She imagined what it must have been like for the first astronauts heading for the moon, just a few years earlier.

The boredom of the long flight, punctuated by meals, drinks and fuelling stops, plus her inability to sleep during the interminably long hours of darkness, had left her feeling jaded. 'Will we ever get there?' she muttered to herself; she was beginning to feel resentment in coming to Australia. But at long last, the words she longed to hear came over the PA system—it was the Captain speaking: 'We shall be landing at Sydney airport in less than an hour.'

The flight path took them over Sydney's famous harbour, and as she looked out of the window at the cluster of high-rise buildings surrounding the beautiful blue waters of the harbour, where boats of all shapes and sizes could be seen, she felt excitement rising in her. She tugged at John's arm, 'Look, there's Sydney Harbour Bridge—isn't it magnificent! I'm sure I've seen a bridge like that somewhere in England,' she said. 'Where was it, do you remember, John?'

'Yes, you're right, it's just like the Tyne Bridge at Newcastle, though of course this is much larger.'

'And see, there, the Opera House. Oh, isn't it magnificent, just like huge sails surrounded by sea. It's beautiful.' She felt a thrill run down her spine at seeing the famous sights on Sydney Harbour, and for a brief moment she thought that living in this country might not be so bad after all.

They had to change planes in Sydney for the last part of their journey, so they followed the other passengers, cabin luggage in hand, through the long corridor and out into the airport lounge. There was a lively hum of voices, English spoken with a quaint twang and a bit of a drawl, with voices going up at the end of sentences. They were unaware that their own accent was seen as quaint by the locals. They sat in the cafe, drinking coffee, Sara making a mental note of the brightly coloured summer dresses that the women wore.

As they tightened their seat belts for the last leg of their long trip, she began once again to feel the near panic of that first night John had told her of his totally unexpected plan. She had struggled to control herself over the intervening months, but now she was tired mentally and physically. There had been so much that was new and exhausting swamping both her body and her mind, that she was ready to give way at any minute. What am I going to do with myself, her tired mind grumbled on and on—a stranger in a strange world? All young people will either have jobs or be married, with children to look after. I can't play any sport really well. I've done a bit of shorthand and typing. I suppose I could brush that up and get some kind of job. I can design clothing, but I'm not dedicated—anyway, I know nothing of the trends out here, and I suppose John will be off to this place he calls the 'bush'.

She turned to look at him beside her as he leant over her pressed against the aircraft window. They had left Bass Strait behind and begun to sweep low over surprisingly thickly wooded country and hills. Suddenly she thought of Miss Judith Roland.

'Do you think she'll come to meet us?'

'Who, the old girl?' he asked, without taking his attention from the window.

'Well, unless you've someone else tucked away.'

'No such luck,' he grinned. 'Won't your Aunt Marion have kept the old girl informed? She could be too old or feeble, of course.'

Then it was over. They were down on the runway and walking towards the airport buildings. She was still at the stage of getting used to the Australian voices which all seemed strange to her, making it difficult to differentiate between speakers. She had noticed this first in Sydney, but already walking among these people hurrying down the aircraft steps to meet their friends by the white railings, she detected a softness and gentleness that went attractively with the strange accent.

And there was a strangeness in the air. She suddenly realised that it was the smell. She had heard that each continent had its own smell, and here was proof of it! Undeniably different—eucalyptus—every breath made it more sure. A man next to her noticed her sniffing and smiled at her: 'This your first time in Australia? Yes, I've noticed it in other places around the world; sometimes the smell's good, sometimes bad, but this is Australia, best smell in the world, gum trees. The pity is that you adjust to it too soon. Another week and you won't even notice it. Anyway, good luck to you!' With that he nodded and disappeared.

Suddenly her attention was drawn to the small, compact figure of a woman who could be any age from sixty to eighty, standing very quietly and watchfully behind the railings. Sara took one more look at the neatly gloved hands and much beflowered hat, then grabbed John's arm: 'John, stop a minute. I'm sure that's her.'

He followed her gaze and smiled. 'My dear, it could be no other. Come on, we'll ask her.'

She too, as they approached, seemed to be aware of them.

John went up to her and said: 'I am sure you must be Miss Judith Roland.'

'I am, and you of course will be John Hilyard and your wife, Sara.'

Instinctively Sara held out both hands and was drawn down to the old lady's soft, thin lips.

'My dear, this is quite an occasion! Now come along, I have a taxi. Too old to drive, you know. John, I expect you will see to the luggage. I'll take Sara with me. You can't miss us. We are just over there in the car park. Come along, my dear.' And Sara found herself being swept away by the frail old fingers in the crook of her arm, while a flow of small, explanatory remarks went on, which, while they seemed unending, had a quaint dignity and determination that made her realise Miss Judith could be someone to reckon with.

The feeling remained as the taxi drove through the parched valley round the airport, and on towards the blue waters of the Derwent below the dominating mountain named "Wellington", clear-cut against the pale blue of the summer sky.

'You're noticing the brown grass,' the little woman said presently.

It was a matter-of-fact statement, but Sara felt uncomfortable.

'All countries are different,' was all she could think of to say, 'and of course this is your summer.'

'You will get used to the differences if you accept them.'

Again the remark was matter-of-fact, but Sara felt herself addressed as a child and was aware of a sense of annoyance. Miss Judith was obviously opinionated and quite satisfied with these burnt-looking hills! But once again she was made to feel foolish by a small gloved hand being placed on her knee, and the same voice saying: 'But then, you appeal to me as a young woman who will accept differences. Look now, there is something English for you—Government House.'

As the taxi raced over the Tasman Bridge, Sara looked obediently at the surprising battlements and almost castle-like appearance of the Governor's residence. She felt her heart lift at the sight of sweeping green lawns with English trees and shrubs with the Union Jack floating at the flagstaff. Here was the serenity and seclusion of Victorian England, although it faced a vast river running to the open sea, and was backed by tiers of modern houses scrambling up the shoulder of the foothills to Mount Wellington itself.

She half turned and caught a twinkle in the keen old eyes watching her. She smiled, and with the smile came for the first time a feeling of relaxation, a sense of kinship with this little woman beside her.

From the front seat of the taxi John turned and said: 'I'm afraid I kept you waiting Miss Roland, but unfortunately—'

'Judith would be more comfortable for us all.'

'Judith it shall be. As I was saying, I was held up by one of the representatives of the Hydro-Electric Commission. He very kindly came to meet us. They brought us out, you know.'

'A most progressive Government department,' Miss Judith nodded. 'You did well to attach yourself to them.'

John could hardly repress a smile at her calm patronage. She was so different from the businesslike representative of the Commission for which he was to work. A man very much what he had imagined Australians to be—kindly, to the point, but a little on the defensive. As yet this old lady did not fit his picture.

'He was explaining about the house they will allot us.'

'You of course told him that you were coming immediately to me before taking over this house.' Once again her way of putting it was a statement, not a question.

Sara watched John to see how he would cope.

'As you must realise, Judith, things could be a little difficult. I gather these houses are not as plentiful as the Commission would like, and reallotting them could present problems. We did not expect for one moment that you would be kind enough to invite us to your home.'

'Come, young man, one thing Tasmanians have never been lacking in—hospitality, particularly to one's own relatives!'

John gave up. 'Judith, I fear I have much to learn about Tasmanians.'

'You have, and you will. In the meantime, this man from the Hydro. You may phone him from my house.'

Sara leant back, hardly able to conceal the laughter in her eyes at John's discomfort. He so hated to be managed.

CHAPTER TWO

In the days that followed Sara lost all sense of reality. She had never before felt so separated from John. The Commission, the means to his goal, seemed to have taken charge of his mind and body. She watched him struggling to be polite, to say the right things when they were alone with Judith, and knew that all the time he was really only interested in getting away, establishing himself.

She told herself this was only natural, the only logical attitude when he had taken such a leap in the dark. He must know where he had landed, but she wished desperately she could have shared the problems with him. She sensed his intolerance of the house in New Town, of which Judith was so proud. Could she have got him to discuss it, she knew he would have referred to it as full of Victorian and Edwardian bric-a-brac. Only because of her did he agree to remain for a short time in this backwater of nineteenth-century Hobart, where red roofs in various degrees of fading tones were crowded, nondescript, one behind the other right up to the high fence of Judith's big stone house.

She knew he was relieved that there was somewhere to leave her safe and cared for when every morning he hurried down the asphalt path leading through the large garden to the outside world of modern buses and taxis. She knew too that more than ever this must be for her a time of patience and quietness, that he must not know of the turmoil, the fears and the loneliness in her. Later, yes; if it became impossible she would tell him, but later, much later.

So almost eagerly she tried to enter Judith's world of yesterday, tried to imagine her affection for the heavy blackwood furniture, the glass-fronted bookcases behind whose doors were leather-bound books by classical authors, diaries and letters collected by other, still older people who had built and lived in this house. She stood looking at the framed portraits of those first settlers who had left their mark on the development of this island of blue hills, deep waters and dark forests.

Early the following week John announced that he now knew his movements. He was to work as an assistant engineer on one of the HEC's projects in order to gain experience of Australian methods. Almost before he had finished explaining, Judith looked at him and said: 'Accommodation?'

'As I explained the day you met us, Judith, a house will be provided, for which we pay a ridiculously small weekly rent.'

The old lady nodded wisely. 'I daresay, but I think it would be better for you if you left Sara with me for a time. You will be free to deal with your new work, and she will have time to meet people and get to know Hobart.'

Sara felt as though she was something being shared out between two owners; at the same time she was well aware of the quick relief that showed in John's face. She made her decision just as quickly; she would get a job as soon as tact permitted. Meanwhile she made no comment, but merely reached for her handbag and a cigarette.

At that moment they heard the distant opening and closing of a door—the front door, Sara told herself. Already she knew the sound the heavy carved door made, could visualise the afternoon sunlight falling on the cedar chest standing on the red carpet of the hallway. The chest, she had been told, had belonged to the sea captain who brought out the Roland family from England in 1900.

As she finished lighting her cigarette she was aware of a tall, spare young man standing in the doorway. She was also aware of the effect he had on Judith. At the sound of a newcomer in the room the little woman had turned her attention from John to the door, and at once her face relaxed into an expression of possessive pleasure.

Comes the blue-eyed boy, Sara decided.

'Richard, dear boy, I knew you would be able to come. This is Sara and John Hilyard. We've talked of them so much, haven't we, since the letter from Sara's mother.'

He came into the room then and Sara could take stock of him. She wondered if he was what was loosely referred to in England as a typical Australian. He was certainly different in some strange way. He was tall and broad, his body so flat and spare that his clothes seemed to hang on it rather than fit it— he made John look almost fat. With interest she waited for him to turn so she could see his face. When he did she felt cheated. He was like any other young man she might have met—except that he had very blue eyes which looked at her casually but comprehensively. For one fleeting moment she felt undressed, knew instinctively that his interest in a woman was purely physical, and for no reason she was intensely glad of John sitting opposite. Then he smiled and held out his hand. 'As my aunt says, we've waited quite a while for you both. Had a good trip?'

The smile changed everything about him, suggested he took life very much as he found it, and had every intention of enjoying what he found. He could be interesting, she decided. Easy—without a great deal of depth perhaps. Almost immediately he settled himself beside John and began to question him about the trip and their reason for coming to Tasmania. Judith got up to make the tea, and Sara decided she was going to offer her services to domesticity. There was an atmosphere of males and females being divided.

'I'll come and help you, Judith.'

The old woman smiled and made no comment until they reached the kitchen. Then—'You are learning Tasmanian ways fast, Sara,' she said.

'In what way, Judith?'

'In England I imagine men and women, in your modern phrase, "get together" more.'

Sara laughed. 'I wouldn't know yet. This is the first time I've really met Australians.'

'Tasmanians, my dear.'

'Is there a difference?'

'Of course. The others are mainlanders!'

Sara still couldn't see the difference, but forbore to say so; something about Judith discouraged opposition. Instead she asked: 'How long is it since you have been to England?'

'Unfortunately not since I left it as a very young child to accompany my sister when she came out to marry her fiancé. He was a scientist, you know, very clever, but much too old for her, as she was only nineteen.'

'It must have been hard for your mother to part with you both.'

'We had lost our mother, which is why my sister brought me. Both our parents were lost in an avalanche in Switzerland. They were intrepid climbers.'

'How dreadful.'

'It is a long time ago, my dear,' Judith said calmly, 'and in those days I don't think children and parents were very close to each other; there were too many servants in between. Besides, we came of old pioneering stock. My great-grandfather was brought out here at the age of three early in the last century; your mother may have told you the family story.'

'A little, not a great deal. You must be the last of the family, Judith.'

'No, my dear, Richard is the last. He is my sister's only grandchild. She and I were one of the few left on the English side from a long-established family. Your great-great-great-grandfather, Matthew, was your original progenitor. You happen to be English because one of his great-grandchildren went back to England in the first war and married your grandmother. Unfortunately he was killed before their child, your mother, was born.'

'Of course there are lots of other relations—all the Rolands seem to produce large families—but they are spread throughout Australia now and we have lost touch with most of them. The men seem unlucky too—so many killed in the two wars, my dear. You and I are two of the few left from the English side, as far as I know.'

'Richard is very well-off, being the last of the family, which is another reason why it is so important that he should marry the right girl.'

Sara wondered what Richard thought about that. Did he too come under the old lady's thumb? Somehow she didn't think so. In any case he could not be a Roland. Judith was unmarried, so Richard must be the last of her sister's husband's line.

At the end of the week John went off to take up his new position on one of the Commission's dam projects, and Sara remained for the moment in New Town. When it came to the point, she had not needed a great deal of persuading. Although he did not say so, she knew her guess at John's relief when the matter had been raised originally was correct. The more she came to think about it, the more she realised they were two people very unsure of themselves, and it was far better for them to be apart until they had worked things out. She also realised the decision was being made easier by her growing fondness for Judith.

Although living so much in the past, the old lady was fascinated by the modern world and genuinely tried to understand it, using all her inborn perception and love of humanity to do so. Also, she did not stop at theory—she was still an active member of at least three organisations working for women's rights and freedoms. She had the innocent curiosity of a child plus a ruthless determination to satisfy it. Social climbers had a rough time at her hands; she was very much Miss Judith Roland, whose forebears had come from well-born English stock and decided to emigrate to Van Diemen's Land as free settlers. As such she had a firm grip on the land and all that it meant.

Under her tuition, Sara very quickly came to realise that two of the most important aspects of the social life for a woman on the island were luncheon and dinner parties, both private and charitable. The latter undoubtedly raised money which would not be acquired in any other way, and gave the ladies concerned an opportunity to display the latest fashions, at the same time keeping up their reputation of being 'so terribly busy'. The second was committee meetings.

Almost as soon as John departed, Judith gave a luncheon party in Sara's honour. She had not given one for a long time, so it required a great deal of thought and attention. But while she took out the family silver, so long wrapped away in chamois leather, Sara took herself into the city and bought one of the latest books on shorthand. She was determined to get a job of some kind. So it was with very different ideas in their heads the two women approached the day of the party: Judith confident that she had selected just the right people in the right number; Sara sure she could persuade some Hobartian matron to come to her aid in the matter of employment.

With this in mind she decided to wear her mother's parting gift—a turquoise jersey frock which fitted her like a sheath. Her mirror told her it gave life to her eyes and was a fine background for her dark hair and white skin.

Judith watched her walk down the thickly carpeted stairs, her long fingers just touching the balustrade as she moved, and the old woman felt a stirring of pride and kinship for this young, quietly spoken girl who had come so unexpectedly into her life. Wondered too, if under all her quietness she might not be a little like that other Sarah who had stooped so low to climb so high—the Sarah who had played such a part in the lives of the Roland family—and she breathed a prayer that this Sara would never know the terrible problems that had faced the other, although for the moment she had a strange sensation that these two were linked, that the young girl walking down the stairs could once again affect the Roland story.

Sara, about to put her foot on the last tread, found herself looking down into a face twisted into such an expression of startled intensity that she had a feeling of apprehension.

'Is anything wrong, Judith?'

The old woman swallowed quickly. 'Of course not, child. That is a very pretty dress you are wearing. I—I shall be proud of you today.'

'Judith, there *is* something wrong. Please, may I help?'

There was a stillness in the square entrance hall where only that morning Sara had filled great vases with hydrangeas of all colours. Then the door bell rang. Judith turned away— the first guest had arrived.

For a long time Sara remembered that party. The influx of well-dressed ladies of Hobart who all knew each other, and all appeared to talk at once with such complete intimacy that she had the feeling this was merely the continuation of a previous like occasion, the tale being taken up where it had been left off, the latest titbits of news swapped as a child swaps stamps. On the other hand she did not feel it was at all vicious, this checking of social events and personalities; rather the getting straight of exactly what people were doing and thinking, the allotting and plotting of positions. There was no small talk in the real sense; the weather had no place.

She was quite sorry when she was firmly edged from one group to another by the old lady. She felt her presence necessitated a switch from the eager pursuit of personal knowledge among friends to the humdrum business of polite courtesy to a stranger. And how courteous they were! She was soon made to feel that this party was indeed in her honour, even if she was unaware of the relationships of those among whom she moved. At the moment that would be forgiven; the future would tell if she could make the grade. Today they would give her the benefit of the doubt, as they asked her carefully what part of England she came from, whether she had relatives here apart from Miss Roland, whether she had children, and being told "no", immediately seized on the idea that it would be good for her to *do* something if her husband was going to be busy on one of those big schemes of the Commission.

In one of the few moments she found herself alone, she happened to look across the room to catch the eye of an

Italian girl some years younger than herself—at least four or five, she decided. Suddenly she remembered seeing the girl arrive among the last of the guests, accompanied by a middle-aged woman. Strangely enough they had been about the only members of the party to whom she had not been introduced.

Watching, she felt that the girl, like herself, was an alien in this room. A fellow feeling made her thread her way through the busily talking matrons, and she realised as she approached that such a girl could be alien in any company. She certainly never would be in men's! Slim, with the resilient slimness of a willow, with small breasts supporting her green woollen dress which then clung to her narrow hips, and with dark, amused eyes framed by a pale olive skin and golden, simply dressed hair, she was a figure to arrest anyone's eyes. Sara wondered if Richard had met her. Together they would be quite a pair!

The girl had obviously been watching Sara's approach. 'You came,' she said simply. 'I hoped you would.' Her smile was as irresistible as the rest—lazy, warm. Sara found herself smiling too. 'We didn't get a formal introduction,' she said. 'My name's Sara, Sara Hilyard.'

'And mine's Arna d'Este. You live with the old lady?'

'Not really. I've only just arrived in Tasmania.'

'So! Me too. Will you like it, you think?'

Sara decided to be cautious. 'It's early days.'

Arna laughed softly, but it was enough; it spoke for her, and Sara felt vaguely uncomfortable; this girl had read her completely. She rushed into words. 'I think I shall get a job. That's the best way to get to know people. You see, to begin with, my husband will be away quite a lot.'

'What kind of job?'

Sara began to feel she was being interrogated.

'I haven't decided yet, and what about you?'

Arna shrugged. 'Maybe I too shall get a job.'

Sara tried to place Arna in a job and failed. Again the other girl laughed. 'You think perhaps I would not be so good at a job!'

They both laughed.

'It would have to be something *artistic*, very artistic.' Her hands, as slender in their way as the rest of her limbs, sketched artistry in the air.

'Clothes, in some way perhaps, yes, clothes, but oh, so— different.' Her eyes moved over the oblivious guests. For no reason at all Sara could imagine the kind of clothes to which she referred. She found herself saying, 'But would there be an opening here for these—sort of clothes?'

The dark eyes met hers. 'But of course, always there is a place for those clothes.'

Sara said: 'Of course I could paint, or try designing again, but I don't think that I'm good enough or could be serious enough. Besides, there is probably no outlet here.'

'You are full of noes, yes?'

'Yes—no, I mean.'

Again they laughed.

'Perhaps we may find a job together one day. So, you design?'

Sara's face grew serious. 'Once, I was quite sure it was what I really wanted to do in life, and then—'

'And then?'

'Oh, then I got married, and only worked at it for a short time.'

Judith came suddenly upon them. 'I am so glad you have met. I expect Arna has told you she has come to live with one of my oldest friends. Sara dear, excuse my taking you away, but there is someone I very much want you to meet.'

Politely Sara allowed herself to be borne away, aware of the amused expression following her, also aware that Arna sensed the patronage in Miss Judith's kindly words.

'I will tell you all about that child, later,' Judith whispered, as they went in search of the "someone".

So, later Sara learned that Arna was the result of an affair between the son of Judith's oldest friend, with whom she had come to live, and the daughter of an Italian countess—the son being killed in a Monte Carlo rally before the affair had been legalised. 'Such a to-do,' Judith confided that night. 'Everyone thinks Edith is wonderful to bring the girl out.'

'What do you think?' Sara couldn't help asking.

Judith obviously struggled mentally with what she ought to think and what she couldn't help feeling. Presently she smiled up shyly at Sara: 'My dear, although you're so young you make an old woman like me feel she can say things perhaps she should not say.'

'Why shouldn't you say things if you really believe them?'

Judith's cheeks grew very pink. 'Well, my dear, I suppose we weren't brought up to say what we really believed, only the right things for us to believe.' Then she rushed on before Sara could speak. 'But she is so beautiful her mother must have been exceptional. I have never seen a fair Italian before, have you? And those Latin races don't think about those things as we do. It must have been so difficult for David, he was such a dear boy, beside the Mediterranean and everything, and I am sure it would have been all right if he hadn't got killed.'

Sara did not trust herself to look at Judith. To treat such a breaking down of traditional thinking with any form of levity would have been an irretrievable betrayal of trust. Instead she said, 'You are a wonderfully understanding person, Judith,' and could feel the gratitude that was spreading through the little figure beside her.

'I hoped you two would get on. You see, I fear it may be difficult for her for a while here.'

'Oh, we will,' Sara said, and just managed to stop herself saying, 'We might even go into business together,' but wild as the thought seemed, she suddenly realised it could be true.

CHAPTER THREE

She began to think more and more about the idea of occupying herself in some way. No matter how fond she became of little Judith, she knew she could not be absorbed wholly into her world. In fact the more fond of her she became, the more certain she felt the break must be made. John had to be on his own for a time—she quite saw that—but how then could she strike out on *her* own without hurting the old lady?

Suddenly she thought of Arna, thought of the excitement she conjured up. If for no other reason it would be good to see her again. Judith was only too pleased to supply the phone number, and within minutes she heard the fascinating, soft sounds of provocation that made up Arna's voice coming from the receiver.

'Hullo, there,' she said. 'It's a lovely day—let's make use of it.'

There was a silence, then the lazy laugh that said so much more than her words. 'Where and when shall we make use of this so lovely day?'

'Wherever, whenever you like. What do you say to our going to look for some of those "different" clothes?'

'We will not find them, but let us look by all means.'

'I'll meet you at the Post Office in an hour.'

To Judith she said: 'Arna is in. I am going to meet her in town and we'll have lunch.' To which the old lady replied: 'It is going to be hot. You'd better take a taxi.'

Sara, however, had no intention of taking a taxi. It was not far to the city, and she always found it easier to think when she was walking. What really was she going to say to Arna, a girl some years younger than herself, and whom she had only met once—'It would be fun if you and I started a business together'? Neither of them knew anything about buying and selling or finance—at least she didn't, and she strongly suspected that all Arna knew about life was employing female flair, plus—or was it? Anyway, it would be fun to find out, and no harm done.

She wondered too if their second meeting would prove as interesting as the first. Perhaps eighty per cent of her fascination had been that she was the one vivid contrast in that room of conventional good taste—brought about by the ease of money. In spite of herself she found she was hurrying down Elizabeth Street in the urgency of her need to know; and as soon as the Post Office steps came in view, she could pick out the vivid splash of colour that was Arna. Subconsciously she noticed the punctuality; somehow punctuality seemed totally unrelated to such a personality.

Later in the day she was to review many of her first impressions of the Italian girl, but what most definitely remained, in fact possibly increased, was her fascination. Without seeming to do so Arna took charge of their expedition, and it was she who showed Sara where to look for the things they sought, only to prove her point that they would not be found. Looking back, Sara realised she knew instinctively on that day Arna was all feline softness on the surface, but underneath was as hard and as astute as any businessman.

For lunch they took themselves underground to the discreet darkness of the bistro, with its small tables, paintings on dimly lit walls, and foreign waitresses.

'You see,' Arna said as they tucked themselves away beneath an Impressionist painting which immediately absorbed Sara. 'There are innovations in eating in Hobart, so why not different clothes?'

But before Sara could answer she caught sight of Richard, and he of her—or was it Arna? At once he came towards them and quite ridiculously she felt nervous, ill at ease and yet quite exhilarated. It was a most confusing sensation and did not please her at all. She remembered how she felt about him at that first meeting—the blue-eyed boy, spoilt, self-satisfied.

She was glad also that Arna was with her, and that she would monopolise him: it would be amusing to watch them.

From the way he was looking at her it was obvious that they had not met previously, so Sara quickly made the introductions and he promptly suggested he should join them, in fact took it for granted by settling himself into a chair between them.

He turned to Sara: 'It didn't take you long to discover our one Continental rather than local attempt at eating.'

She smiled at Arna. 'Oh, it was Arna who brought us here. I don't know my way around yet.'

His eyes slid over the Italian girl, not missing a point, Sara decided, but she also noticed the difference between Arna's reception of it and her own. Arna took it quite calmly and in fact, in a completely feminine way, returned it. Here, Sara told herself, are two of a kind.

'And how long have you been here?' he asked Arna.

'A month perhaps. Does time matter in a place like this?'

'You see us as somewhat remote from the rest of the world.'

The flick of sarcasm made her laugh. Laughter was never far from Arna.

'Are you?'

'If so, delightfully so. Remind me to prove it to you sometime.'

'I will.'

They seemed so at ease that Sara wished there were some way to remove herself invisibly, but in that moment two things happened: Richard turned to her and the waitress came to take their order. Once again she was aware of the discomfort of her reaction to him, so that she was glad to immerse herself in the menu.

'I take it that John is still away?'

'Oh yes, and will be for some weeks this time.'

'That will please our Judith—I mean having you round the place.'

'That is nice of you. I like being with her.'

'Good for her. Not perhaps so good for you.'

Before she could think of a suitable reply he continued: 'In spite of the fact that we've an expert in our midst, girls, try the ravioli.'

The luncheon turned into a very pleasant affair, and after a few glasses of wine, some of Sara's inhibitions fell away and she felt herself almost as much at ease as the other two most certainly were. In fact it was she who said jokingly when they had reached the coffee stage, 'You know, Arna and I feel we should have some suitable occupation. Any suggestions?'

Richard sat back in his chair, looking at them both in turn before he said solemnly: 'Don't, please don't tell me that you can both type and do shorthand and want to be somebody's secretary!'

Sara conjured up a picture of Arna as a secretary and started to laugh before the other two joined her. Heads turned in their direction. This romantic dimness and pseudo-cultural atmosphere did not at all fit the ringing laughter of three young people. It was Arna who stopped first. 'But seriously, Richard, we do indeed require employment—that is,' with gracefully waving hands, 'we need to employ ourselves.'

'A different story.'

'Ah, yes,' she sighed.

'Obviously it is you two who have the ideas.'

'They're dreams more than anything,' Sara said hastily.

'Such as?'

'Well, I suppose really you would call it a boutique—'

'With a difference,' from Arna.

'Naturally!' from Richard.

'Sara knows about design. I know what we want. I have a friend in Italy, very very clever with her sewing, very quick—we would need to make her emigrate.'

'We'd have to find somewhere—the right position.'

'Battery Point, of course.' Arna answered without hesitation. 'It is so romantic.'

'What do you know about Battery Point?'

'Quite something, I read.'

'But finance?'

'There are ways,' Richard said.

'Stock.'

'Imports. We'd have to start with some really exotic models.'

'What about Customs, and— how would people react?' dubiously from Sara.

'Stop a minute,' Richard said. 'You're going too far and too fast. Are you really serious?'

They looked at each other and nodded. 'We'd like to be, but—'

'There's my husband.'

'There's whether I shall stay.'

'There's money.'

'There's the right connections to get the right exciting things.'

'We'd have to call it the 'Boutique Satanas.'' Arna stopped to point a finger at Sara. 'Your decor, it would have to be way out, way out.'

'You're off again,' Richard stopped her. 'There's one thing that would have to be joined to the list—a manager!'

Arna held her hands across the table. 'But of course, dear Richard, that would have to be you!'

He picked up one of her incredible tiny fingers between his own forefinger and thumb and matched her brown eyes with his blue ones. 'I would have to be out of my sweet mind to accept!'

Surprisingly, Sara heard herself say: 'I would take care of you, Richard,' and decided immediately she had drunk too much wine. She remembered a long time afterwards the expression in his eyes as he turned to look at her.

That night when she and Judith were having their coffee in the little study opening onto the garden, the old lady told her with delight that the luncheon party had brought in a splendid harvest of return invitations for her.

Because she knew it meant so much, Sara said: 'People here are very kind, aren't they?'

'Only if it suits them,' Judith said quite sharply.

Sara felt it difficult not to smile at the old lady's egotism, but managed to sip her coffee instead. She was enjoying it, although the night was hot enough for the french windows on to the lawn to stand open, thereby causing Judith to grumble about the odd mosquito that was brave enough to venture into the room.

It was then that once again Sara felt conscious of the old lady studying her surreptitiously. That decided her! She must have this thing out. Putting down her coffee cup, she said quietly: 'Judith, I feel sure I remind you of someone.'

There was quite a silence but she did not repeat the question. She knew she had been heard.

At last: 'You are quite right, my dear. Her name was Sarah too, but spelt with an "h". How much did your mother tell you about her, indeed about us all, before you came out?'

Sara felt embarrassed. 'Well, not a great deal really. Nothing about the other Sarah, except to comment on the fact, as you have just done, that her name was spelt with an "h". There is only one family of Roland, isn't there?'

'That is so.'

Again Sara waited. Judith began to rock herself slowly back and forth, her hands crossed on her lap, her little feet tapping rhythmically on the polished floor beyond the edge of the carpet. Her eyes lifted to a large painting over the mantelpiece of a young woman with aquiline features and a wealth of Titian hair dressed high on her head. Her voluptuous, small-waisted figure was clothed in deep hyacinth-blue material, the skirt of which was gracefully swept away from the figure by a most beautiful hand. Ever since she had first come into the study, Sara had been fascinated by the portrait, and often wondered about it. Now she followed Judith's eyes with here own and said: 'Who was she?'

'The other Sarah,' Judith replied, so quietly that Sara had the feeling she was about to discover something strange and compelling. 'She was transported from England as a convict in 1826.'

'A woman like that, a convict!' Sara said in utter astonishment.

Judith continued rocking. 'We often talk about our own times being strange to live in. Sometimes when I read what England and her people must have been like, I wonder which were stranger.'

'But how—'

'Oh, it was quite simple, I imagine. You see, she was born on the wrong side of the blanket. Her father was an earl, her mother a lady's maid who made him promise that Sarah would be brought up in the household in some capacity and given an education. Anyway, Sarah was born about the same time as his legitimate daughter.'

'The old beast!' Sara interrupted.

'My dear, you young people of today who try to ignore most conventions, to say nothing of morals, lack a sense of proportion. The story was not an unusual one in the England of those days, or today for that matter. The only unusual part was that the earl *did* keep his promise and had Sarah taught her letters. However, to continue: the two girls grew up together, and Sarah eventually became personal maid to her own sister.'

'Did they know they were sisters?'

'Not until the time of the transportation. Apparently they were very fond of each other. You must remember, in fact you should know, in those old families where generation after generation served with the same masters, the children of each did grow very fond of each other without the station in life of either being involved. The position was perfectly understood: one was to serve, the other to be served.'

Sara made no comment, so Judith continued: 'However, there was one person who did know the situation—the housekeeper, who had always been bitterly jealous. One night, when the young countess had gone to a ball in London, this woman found Sarah trying on her sister's famous ruby necklace and tiara. She gave the alarm and swore she had caught the girl stealing the famous jewels. The result was a foregone conclusion in those days—hanging, but—'

'But surely her father—'

'Could do nothing without telling the truth, and why would he do that? Probably he thought the whole thing a release from what could, in time, prove a difficult situation. But he did secure her transportation instead of the death penalty.'

Sara sat staring up at the portrait in silence.

'What happened to her in the end? How and why was that portrait painted?'

'It is a long and, in some ways, dreadful story, my dear, and I'm tired. Some other time I'll tell you, or better still I'll give you the journal she kept faithfully.'

Sara was so fascinated that she would have pleaded for the whole story, but, on turning towards the old woman, saw that she did indeed look very tired. 'It might be a good idea if we both had an early night,' she said instead, and got slowly to her feet.

Outside, in the garden, the moon was shining on the roses, and as the sprinkler was still going, its spray fell over their white blooms like scattering diamonds.

'Shall I turn off the sprinkler, Judith?'

'Oh dear, I must have forgotten. That will tell you how tired I am. I can't bear the heat, I never could. Yes, please, then I'll be glad of your arm upstairs, my dear.'

Sara went out through the french windows and could feel the wet grass through her sandals. As she walked towards the tap on the lawn, she looked up at the vast depth of the sky with its scattered stars and was aware of a great peace for the first time since she had left England. She wished above all that John were here to share this moment with her; wished that she could tell him now, this instant, she knew at last he was right in coming to this place.

In the study Judith had got out of her chair and was waiting. Sara closed and locked the french windows behind her and looked up once again at the enigmatic expression of the other Sarah above the mantelpiece.

'I can't see why I reminded you of her. We're not at all alike, not even in colouring, and I believe the likeness you thought you saw worried you.'

The old woman slipped her hand in Sara's arm, and together they stood looking up at the portrait.

'I didn't say I was worried.'

'No, but you looked it.' Sara laughed. 'Perhaps it's because the names are the same. Come to think of it, I wonder if Mother did deliberately call me Sara after her? I'll make her tell me one day. I can't think why she never told me the story, it's so exciting. She must have known it.'

'I'm certain she did. This Sarah was a convict girl who was sent to a family in the country as a servant. I don't seem to recall all the details at the moment, but she was greatly valued by them—once you've read the journal, it will become clear. I would imagine the story has been kept quiet for so long because she *was* a convict, although she obtained her freedom eventually.'

'Surely you don't imagine the other Sarah and I are alike in that respect?'

'Of course not, my dear! And after all, who wants to be likened to a convict? Let us go upstairs.'

In spite of herself Sara felt she could not let the subject drop. The thought of it excited her strangely. In some way she felt she must reassure the old lady, and at the same time herself.

'You must never worry about me, Judith. I may be Sara in name, but the other Sarah had no future to count on. I'm married, I have John, and we both came out of our own free will.'

'Of course, my dear. It was just my foolish fancy to link the families, the names, the fact that you two girls came here to this country to start a new life.'

'So now you go to bed, have a good sleep and forget all about me,' Sara said as she walked slowly upstairs, easily supporting the frail little burden on her arm; 'but you will lend me that Journal, won't you? I must know the whole story and work out all the relationships.'

'I shall give it to you tomorrow. You may keep it.'

'Oh, no,' Sara said quickly, 'I couldn't do that. I—'

'You will do as I say!' Judith said with a sudden return to her usual manner. 'Now, my dear, I am very, very tired and must go to bed. Remember that the journal is yours to keep. You may begin reading it tomorrow.'

In silence Sara kissed the little old woman and went slowly from the room.

The next morning they found Judith with her face turned peacefully towards her rose garden and the early morning sun. She had finished with being an autocrat.

On the dressing table was a large heavy leather volume with an envelope on it simply addressed to Sara. Inside was a short note: 'I leave this to you, Sara. It is years since I opened it and I have undoubtedly forgotten many aspects of the story it contains. However, may you learn from it the strength of human courage demonstrated by the woman who wrote it.'

CHAPTER FOUR

John was faced with problems he hadn't expected. In leaving England he had considered only the business of immediate survival and future prospects. His primary objective had been to get away from the bureaucracy of the old world. What he had not considered was that, in handing himself over to the new, he would come up against any serious criticism of the old from others than himself. When he did it came as a shock to realise that he possessed a hitherto unsuspected deep loyalty to the country that had bred him and equally deep anger that he was expected to make excuses for it.

He had taken Australia for granted—had expected it to be a young, uncultured copy of England overseas. Instead, he found the people had minds of their own and a way of thinking and living that was only basically English. They liked to travel if they were sufficiently wealthy; to visit the old world in the hope that a little of its ancient prestige would become a part of them, an experience to carry back to their modern villas, to boast of gentility. To travel was all very well, but give them Australian sun and comfort, to say nothing of Australian beer. This was considered the best that life had to offer.

This judgment of a nation by its mere appeal to the senses shocked John. Further, he realised it was a situation with which he must come to terms if he were to succeed among these men, and failure he was not going to accept. These thoughts were in his mind when Sara rang: 'John, it's Judith—she died in her sleep this morning.'

'Hold on a minute, I can't hear with all this racket going on.' He reached over to slam his door. 'Did you say Judith had died?'

'Yes, this morning. John, you will be back on Saturday?'

'Of course. I'll see if I can get away sooner. Anything I can do?'

'No, dear. Richard is here.'

'Poor old girl! Pretty sudden. You all right? Sure?'

'Quite sure. It—it was such a shock. Only last night we were sitting talking together. She—I don't know—she seemed so like our own—'

'Look here, my dear, I'll come as soon as I can.'

When he had hung up he thought suddenly: this will mean Sara must come and live out here. He wondered if it would be a good thing, wondered what she would do with herself and how she would get on with the other wives. She would probably strike the same problems as he had but it wouldn't matter so much for her, or would it? It came back to him how she had always told him he was too unobservant of people, too uninterested in their feelings, beliefs, wants, and he had laughed at her, told her that she for her part dramatised people. It would be interesting to see how she answered up to these Australians and their blunt determination to make their own society and their own standards.

Later, before going to the funeral, he saw the senior engineer, David Lint, and told him what had happened. Lint was most sympathetic and helpful. 'As a matter of fact, Hilyard,' he said, 'Steve Boston is going on three weeks' leave tomorrow. How about my asking him to let you and your wife take over his house while he is away?'

So it was arranged, but from further conversation John realised that, the original house allotted to them having once been refused, its replacement could take time. He detailed the conversation to Sara the night before the funeral, and she knew the situation worried him. She watched him thoughtfully as she got into bed.

'John!'

'Yes, my dear?'

'Is it going to cause trouble, my coming to live with you on the camp?'

'Of course not. Even if it did, I wouldn't accept such a situation. You are my wife and it's our right to live together just as any other married personnel.'

'But we—haven't any children. If there's trouble it'll probably be because we are occupying a house someone with a family needs more!'

'Oh please, Sara, do stop making children the be-all and end-all of everything that happens in our lives!'

She drew the bedclothes up to her chin and stretched her toes as far down the bed as she could. He switched off the light and got in beside her. She felt his arms round her.

'Sorry, dear. I didn't mean it like that.'

'I know.'

'Out here things could be different. We might still have them. You mustn't let it become an obsession—promise?'

'I promise.'

She could feel him relaxing. He had said the things he knew he ought to say, and was pleased with his own good sense. She smiled in the darkness and said: 'What did you think of Arna?'

'The Italian girl?'

'Mm.'

He lay still. The question took him back abruptly to the moment when he and Sara had walked into the study that morning after he had arrived. Arna was sitting in a chair by the garden window, her incredibly thin olive fingers flicking idly at the pages of a magazine. She did not look up immediately but when she did he was guiltily aware that this young woman was one of the kind men dream of possessing, from adolescence to the grave. To Sara he replied: 'I would think she'll cause a lot of claws to be sharpened!'

She turned wholly to the warmth of his arms, smugly aware that for all her beauty, Arna had not yet achieved this freedom that was hers. But her triumph was somewhat spoilt when she had another thought, that perhaps it wasn't necessarily marriage that Arna wanted.

Next day she was more depressed by the funeral than she had expected. For no apparent reason she felt the ground had been cut from under her feet, and she felt she wanted to scream when wreath after wreath piled up in the silent house. All the rooms seemed to have an atmosphere of waiting, of knowing that their end had come, that the little old lady lying in her silk-lined coffin had taken their life with her.

Richard noticed her wan quietness, saw her almost flinch as each ring came at the door bell and yet another floral tribute was laid gently, maddeningly gently, on the growing stack waiting firmly for the hearse in the now heavily scented drawing room.

He came and stood beside her. 'Smile, Sara. She didn't like gloom.'

She made an effort to brighten up. 'Sorry. I just never realised how depressing flowers could be.'

'You know, I think the old Irish idea of a jolly good wake with masses to eat, drink and get merry on, was first rate. Read somewhere the other day of an old boy who was dying, and to pass away the time organised his own wake—in fact sent for some of the pork he could smell cooking in the kitchen.'

Sara did laugh then, in spite of herself.

'Incidentally, I'm organising a party on *Sunbolt* on Saturday. I want you and John to come.'

'*Sunbolt?*'

'My—or at least "our" yacht. My father owns her officially. The big idea is to race her in the Sydney to Hobart race.'

'We'd love to come.'

But John, when he was told, said: ' I can't possibly. I must get straight back after the funeral. I've taken the day off today, take over Steve Boston's house tomorrow, and if this weather holds we'll all be working on Saturday. I can't very well ask for that too, but there's nothing to stop you. Couldn't you stay the night with Arna and I'll pick you up first thing on Sunday mornin?'

So after the funeral cortège had moved away from the New Town church where Judith had worshipped for most of her life, Sara went with Arna to Sandy Bay.

The harbour was ruffled by a late-afternoon southerly, and scores of little boats round Wrest Point hotel were dancing and nodding in time to the waves. Even the big thirty and forty-foot yachts, their sails furled, were swinging and bowing clumsily to their moorings. It was a sight for the young in heart, for those who could take time off from the everyday tedium of home and livelihood to listen to the wind of the free places, the slap and gurgle of water on wood, and maybe to dream a while without knowing they were dreaming.

When they got off the bus Sara leant on the rail for a moment, looking across the blue-grey water where some of the white-winged yachts were tacking home, their canvas filled, their sleek sides heeling out of the water. She looked too at the young people strolling in the sunshine in their tight jeans and long sloppy jumpers; wondered if they were happy in this island of theirs where both the young and the not so young seemed to live in the water, in boats, on water skis and surf boards (it seemed to her that every car that passed either trailed a boat or carried one on a roof rack) or on tennis courts.

Yet so many of them, the girls particularly, went round in droves, all looking the same in their jeans and jumper uniform, parading up and down as though looking for something they never quite found.

'I'm looking forward to tomorrow. I've never been on a yacht,' she said suddenly to Arna leaning on the rail beside her. 'I wish you were coming.'

Arna smiled her secret little smile. 'Me too, but it wouldn't do for me to interfere with Mrs Neepers' plans. To me she has been very kind. And you know what they say, Sara dear: two is the company, three none!'

Sara turned abruptly towards her. 'What do you mean?'

'Just that we must get to know Richard one at a time.'

It was Sara's turn to smile. 'I fear that particular dream will definitely be only "one day"—especially now, but it would have been fun.' Unconsciously her smile turned to a sigh.

CHAPTER FIVE

On the Saturday morning Richard called early for her.

Somehow he seemed different, alarmingly athletic with his long, hard brown legs supporting the briefest of shorts, a sloppy green jumper covering what she suspected to be a body every bit as hard and brown as his legs.

'Good morning to you,' he said; 'it's best to get going early on an outing of this kind. Generally the wind's not so good at this hour on this kind of day, but it gives us time to get ourselves sorted out.'

'I'm all ready. Unfortunately I've no real outfit for this, never having done it before.'

He looked her over. 'You'll be OK, but you need a jumper.'

'Sir, an Englishwoman never moves without one.' She was glad to bypass his scrutiny and climb into the car. 'Is this the famous Holden?' she added.

'It is. Don't tell me you've heard about it in England.'

'You forget. Australia House is in England.'

'The shop window—it's pretty likely I'll be going there myself the year after I get this race sewn up—London, I mean.'

'What, you!' She turned quickly towards him, more eagerly than she knew.

'I believe you're homesick already,' he teased her as he swung the car out and drove fast toward the yacht club.

'Not really. It's just that I still can't believe I'm here and not there. It all seems to have happened so quickly.'

'What made your old man do it?'

'Come here? Oh, I think he just got fed up with the difficulties in England. Wanted a change basically, I think, and, well, you see it is so easy with no children for us to do a thing like this.'

She knew he was looking at her again, knew he had read through her attempt to speak lightly, and resented the feeling of intimacy he always managed to convey to her. For one uncomfortable moment she imagined him making some comment about children. Instead he said: 'So you've never sailed before? We'll soon break you in.'

'Now, this race you were talking about.'

'The Sydney to Hobart—the ultimate? Winning the Sydney-Hobart is not just winning at a sport; it's a life's achievement. Put it this way: you spend most of your young life preparing for it, and the rest of your existence living up to it. Boats and water stay with you all the way to old age. Anno Domini takes a hand with the other kinds of sport.'

'I don't think I'd care for anything so possessive.'

'Quite right. It isn't a woman's sport.'

'Nonsense! Women sail.'

'Amuse themselves on the fringe of it.'

'We're getting very argumentative. I don't care for that either,' she said as he smiled down at her in his quick way that seemed to change his whole face.

'Don't be so prim, Sara; we'll probably always argue, so you'd better get used to it. There's a bunch waiting for us, and there is Madam herself. To you a thirty-eight-foot masthead sloop, which won't mean a thing at the moment. As for the race, it was begun just after the last World War by two businessmen in Sydney who discovered over lunch one day that they both had appointments to keep in Hobart. On the spot they decided to race each other in their yachts to Hobart, thereupon starting a race which is every yachtsman's dream to win.'

'You make it sound really something.'

'That's for sure. Well, come and meet some of the sailors. You won't be meeting all the crew members today; two of them have urgent domestic problems.'

The bunch turned out to be twenty-two-year-old twins, Michael and David, two girls, Sally and Mary, whom Sara remembered meeting at New Town, and also one of the official crew, Mick Ross, and his wife Angela. Like Richard, they all wore shorts and all looked very efficient, although the girls, she noticed, managed to look very feminine at the same time.

She was conscious of being the only one in the wrong kind of clothes, and wished desperately she could do something to convince them that she was not quite as useless as she must appear. What she did not realise was that the girls thought her anything but useless in what mattered to them.

In fact, when they had met her at New Town they had mistaken her quietness for aloofness and had decided she was too poised, too sure of herself, too English. Also, they wondered why Richard had brought her at all. He had been on the marriage market too long and was too obsessed with this yacht. Indeed, although good at crewing, they had only become so because they knew *Sunbolt* was their enemy. She possessed Richard, therefore the only chance they had was to join the queue and make her ways theirs. At first it had been fun, particularly being ordered about and trained by Richard. But gradually they had come to know she had won again. In Richard's eyes they had fallen into place, become part of the unofficial 'runabout' crew. Therefore it was positively unfair for any woman, relation or not, to butt in on the picture.

However, the introductions were soon made and everyone was busy with ropes, jobs and orders, all of which were entirely foreign to Sara, who once again was at a loss until Richard sized up the position and shouted at her: 'Hi there, Sara, you're in charge of rations. Get them into the galley, sorry, kitchen to you, and don't lose that beer or we'll dismember you!'

Thankful to be busy at last, she was only too glad to gather up picnic baskets, towels, odd clothing, cartons, and of course—beer. Already she knew what Australian beer meant to Australians. Actually, hurrying up and down the few steps connecting decking and cabin, she thoroughly enjoyed herself. Already she liked the slight, live movement of *Sunbolt* tugging at the jetty as though she wanted to be done with all this and away, skirring over the water. She loved the shine of woodwork and the neatness of slim-fitting bunks; the economy of planned space. On a sudden impulse she kicked off her shoes and stooped to put them out of the sight, then made her last trip out on to the smooth, sunlit boards in bare feet.

That also Richard did not miss. He smiled to himself as he and David cast off fore and aft, and *Sunbolt* slid away from the jetty like something released from bondage. As soon as they stood well away from land, a breeze sprang up to meet them. Richard gave the order to stop engines, the sails were bent and proudly *Sunbolt* came alive.

Sara was to remember that day for a long time: the feel of the wind battening itself against her face and throat, sweeping her hair back from her head until the roots were tugged; her toes scrabbling on the bare deck as it slipped away from her; the feel of her outstretched body in company with other stretched-out bodies as they lay back and looked up at the taut canvas straining against the sky and the few puffs of clouds. She was filled with a wild, exultant gladness that matched the tang of salt on her lips and the hiss of water being sucked along the bows beneath her.

Richard watched her covertly, knew how she felt and wished he did not know; knew that this quiet conventional English girl, who had so obviously lived a simple, unawakened kind of life, was being stirred in a way that could be dangerous. It occurred to him too late that it would have been better not to have asked her, or at least made sure she was accompanied by the self-confident, worldly young Italian. So he looked away and busied himself with *Sunbolt*, which was beginning to abandon itself to the stiffening wind as they approached South Arm.

Having a newcomer to educate, they told her how, past where they were now sailing, the two brilliant explorers, Cook and Bligh, had both missed the harbour entrance by sailing straight past it. They told her of the unfortunate young English Lieutenant Bowen who in 1803, with no superior officer to give him counsel, plus fear of the French whom he believed to be close on his heels, had gone ashore at Risdon Cove and, in the name of the British Empire, claimed the land and tried to begin a capital city out of canvas tents, mutinous sailors, suspicious natives and sulky convicts. They re-created for her the two and three-masted sailing ships which had come into this harbour carrying the vicious, the desperate, the sad and the hopeful, free settlers and convicts alike, until she had shivered in the warm sun and gladly joined in the first ration of beer for the day.

They anchored to dive off the deck, the cold water taking her breath as it had in England. Then they had swum ashore to where the men brought the luncheon baskets in the dinghy. The afternoon passed with laughter, radio music, eating and drinking, until she felt one with the bunch. The girls seemed to have lost their hostility and lay beside her in the sun while they talked of fashion, life in England and Australia, and the men talked yachting 'shop' or slept or wandered away.

She was more than sorry when the time came to pack up and start on the homeward run. But now the wind had dropped and the water had lost its life; *Sunbolt* floated rather than sailed. It was as though the spirit which had driven her in the morning had gone out to the open sea and left her to turn about and creep to the safety of home.

It was Sally, the younger of the two girls, who suggested rounding off the day with dancing at Wrest Point. For no reason at all Sara and Richard looked at each other, but it was she who looked away first.

The party took up the idea. Just what was needed after such a day. No one wanted to do mundane things like getting meals. Everyone wanted to carry the day into the night. So it was decided, and much to the chagrin of *Sunbolt*, her engines were started, her proud sails furled, and willy-nilly, slim and naked, she was driven home by petrol instead of wind.

Strangely, since it is not often one good experience can be extended to make an equally good second, the night became worthy of the day. Sara loved dancing and, knowing it to be one thing at which she excelled, relaxed completely, thereby losing any trace of self-consciousness. To her utter delight she found Richard too was a dancer. Without comment they went from modern to tango, to Latin dancing, until she was aware of being impatient at having to dance with the other members of the party. On the trip they had all merged together as part of the yacht. Here, alone with each other, there was the effort of obtaining a mutual topic they could both approach with the same understanding. With Richard it was different. They just danced, and in doing so both knew each satisfied the other; there was no need to force a conversation.

But suddenly in the middle of the one and only waltz of the evening, for which he had made sure of asking her, she knew she must come out of her dream and end this evening. In spite of herself she sighed; nothing could ever be perfect.

'What does that mean?'

'What?'

'The sigh.'

'Oh—well I was just thinking there is always a hitch in the most perfect experience, and today has been perfect.'

'What's the hitch in this case?'

She hesitated, then hurried on. 'Just that I'm more tired than I thought after my first day's yachting, and John's coming early in the morning.'

'So?'

'Would you mind taking me home? I must get some sleep.'

'Suppose I refuse?'

'Please, Richard.'

'You know, it's time you stopped calling me Richard. Everyone else calls me Rick.'

'It was Judith—she always called you Richard.'

'She belonged to the past. You don't.'

'I'll call you anything you like if you'll take me home. Or get me a taxi.'

He stopped dancing and led her by the hand back to their table just as the music ceased, and for no amount of clapping would the orchestra continue; it was time for their interval and beer.

As they drove out of the entrance to the hotel Richard said with a grin: 'So my dear Sara, you're a coward after all!'

'I'm not even going to try to answer that.'

'Yet it would be wiser if you did.'

'I'm not a very wise person. John could tell you that.'

'Does John have to come into everything with you?'

'He does. Now, here we are. Just put me down on this corner and you won't have to turn in the narrow street.'

'You're passing the buck again, Sara!'

She began to laugh. 'Rick, you're absurd.'

'On second thoughts I'd prefer you to call me Richard until I can educate you to pronounce Rick with the right sound.'

'All right, Richard-Rick, but just stop the car.'

'I always deliver my partners safely home.'

Again she sighed. 'Yes, it was a wonderful evening of dancing and I did love it. In fact,' she added hastily, 'the whole day was something I shall never forget. Goodnight and thank you.'

He did not answer but leant across and opened the door for her. For one moment she was very aware of that hard, strong body of his, then she heard the catch click under his fingers and saw the door moving outwards. She quickly swung her legs on to the road and drew her coat closely around her.

As she stood up she heard him say behind her: 'Take care of yourself, I'm still thinking of that boutique affair you girls were planning.'

'Oh, things are different now,' she replied hastily. 'I shall probably be going to John's camp to live.'

'I see.'

Then, with a wave of his hand he turned the car and roared up the road, shattering the peace of the houses behind their neat, dark gardens.

So Sara went to join John in a small, modern house on the dam site. But although it had everything a young couple could require, it was to her a foreign place. To begin with, she had never lived in a house on one floor in her life; it had not the shut-in feeling of a flat nor the spaciousness of a two-storey house; therefore she found it difficult to place in her awareness, and to Sara a house had to be placed. Then she had never before been faced with the everyday living of a close-knit working community; never been so close to other people's washing, or the problems of newborn garden plots whose unyielding soil was swept by hot winds; dust forcing its way through closed doors and windows; the sound of children crying, playing, squabbling; the sudden blare of radios.

It fascinated her and made her feel indescribably lonely at the same time. More than ever she felt she was on the outside looking in; everyone was so busy, so purposeful; everything, even if it was quarrelling, led to a reason, and the reason was intrinsically family. Always, always the vicious circle. These people had to be busy because they were caught up in the whirl of creation. If *she* wanted to be busy she had to look for things that really had nothing to do with her being, things that were man-made—pottery classes, play-readings, sewing circles, penguin clubs; they were all time-fillers, excellent ways of getting through life. She had no personal contribution to make, and sometimes it appalled her when she looked along the road ahead—the mundane tramping through life, mechanically doing the everyday things that fed the body to keep it alive and enabled herself and John to live up to a common social code.

More and more she worried over the problem as the time allotted to them slipped away, until she faced the fact that it was something she and John must sort out together. Her chance came one evening when he arrived back very late from work. She was just beginning to worry that something unforeseen had happened, when she heard the car being swung round the back of the house, while a scatter of loose pebbles hit the foundations.

Relieved, she pushed open the swing door on to the back verandah and called down to him: 'I was beginning to worry.'

'Never do that. If anything was wrong you'd have heard hours ago.'

He smiled up at her as he came up the steps, and not for the first time she thought how different he looked—happier, fitter. A pang of envy went through her.

'I suppose so.'

He put one arm round her while he opened the door again with the other. 'You're just not used to having a bushman for a husband yet. That's a good smell! I could eat a horse.'

'It'll be ready by the time you've had a shower.'

Presently, through the splashing of the water, he shouted out to her: 'I don't think we'll be able to get our own house for quite a while.'

'Why?'

'Oh, usual reasons—all the present ones are full, the building programme's behind time; then of course this is only a temporary job for me, and we didn't help by refusing the original house.'

'I see.' She went on stirring the gravy, not sure whether she was glad or sorry, ashamed of her own attitude.

He came and stood in the kitchen doorway, towelling the back of his hair. 'Not to worry. We'll solve it somehow.'

It was then, as he went into the bedroom to get his clothes, that the idea came to her, at least the beginning of the idea. Thoughts flew into her head with exciting suggestions, not all of them linked up; some were ridiculously impractical, but in an amazingly short space of time they were beginning to present a picture. They were so intriguing that she was only brought back to a sense of reality by the vegetables boiling over.

'You needn't have speeded things up that much,' he said from the doorway. 'Half a jiffy, I'll wipe it up for you.'

Putting the dishes in front of him at the table, she said almost breathlessly: 'While you were changing I had a sudden idea.'

'Is that why the vegetables boiled over?'

'Could have been, but just listen. If it's going to be quite a while till we can get a house, why don't we buy one of our own in Hobart, as a headquarters? It would give us a feeling of belonging, something of our own.'

The words were eager, tumbling over themselves to be said, and he considered them as he carved the meat.

She sat down, facing him. 'There's the money from "Little Compton" (later she realised she had referred without a pang to the eighteenth-century cottage on the edge of the Surrey common) and you know Granny gave me that cheque for £2,000. If we were clever about it, it could be an investment, you know.'

'It could be,' he said slowly, handing her her plate.

'And there's another thing. Before Judith died, Arna and I talked about doing something together. You know, she's at a bit of a loose end like me—that is, neither of us has anything to do really; let's face it, I'm not much good to you if we can't get a house together.'

He made a sound like agreement and she rushed on again before he could make a further comment. 'Well, she'd like to start a really modern sort of boutique, and I could do the décor and the designing. All we'd have to do is find some quaint old cottage in a side street in a good area. It would be such marvellous fun, something to stop me being lonely when I can't be with you, and at the same time it would be our home, and you could come up every weekend.'

He looked at her excited face, the light in her eyes that he hadn't seen for a long time, and he knew that her fingers were tight-gripped under the table.

'Don't tell me,' he said, 'that all this transpired as you made the gravy!'

For a moment the tension was relieved.

'Yes and no. We had talked quite a lot about it. Then Judith's death and coming up here put it out of my mind. It was when you said we probably wouldn't get a Commission house for quite a long time that it came back.'

'Flooding back by the sound of it!'

She realised that she was almost trembling in her excitement and longed for him to agree, but something warned her to keep quiet for the moment, to let him digest in his own way the overlarge project she had flung at him suddenly.

Bit by bit his methodical mind considered what she had said, saw at once problems she would not even think existed. At the same time he saw that a mistaken decision on his part would be disastrous, not only financially but also for their personal relationship. He was well aware of her boredom in this outback existence, that there was little to do to fill her time and that eventually it would affect his own work if he were always conscious of her discontent.

At last he said: 'Apart from the idea of buying a house in Hobart as our headquarters—it's a good one—what do you two girls know of business, of handling stock, buying and selling? You and I might finance the house, but we would be hard put to it to stock a boutique. What has Arna to put into the venture?'

'We hadn't got that far,' she confessed, 'but we did talk it over with Richard.'

'Oh.'

She found herself hurrying in her speech again as she gave him an edited account of the luncheon conversation on the day Judith died. She was a little shocked to realise she was editing it, making it sound very casual, an ordinary conversation in which three people had discussed a commercial proposition quite by chance.

'And did you actually suggest he should put money into such a venture?'

'Heavens no! But I'm sure he would.'

'Why?'

'Oh, come to think of it, Arna did mention there would be the problem of finance, and he said there were ways.'

'There always are—of a sort.'

She got up then and went to make the coffee, talking over her shoulder. 'I don't think he meant anything shady. After all, he needn't resort to that. Both he and his father must be pretty wealthy. I hate to think what that yacht of his cost. Nothing is being spared to give it every chance of winning this Sydney to Hobart race.'

He forbore to point out that two wealthy men might be determined to pour money into what was a life-long ambition, but would think very differently about financing two inexperienced young women in such a doubtful venture as a boutique, unless—suddenly the exotic figure and face of Arna floated in front of him. Yes, that picture could be enough to inspire a man such as Richard to put money into a boutique. Whether it succeeded or failed it would be well worth the price. Half his luck! Almost with a start at his own thoughts, which gave him a distinct feeling of guilt, he too got up from the table.

'Did you say something?' Sara asked eagerly as she came through the door with the coffee tray.

'No, but I'm about to—I can't see that a few careful enquiries would do any harm. As you say, a headquarters for us could be a good idea.'

'Oh, John!' The joy in her voice made him feel good. 'And the boutique?'

'That I feel could be another matter, but there again, there's no harm in enquiring.'

So the evening turned into an exciting one. By the end of it John had even caught some of her enthusiasm, and that night Sara went to bed happier than she had been for many months, which brought them closer than they had been for a long time.

The next morning Sara went in search of writing paper and envelopes to write to Arna to tell her the good news, and say that they hoped to come up for the weekend. In doing so she came across the leather-bound journal belonging to the other Sarah. The fact that she had only now remembered it gave her a shock. How could she have forgotten? The memory of that last evening with Judith came flooding back to her. The strange tale the old lady had told her, and the almost prophetic manner in which she had linked the fascinating convict of 1826 and herself, made her forget everything, even the letter to Arna, in her desire to discover what these old pages could reveal; above all to discover any connection between Sarah and herself.

Going out to the kitchen she switched on the kettle to make herself a cup of coffee, and presently, carrying it and the journal tucked under her arm, went out to sit on the back steps in the sun.

For a moment she sat there, savouring the moments of anticipation, recalling the portrait over the study fireplace of the woman with the Titian hair, the beautiful hand that so disdainfully swept aside the long blue frock, and the eyes that followed, whoever looked at them, from every angle of the room. Remembered too how Judith had been afraid for her, the Sara of the twentieth century. Why?

Very carefully she put down the cup of coffee, and laid the journal across her knee. And as she turned back the leather cover she was aware of a sense of excitement such as had not often stirred her.

CHAPTER SIX

'Ardrossan'
In the Colony of —
Van Diemen's Land,
In the year of our Lord, 1827.

To:
  The Lady Anne
    Deerbrook Park,
      Somerset,
        England.

My dear Sister,
   Yes, I have now no fear of addressing you in such a manner, now that we know our true relationship and I shall be of no further embarrassment to you. That we shall ever meet again is more than unlikely — you who live at the heights of society, I who have fallen to its depths. Yet I write this Journal for you and you alone, with no sense of disgrace nor self-pity. Our childhood together, the beginning of our youth, will ever be my inspiration, now that I must follow the strange, exciting path of my womanhood alone, with courage, ruthlessness and determination.
   I will admit to you that at the time of the trial and my final interview with His Lordship I was so embittered I wished

only for death, yet those dreadful hours have passed and I would have him know he has my gratitude.

Through his perhaps understandable belief in the lies of Mrs Turner (the Devil rot her soul) that I stole your jewels (as if I would as much as steal the combings of your hair!) he sanctioned my entrance into a new and amazing world, albeit a hard one; but my dear sister, it is a challenge I would never have known in your service, dearly as I valued you.

True, for weeks I lay in that rotting barge in the Thames and cursed you all. Cursed the cruel fate that made my Mother, poor honest gentle fool, fall prey to His Lordship's charm, so thrusting me into a world in which I could have no place. Being of his blood, I was contemptuous of the scum around me in that noisome place. Being of hers, I must face them and it or cease to exist. Thus I believe the mixture of these two bloods will give me the strength with which to survive this existence of crime and adventure into which I find myself pushed.

Enough of moralising! This Journal is to relate to you all that befalls me. Before God, I shall endeavour to be honest in these pages. I shall not lie, no matter how bitter the truth.

As you know, on the 29th day of August, 1826, I was sentenced by Justice Goff to transportation — the death penalty commuted by the good offices of our joint Father. He came to see me in my cell. I can see him now: his broadcloth and cape, perfect with the perfection of material and tailoring, stood out as untouchable even in the dim light of that evil place.

He told me he was disappointed in me, that he had striven to keep his promise to my mother to have me brought up in his household, even allowed me to be taught my letters, that because of my wickedness he should really have allowed me to go to the gallows, but seeing that I was my Mother's daughter and passing young, out of his regard for human nature he had done all in his power to get my sentence commuted to transportation.

How I hated him as he stood there, balancing his malacca walking cane in his gloved fingers. How I sensed his relief at getting rid of an obligation, of being able to put the world between him and me, a scandal of his own making that would be buried in an unknown country.

Doubtless he thought, as I stood there in front of him with bowed head above my prison-soiled garments, that I was overcome with shame. Little did he know of the murder in my heart; of the already strongly formed, though seemingly hopeless notion, to make him regret what he was doing. To take my shame and make it his. At that moment, did he but know it, his blood was truly mine!

I was then removed to the barge floating on the Thames with its load of miserable human beings, to await the sailing of the Elderburn to Van Diemen's Land. To my dying day I shall remember the smell of dirty bodies, dirty clothes and stale urine. Remember the shabby, mean little tricks of humanity on the run. They were not loyal, even to themselves, and would not hesitate to steal the remaining crusts from their starving, so-called friends.

I made one friend in the darkness of that gently rocking den of thieves and vice — a prostitute. You see, I have learnt a word never taught to us at 'Deerbrook'. Yet it signifies to me someone who has taught me much in the way of ordinary common living, someone who knows better than any of us the ways of the human mind and heart. It was she who gave me the courage to lift my head again, to plan how to live and fight.

So much so that when the day came, a grey cold day with biting winds, that I climbed aboard the Elderburn (clutching my cloak about me with one hand and in the other a basket containing the few clothes and personal belongings I had been allowed and had managed to keep reasonably clean), I had already planned my course for the future and had become calm with the calmness of resolution.

I stood on that deck in company with my fellow convicts waiting to be marshalled to our quarters, and watched the confusion of loading going on around us, accompanied by the swearing of the sailors, the frightened bleating of sheep and squeals of pigs, to say nothing of the shambling cows being beaten and pushed aboard. I looked up too at the spars, rigging and great furled sails, and knew there was not a soul in the world (save perhaps you who are powerless) who cared whether I lived or died, failed or succeeded, that I would do anything I could get away with, that I had fallen so low nothing was now expected of me save that I remain within the letter of the law. It was a sobering, challenging thought. For the first time I was proud of the noble blood that ran in my veins, and resolved it should prove itself along the way ahead.

'Move on there, me Redhead,' one of the men shouted, 'there'll be other ways for you to pose!'

His remark was greeted by coarse laughter and other comments among themselves, which though I could not hear, were easy enough to guess. Already in these months I had learned men were basic in their relations with women.

I felt annoyance, contempt and pity so equally that these men and their remarks were as nothing to me; I would have stared them out of countenance had my eyes not discovered the presence of a man standing alone, watching the scene as I watched it. A man who wore the uniform of a ship's officer.

I guessed him to be the captain by the air of authority about him and the fact that, among the activity of all about, he alone stood still. For a moment our eyes met before I was hustled below decks in our long, untidy line, necessarily slow as many of the male prisoners were in chains. The expression in his eyes was so obvious, I was fully prepared for the summons that came later that night when the Elderburn had spread her sails to the chanting of the sailors and the pressure of a strong westerly driving her down the Thames.

They took me to his cabin along the narrow companionway, where already it was difficult to walk as the creaking ship raced down the river. I could hear the night wind singing in the canvas, and it answered a wild surging in me. I could have wished this passage was not one of shame. I wanted to go out on the decks free as that wayward wind, free to adventure as I pleased. I knew what it was to envy one's right to travel unhindered when and where one pleased.

They threw me through the cabin door, so violently that the raised step across its entrance nearly tripped me. As it was I fell across his desk, and it took me some seconds before I could stand upright before him with dignity. Then, as I brushed the hair from my eyes, I saw he was leaning against a porthole, his hands clasped behind his back. He had removed his braided jacket and I could not but see he was a fine figure of a man.

Suddenly he flicked his fingers at the men who had held me, and they backed out hurriedly, closing the door. He came and walked round me as one would when selecting an animal in the market place.

'They tell me you have the name of Sarah?'

'That is so, sir.'

'And a history to go with the name.'

I did not answer until I saw more clearly where his conversation was leading.

'Well, come, what say you? I'd not think your tongue is lacking — never knew a quiet redhead yet.'

'That depends, sir, on what you would call a history.'

'Do not trifle with me, Sarah. We have a long journey ahead.'

He stood in front of me straddling his legs, his hands still linked behind him. I believed suddenly that had we met in different circumstances he could have been a kind man.

'What, sir, would you have me tell you? That I am my Father's natural daughter, and that he feels a heaven-sent opportunity has arisen to rid him of me?'

'And of course, you would have me believe you innocent of any crime?'

I did not answer.

He crossed the cabin, opened a cupboard and took out a whisky bottle, pulling the cork with his teeth as he returned, this time to sit astride the corner of the desk.

'I have just told you I expect my questions answered.'

'I can see little point in answering, sir, since whatever I say you will condemn as lies.'

'A female who argues! Detestable! Have you any idea why I had you brought here?'

'Perhaps, sir.'

'Well, I shall tell you. Do you know what happens to women aboard a convict ship?'

'No, sir.'

'Each and every one is selected by a sailor as his "wife" for the duration of the voyage. Selection of course begins with me, the others in order of rank. You had the only clean looking head of the noisome bunch coming aboard.'

As I watched him upending that bottle and sucking from it, for all the world like a calf from a teat, I felt all the blood in my body surging in revolt. You know, dear sister, my temper was ever my trouble. So, before I could think what I was about I picked up a ruler lying on the desk and struck at his face. Unfortunately his reactions were too fast, and without moving the bottle from his lips his other hand grasped my wrist in mid-air with a grip of steel. There we remained until he had had his fill of whisky, when he put down the bottle and let go my wrist.

'Your coloured hair always signifies a difficult woman, but, as I said earlier, your head is unusually clean, the only clean one. Get into the inner cabin, make up the bunk and don't let me see you put foot out of there until I give you leave.'

So it began, that long and arduous trip. When I think of it it seems like an impossible dream. Yet where would I have heard such things as these to compound even a dream, had I not experienced them?

When he discovered that I was indeed a virgin it pleased him not at all. He would have made me the butt of his unbridled temper and foul-mouthed vocabulary had I not withdrawn into my coldest mood, closed my ears while my whole being was filled with the most bitter humiliation and misery. I knew that I was enraging him further but cared not at all. What did it matter?

Then he was gone, and in spite of everything, I fell asleep in the bunk; it still amazes me when I remember that sudden deep sleep from which I was awakened by broad daylight, the violent movements of the ship and a small cabin boy who didn't seem either suprised or embarrassed by my presence. I realise of course that he must be quite used to such a scene, so drawing the scanty blankets around myself I accepted the dry bread and mess of gruel he handed me.

Jerking a dirty thumb over his shoulder he said in a friendly fashion: ''E's gawn! Right proper mood 'e's in!'

I made no comment but tried to swallow some of the bread. 'What's your name?' I asked at last, since his main contribution to domestic duties was kicking his foot aimlessly against the chairs and cases.

'They call me Nobs. S'cuse me, Miss, but I ain't never seen 'air like yours.'

The reference to my hair was an unfortunate one. I pushed the plate at him and said sharply: 'Now, you get about your work, Nobs. These two rooms or whatever you call them are a disgrace. You get started next door while I dress, then I'll help you.'

'Don't you feel seasick, Miss?'

'No, of course I don't. Off you go.'

'But I was awful sick the first time I went to sea.'

'Well, that was you, not me.'

He lurched his way through the doorway, staring at me over his shoulder as though I were some kind of exhibit, then he was gone, shutting the door forcibly behind him. I got out of the bunk as well as I could against the shifting floor, and somehow managed to get clothed.

For eternity itself it seemed Elderburn fought the elements. Day after day, night after night she careened, rolled and leapt as though she were on thousands of springs. Water poured over her and each time I felt her shuddering frame being thrust down under the weight of the waves I felt her agony in my own body, but there was no fear in me.

I counted the interminable time before my "husband" returned, then it was with such a growth of beard on his face that I hardly recognised him. He came into the cabin as though he did not expect to find me, indeed as though I had never been. Almost I felt it incumbent on me to explain my presence. As on that other occasion, he threw aside his braided jacket and opened the cupboard where he kept the all-important bottle.

I wondered if I might find my way to the door unnoticed. I was curious to see how my fellow convicts had weathered such a storm, and indeed how the poor animals had fared. But I was wrong in thinking he had not noticed my presence. Although his back was turned he removed the bottle from his lips long enough to say: 'I have already told you not to leave this cabin without my permission!'

'Now the ship has quietened I would greatly like to walk in the fresh air.'

'I've no doubt you would.'

'Then — '

'No!'

I decided not to degrade myself by arguing with him, but turned back to the inner cabin. To remain in silence watching the steady emptying of that bottle was more than I could bear. Also, I realised instinctively that silent contempt impressed him far more than words, and indeed in a few days time I did receive permission to go out on the quarter deck. This was relayed to me by the First Mate, a Mr Ronson by name, together with a warning not to take any liberties. 'A strange man, the Captain,' he said. 'No finer sailor put to sea, but he'll not brook opposition. Not that I blames him, with a crew like this.'

'What do you mean by that, Mr Ronson?'

'I mean, they've only signed on to get to the other end, then they'll desert like rats. Half of them don't know the difference between a mainsail and a jib. A free passage, that's what they want, to a new life...'

I searched his wrinkled, weathered face, the grizzled hair sticking out in thick tufts under his seaman's cap.

'And is it, Mr Ronson?'

'Could be for the likes of them what has some money put by, I s'pose. I don't fancy putting up with bushrangers and them murderin' blacks. And clearing bush doesn't appeal to me neither. I'd rather splice the mainbrace.'

'What's that?'

'Grog up — rum. Now don't ask no more questions, I've got to get up on watch. And don't go no farther than here.'

'I won't, Mr Ronson.'

As he walked away in his leaning, shambling way I held up my face to the wind and the scudding clouds, and noticed a huge white bird which I was later to discover was an albatross, seemingly bound by an unseen line behind and above the ship. It fascinated me as presently I watched it change direction with a long, low dive, its wings taut and strong. I felt clean, free, strangely at peace.

But within the next few weeks I knew there was little peace in that ship. I was cursorily ordered by "my husband" to go to the ship's doctor. Just the brief command, no explanation. Dearly I would have liked to ask for what reason, yet at the same time I was half afraid of the reply. Nor would I sacrifice my pride to ask. Better to go forward in ignorance of whatever trial awaited me. So with a beating heart, and head carried as high as I could contrive, I followed the talkative Nobs down narrow ladders and along foul-smelling, creaking, lamp-lit corridors into the very bowels of the ship. My stomach retched and twisted, yet with all that was in me I bid it be quiet. At last we stepped into the somewhat cleaner domain of the surgery.

In the outer cabin men and women were packed, and the smell was indescribable. Through a doorway I could see the doctor working, his shirt sleeves rolled above his elbows.

I went into him, but he seemed not to see me. At last I went close to him and said: 'The Captain sent me.'

He moved then, looked up at me in a short-sighted kind of way, and I saw he was working on a child — a child so emaciated and covered in running sores that I felt sick and faint.

'Sending you is one thing, whether you're any use to me is another.'

'I can try, sir.'

So began the long days and nights — time was not. I became so weary that I almost wished I too could be ill so that I could have the legitimate excuse to lie down and sleep. All fresh food had gone, and most of the water. Half the cows and goats had been washed overboard during the first storm, so that there was practically no milk for the children; there was little else save salt pork and gruel, and a fear that too would run out before we reached the South American coast. Dysentery became rampant; indeed there was scarcely one who was not affected, including myself. Soon after leaving Rio the much dreaded scurvy raised its head. The Captain may have been a good sailor, but he was far behind others in dealing with that scourge of the sea. I had learnt, as did you my sister, that sailors like Cook and Bligh had learnt to eliminate it forty or fifty years ago. The secret lay in fresh fruit and vegetables and here my education paid off. When we re-victualled in Rio I begged my "husband" for some oranges and vegetables, which I got, but he — a so-called fine sailor — did not understand why. Thus, while most of the convicts and not a few of the crew succumbed to the disease, I, aided by my knowledge and a good constitution, remained free of it.

Being of natural good health and strength I grew used to my daily labours, even grew proud of my work and that I had been chosen to do it. Proud of the way in which I could come and go unmolested. There was not one amongst them would dare to lay a finger on the Captain's woman.

Of him I saw little for weeks. At night when I returned to his quarters he was either sprawled drunk across the desk, or was on the quarter deck. He knew only these things: the command of his ship, his whisky bottle, and me at his beck and call. Yet when we were becalmed he gave us hope, and when hungry, he promised us food. We believed him, even though our common sense warned us we were running out of time.

But everything, dear sister, must come to an end, so after a week or so re-victualling at Cape Town, nearly seven months later we swept up the great neck of water known as the Derwent. It was early in December, summer in Van Diemen's Land. We glided up the channel in hot sunshine, a full breeze holding out our canvas; and so I had my first sight of this country I have come to call my own.

Mr Ronson found time to point out the trees growing thickly right down to the sandy beaches we were passing.

'There's your first eucalyptus,' he said; 'you can smell them from here.'

And so I could.

My "husband" too came and stood for a moment beside me, let me look through his telescope at the densely packed trees.

'That's it, Sarah, the land of convicts and opportunity. It's up to you from now on.'

'Will I have any choice?'

'It will all depend on how you handle your first assignment — you will be an assigned servant of course.'

'To what kind of people?' I lowered the long cumbersome instrument he had given me, leant on the rail and looked up at his powerful shoulders and frame, his hands as usual clasped behind his back, his eyes with speculative expression watching the land and water slide by. I wondered what his wife was like, if she could at all visualise him as he was when he was away from her like this. Did she know the life he lived — guess at the women he took to himself as his right?

There are families who come out here because their investments are failing in England, therefore they are unable to live in the style to which they are used. Providing they have still some capital left, or hold military rank, the British Government will give them free grants of land. Big grants too, a thousand acres or more. Clever when you think of it, getting ambitious people to provide food on the spot for a community of prisoners. But to these settlers it is a chance to make something of their lives, to have the voice of authority again, because they believe they will have no moneyed opposition. So they can mould a society and rule it at far less cost than in England.'

'You are cynical, sir.'

'Life is a cynical affair, Sarah.'

'And you propose I be a good girl and serve one of these families for the rest of my life — become a family retainer?'

He leant one elbow on the railing and smiled down at me. I could not recall having seen him smile before.

'All I have seen of you on this journey, Sarah, does not lead me to suppose that you will fall into any recognised pattern. I merely suggest you use your wits, control your temper, and I have no doubt that at some stage in your career you will manage to persuade someone that you are a wronged and innocent woman. Get a remission of your sentence and this is a new land with new ideas, new values — the rest is up to you. With this in mind I am sending a note ashore concerning you. Some years ago, I brought out several families of settlers with all their possessions. There is one family I am thinking of in particular, the Rolands. They acquired a very large grant of land and I believe are doing very well in some remote area. As I remember her, Mrs Roland could do with someone such as yourself. I am recommending that you be sent to them, that is if they care to take up your assignment.'

I swept him a curtsy, I could do no less. My heart began to pound with hope. How easily can one be swept to the heights, dear sister.

'You are more than kind, sir.'

'Not kind, Sarah; let us say I have an uncomfortable conscience and I am not a man who likes to be uncomfortable in any way. The manner in which I live in this ship is my just due for the years I traverse the seas and fight them. The women I pick to share my cabin are as necessary to me as my bottle of whisky. I believe for such women I am equally necessary. There would be mutiny on these ships if there were any other laws. But you were unexpected. I have no truck with virgins, even hot-tempered scheming ones, as you indeed are, my dear. I regret what I did where you are concerned; this is the only way of repaying you in some slight measure. It's up to you, as I said, to make the best of what comes your way. You will remain on the ship until such time as Roland finds it convenient to interview you.'

I could not speak for I would not have him know how near I was to tears. So he strode away and I did not see him again, except in the distance where he stood on the quarterdeck watching the convicts being herded ashore and *into bullock drays, which for all the world looked much as I imagined tumbrils would have looked going to the French guillotine...'*

Sara became aware of banging on the front door and, putting aside the journal, went to open it. Outside the postman was standing, wiping his hot forehead. He put away a none-too-clean handkerchief and handed her a registered parcel and several letters. One she saw was from her mother; the other in a large, artistic hand she did not recognise, but instinctively felt might be from Arna.

CHAPTER SEVEN

The letter was indeed from Arna. An Arna at a loose end, discontented and not sure she wanted to stay in Australia, and to make it worse, not sure she really wanted to go back to her old life. 'But for Rick,' she finished, 'I think I would not be at all happy. I hope that you too will soon come out of this "bush". Now that the casino is up and running you will see our "boutique" would have been just right for the new spirit moving in the town...'

Yes, Sara thought, as she put down the letter, little did Arna know it, but the boutique was alive again. Yes, it would fit in with the casino. Poor little Miss Judith had been so indignant about it. 'It will bring us quite the wrong tourist,' she had said with tight-shut lips. But like Arna, Sara thought it was bringing just the right tourist for the boutique they had planned; would in fact give it real commercial value.

Almost, Fate seemed to be on their side.

All the week she could hardly contain herself as she made the house ready to receive back its rightful owners; packed, made sure all John's clothes were washed, ironed and mended. And occasionally Arna's written words danced in front of her eyes: 'But for Rick I think I would not be at all happy.' So it was Rick, now, no longer Richard.

With a pang, for which she was in no way prepared, Sara wondered how much more had been broken down than the name. Suddenly she realised she was jealous. To keep her mind away from the nagging questions which persisted, she returned to the journal as soon as her everyday chores were finished. She was anxious to immerse herself in a world long since dead, to discover how, with every code of society against her, this other Sarah dealt with the problem of freeing herself to live the life she was determined to have. So she leafed back the pages to where she had left Sarah standing on the

Elderburn watching the departure of her fellow convicts after their long journey together.

And so, dear sister, I wondered greatly what manner of family this was to whom the Captain had done his best to assign me. That he would keep his word I never doubted. He would not tell me of such a scheme did he not intend to carry it out. However, a week passed and my captivity was more irksome than the many weary months of the journey itself. Particularly as I was now completely confined to the cabin, in the sole charge of Mr Ronson, whose business it was to see the ship was made ready and provisioned for her return journey to England.

There were no more walks on deck, and the slow-moving hours seemed unending. Suppose the Captain had been unable to contact the family of whom he had spoken? Suppose that even though he had they now had no need of me? He had said that I must be assigned to someone, of course, but in speaking of this family he had managed to convey to me that they were both wealthy and of good standing. For my future plans it was necessary to be attached to just such people.

So my impatience grew exceedingly, and I became tired of my limited view of Hobart Town through the cabin porthole, which consisted of what I had been told was St David's church, and behind it the towering blue mass of wooded mountain. But apart from this and the great river on which we were anchored, the wharf itself and some slight movement behind it of horsemen in the distance, there was nothing.

Also, since the ship was no longer moving there was no fresh air in the cabin, bringing back memories of the becalmed, waterless days of the tropical period of our journey, when children first screamed for water, then became too weak to make any sound as they slipped into unconsciousness. Cattle had died and been flung to waiting sharks, and I had seen in the eyes of many men that it was only the grim picture of the dead cattle being seized upon by those scavengers of the deep that kept them too from springing down into the tantalising world of translucent water.

But at last, on one glorious summer morning that made my whole body long to explore, and had kept me over-long at the porthole, I saw approaching along the shore towards the wharf an exceedingly handsome pair of greys, drawing a carriage of passing good style for a country such as this. Indeed I had not thought to see such evidence of good taste and breeding. My heart-beat quickened, I knew, indeed I felt sure the figures I could see in glimpses through the carriage windows were those of the people to whom the Captain had suggested I should be assigned. At least I was to be interviewed!

Quickly I scrambled down from the porthole and made haste to smooth my hair and make tidy my person so that I should be as composed and as ready as possible when I was sent for. Nor was I wrong. I did not have long to wait before Mr Ronson appeared.

'They've come to look you over,' he said, 'those gentry what his Nibs brought out. You just mind your manners, my girl, they look right and proper folks. Those greys of theirs 'ud cost a pretty penny; maybe there's something in settlin' roun' these parts after all.'

I swept in front of him without a word. I needed no instruction from such as he how to present myself to my future employers.

I felt like running, so gay was my heart, so eager was I to take hold with both hands of this new life stretching out before me. But you will be glad to know I controlled my deportment both in the boat while Mr Ronson rowed me ashore, and when I climbed on to the wharf. Oh, how good it was to be standing on dry land once more.

Mr Ronson had taken off his cap and tucked it under his arm, thereby disclosing his thick thatch of grey, stringy hair, and walking decorously behind him I could sense his great discomfiture. Round his back I could observe that one of the biggest men I had ever seen had got out of the carriage, and was watching our approach.

'Your Honour,' said Mr Ronson, 'this be the girl I was told to bring 'e.'

I thought he would never stand aside, so anxious was he to take in all details of the carriage and its occupants. But at last he made a half gesture towards me, and I took the opportunity to make one of my best curtsies. When I arose from it I saw the big man was in front of me and I was more than ever aware of his size.

'You are Sarah,' he said, with such authority that had that not been my name at the present it would have been henceforth.

'I am, sir,' I replied.

'My wife will speak with you.'

He opened the carriage door still wider and I moved forward until I could see a lady was seated in its dim interior. Once again I curtsied and waited. I now had a full view of my future mistress. She was a small, round person, tightly laced into voluminous skirts, her hands hidden in a silken muff on her knee. But as I raised my eyes I saw that her face was soft and gentle under her bonnet, belying the fashion of her dress. She gave more the impression of nervousness than ease, also that she was very aware of her husband's presence, which I could feel rather than see behind me.

'You will be Sarah,' she said, and her voice, like her eyes, was soft and gentle.

'She has already told us so, my love,' her husband replied for me.

'Yes, of course. The Captain — that is Captain Norton, tells us you comported yourself well on the journey from England. What experience have you in domestic matters?'

'A fair experience, Madam, and willing to learn further.'

'And what, to you, young woman,' the voice behind me said, 'constitutes a "fair experience"?'

I made a quick decision. Even if I stretched the truth a little, it was better at this stage that I impressed the Master than the Mistress. Without looking in his direction I replied: 'Not only am I a fully trained lady's maid and companion to my mistress, the Lady Anne, daughter of the Earl of Bede, but I also received further training in the care and housekeeping of a nobleman's residence.'

'Which apparently did not include the lesson of loyalty!'

Keeping my eyes still unflinchingly on Madam I held my silence, but was aware this interruption greatly embarrassed her. This mistress should not prove difficult to handle. Her husband was another matter. He would need very special study.

Clutching firmly with heavily ringed fingers on the silken muff, she said with sudden determination: 'Please, Matthew, I should like to speak alone with Sarah for a moment.'

I was greatly surprised, and wondered if after all I had cast my future mistress in too weak a role.

'My dear, I can give you just ten minutes. We must be then on our way to Woolley's for luncheon.'

'Ten minutes will be sufficient, Matthew.'

Whereupon he turned away, and out of the corner of my eye I saw him saunter down the wharf, apparently giving his full attention to the Elderburn.

I waited, knowing instinctively Madam was desperately afraid of taking into her home a woman born out of wedlock and transported from England as a thief. For it was obvious from her husband's previous remark that the Captain had at least given them the bare details of my plight. At the same time the fact that I had been in a nobleman's home was a great temptation for her to acquire me, in spite of the fact she knew what the consequences could be were I truly what I was supposed to be.

Were I not so determined to enter her household, I could have felt it in me to be sorry for her.

She interrupted my train of thought to say: 'The Captain has told us of your — er — unfortunate story.'

'Yes, Madam, he would naturally do so.'

'I — I believe, Sarah, he thought you innocent.'

So I was right! Curiosity and the love of prestige had both combined to make her persuade her husband to bring her here today.

'Madam,' I said, with as much sincerity as I could put into my voice, 'I would give much to bring you to the same belief as the Captain.'

Then, before my eyes she became a child, a grown-up child. Withdrawing her plump hands from the muff, she made as though to clap them, only remembering in time to clasp them instead upon her lap, and her eyes, amidst their premature wrinkles, smiled with the spontaneous delight of the very young.

'I do believe you shall, Sarah. I am sure of it, in fact. Mr Roland will agree with me in time. We will not keep him longer. Can you see him on the wharf?'

Upon assuring her that he had already turned back towards us, she hastened on: 'We had to dine with the Lieutenant Governor last night, Governor Arthur, you know. Such a fine military gentleman. So we decided to make this our annual trip for stores, and send the bullock drays ahead, with our cattle man, James. Will you kindly go and tell my husband to come? There is no need to delay him longer. There is so much to do, so many calls to make. He gets quite impatient, you know.'

'I will go at once, Madam.'

'Oh, and Sarah —'

'Yes, Madam?'

'Be ready to accompany James and his wife when they call for you at five o'clock tomorrow morning. It takes the bullock drays four days to reach Ardrossan, our property. I am sure I shall be able to persuade Mr Roland to take up your assignment.'

'Thank you, Madam.'

I swept her a curtsy and walked with all my dignity towards the man who was now impatiently pacing along the wharf towards me. I had won my first battle.

That night I went early to bed in the airless cabin, and slept long and peacefully, the first time for many months. I wakened early as the first light crept through the porthole, and the immediate realisation gripped me that this was the first day of my next, perhaps greatest adventure.

I knelt on the bunk to look out, and there, sure enough, in the grey light of the early morning I could see the bullock drays coming slowly on to the wharf. I dressed hastily, gathered my few belongings into the wicker basket, and waited for Mr Ronson's summons. I am afraid that when he rowed me ashore my mind was so full of the excitements ahead that my remarks to him were of the briefest. A circumstance which afterwards disturbed my conscience not a little. In his own way he had been kind to me.

When we clambered on to the wharf I saw that there were two drays, both piled high to their covers. On the driving seat of the first were the cattle man and his wife. The second was driven by a much younger man who, I could not help noticing, eyed me covertly.

'Morning,' Mr James said. 'I take it you're Sarah.'

I said good morning to them both, and with Mr Ronson's help I soon established myself and my wicker basket among the banked-up bags of stores and produce. A word of thanks and goodbye to Mr Ronson and we were off, Mr James calling to the slow and lumbering beasts.

Mrs James, I could see at once, was not of a talkative disposition and I could sense hostility to my addition to the staff by the way she settled herself more firmly beside her husband, and kept her eyes determinedly on the road ahead. This did not worry me; I had grown used to contempt.

Besides, there were so many things to see and think about that these two human beings as yet did not exist for me.

Indeed, the next four days will not readily leave my memory. First, Hobart Town, and one last glimpse of the bare spars and masts of the Elderburn as she lay black and strangely deserted down in the harbour. I found that some of me was with her still. To begin with she had seemed like something out of Hell, yet on her I had learnt many lessons, discovered many things about life and people.

With a sigh I turned to look about me. Doubtless, if household stores were only obtained once a year, this might well be my first and last journey through Hobart Town for a very long time. It was a much more pleasant place than I had dared to hope. Up to date I had thought of it as a penal town, its main activities divided between those who served and those whose business it was to see they served, but I was delighted to see pretty cottages and gardens spaced commodiously among trees. Mostly they were built of wood and were of one storey, though there were also some built of soft golden stone. There were well set-out, if muddy, streets, along which tree stumps still remained. As for shops, there were a fair number, mainly ship's chandlers and saddlers as well as some general stores, but there were also some hatters and clothiers. These would appear to indicate that somewhere there must be a community of cultured society.

There were few abroad at this hour, only a small number of well-dressed gentlemen returning from some party that had obviously gone on until the small hours, and as the first sun broke across the harbour and splashed the grey clouds resting on the towering mountain and its foothills, I twisted round the side of the dray to stare up at it in wonder.

'You have a passing pretty town, Mr James,' I could not help remarking.

'Maybe, for those what's eyes to look, without minds to wonder.'

But I was in no mood to have moralising interfere with my new-found content.

'Then please tell me something of where we are going,' I said.

'There's not a deal to tell. We'll plod on like this through the bush for three days, and pull in on the fourth, God willing.'

He tipped his cap to the Almighty and flicked the leading bullock with the extreme tip of his whip. 'Get on there, Brutus, get on.'

'What is this "bush"?'

'Those there eucalypts, tight-packed as poles, 'cept for the track, that is once we get over the ferry.'

'Don't the bullocks mind going on the ferry?'

'These here beasts don't seem to mind nought. Wouldn't be no good if they did. There's work to be done and they're the ones to do it. Work here's too heavy for horses. Oh, they'll plough right enough when these chaps 'ave broken up the ground for them.'

I thought of the horses at Deerbrook's home farm. 'Horses do all the heavy work in England,' I argued.

He gave a short laugh and spat ruminatively at the off-side wheel. 'I'd like to see even Clydesdales or Shires pulling the great loads of stones these beasts do from the quarry where there's stone for this fancy house of the Master's.'

'But where would he get stonemasons and workers for that?'

'You should know!' he said slyly.

In all the excitement I had temporarily forgotten I was branded.

Presently I asked: 'Did you and your wife come out with the Master and Mistress?'

'Aye, her and me and Cook 'ud not let the family come to a heathen place like this on their own. The others are all convicts, twenty of them — "assigned" they call them, same as what you are.'

He did not seem averse to answering my questions, so I pressed him for as many particulars about the family as possible.

'Well now, apart from the Master and Mistress there's Master Matthew, he's gone twenty-four, Master Donald, he's twenty-one — I don't think he'll stick, all set he is for the church, reckon he'll go back — then there's Master Richard, he's nineteen, Miss Charlotte, she's twenty, Miss

Patricia, fifteen, Miss Jessica, twelve, Miss Dorothy, eight, and Master Bruce, five. Would that be right, Mother?'

The graven image beside him nodded.

'Eight!' I said. 'That must have been quite a large family to bring to a place like this.'

'There were two more, only they died at sea, but there weren't no stoppin' the Master. You'll know it when you've a deal to do with him.'

The memory of my interview the previous day made me silently agree.

The hours went by and I lost all sense of distance. The steady, powerful pulling of the oxen acquired a rhythm that made time the plaything of eternity; on, on, their horned heads moving in unison, their feet padding forward.

It must have been approaching mid-day when we reached the ferry, for the sun was high, and it was hot perched up amid the sacks under the canvas covers, but I watched with great interest the loading of our two drays on to the barge-like ferry. As Mr James had prophesied, the bullocks offered no opposition to such a mode of transport. Having been driven aboard, they chewed steadily at their cud during the crossing, and with their long, powerful tails flicked away the flies that tended to settle on their warm and shining flanks.

I asked permission to get down from the dray during the crossing, as like the bullocks I was attacked by the flies and found their attention more than I could abide. The noisome insects seemed everywhere upon my person, in my eyes, even in my ears. However, Mr James was adamant, he would not allow movement of any kind. 'I'll not take no risk with Master's goods,' he said.

Once over the ferry we were on our way again, and now the bush became thicker, seemed to close down on the track which had also become rougher, and threw us about with a slow, flinging motion that I found exceedingly tiring, so I got down and walked more often than I had need to. Although at times we all must walk, so steep did the track become in many places, when it would take all of Mr James's urging, and the determination of the beasts themselves, to reach the summit with their heavy loads. I began to see why this journey was only undertaken once a year. To traverse such a track in winter with heavy loads would be well nigh impossible.

At first I found the walking pleasant, having time to see the beautiful undergrowth and wild flowers; to watch the brilliantly coloured and strange birds flash like shafts of sunlight through the dark stillness of the trees.

Whenever we left this dark world of trees with their strong smell of eucalyptus there were hills and steep valleys — gullies I was told to call them — up and down, mile upon mile with not sign of habitation. Fortunately, late in the afternoon we came upon a homestead made of logs standing back from the track. There were fields cleared around it, from which a good harvest must have been cut, judging by the great heads of wheat in the stacks standing about. Smoke rising straight and high was a heaven-sent sight, a promise of food and rest.

Mr James pointed with his long whip. 'There be Captain's homestead. We always sleep in his barn for the night.'

After helping to gather firewood and assisting Mrs James with our simple meal, I fell asleep almost immediately among the warm sacks in the dray. No bed before or since has felt so wonderful.

The next day we journeyed on in much the same fashion, meeting only a mail-man cantering leisurely down the track, with whom Mr James stopped to talk and collect news of settlers living hidden in this world of nature.

That night, however, there was a difference. As the afternoon drew on and the shadows lengthened, Mr James explained that tonight would find us near no friendly homestead.

'This night we light a fire and sleep by it,' he said.

'It was not cold last night,' I pointed out.

'Cold's naught to do with it,' he explained as he called to Brutus to stop, at the same time throwing his long whip back into the dray, 'it's them perishing blacks.'

'But surely they're harmless?'

'Sometimes they are, sometimes they aren't. It's the times they aren't you gotta look for. Get busy, young Jack, we're late.'

Soon I realised that this was a regular staging post. Below us, not far from the drays, a narrow creek bed pushed its way through the bottom of a gully. It was so deathly quiet that the smallest twig underfoot cracked like a report. I had never known such silence, it seemed to have weight that pressed upon me, and I looked about in the thick undergrowth for I knew not what.

Mr James handed me a pitcher and told me to climb down to the creek for water while he and Jack made ready the bullocks for the night. At least, I told myself, as I climbed carefully down the steep slope clutching at trees and undergrowth as I went, no one could approach without my knowing. In this I was wrong! When of a sudden I looked at the creek to get my bearings, I saw a black lithe body lying gracefully on the bank, obviously drinking from the water. At first I thought it to be some strange animal, then saw it was a human form, its only resemblance to an animal being that it lay drinking straight from the water rather than from some utensil, and with such natural and beautiful posture that obviously it always drank that way.

I stood quite still, hardly daring to breathe. But apparently I had not the perfect gift of stillness as had this child (I could now see she was a young girl) for suddenly she lifted her eyes and looked into mine. They were as dark as her skin and mass of curly hair, and their whites shone up at me like lights. Then, in one movement she had gone into the undergrowth without a sound. I was ashamed of the noise I made covering the rest of my journey and told Mr James so when I returned with my pitcher.

His only comment was: 'So the varmints are around! I guessed they'd be.'

After we had eaten and sat a while by the sweet-smelling fire, I watched him reach for his rifle and flint and begin to ram powder wads and shot into the barrel.

'Why do you call them varmints, Mr James?' I asked.

'Because they are. Just varmints.'

'Doesn't anyone try to get to know them?' The great beauty of the sight I had seen earlier was still in my mind.

'Not unless they want spears in theirselves. There's this Mission man, Robinson they call him, what claims he understands them. Meself, I believe in shoot first and understand afterwards.'

'Have many people been speared?'

'Too many — and murdered in their beds.'

I shivered in spite of myself. 'Do you think they will attack us?'

'They'll get a bellyful of this shot if they do! It's all the fault of those lilly-livered settlers giving them tea, sugar and flour to bribe them. Now they've got a taste of the stuff, they'll thieve 'n spear to get it.'

'Perhaps they do not know right from wrong and are hungry. They may think that because we have it they also should have it.'

My only answer was a sneering sound from Mrs James, and such a strange look I did not pursue the subject. I realised she must think my reasoning peculiar indeed since I too was supposed to be a thief. So I leant back against a tree trunk and watched in silence as her husband finished loading the gun to his satisfaction, then laid it across his knee. A position in which, I discovered next day, he and it remained the entire night.

Next morning we had to draw off the track to let the Master's carriage pass. He did rein in for a moment to speak to Mr James, but almost immediately was away again, covering us and the patient bullocks in a cloud of dust from which there was no escape.

However, a few hours later we came upon them in trouble. A wheel from the carriage had struck a boulder and pulled off, and as we rounded a turn in the track we could clearly see the Master's big frame marching up and down, obviously awaiting our arrival.

'The Master!' Mr James exclaimed. 'Now, what's to do?'

He came striding up to us before the little man had properly brought his team to a stop; in fact caught hold of poor Brutus by his horns and nearly stopped him in his tracks.

'James, that damn wheel has broken two spokes. You'll have to do something.'

Mr James handed the whip to his wife and walked across to his Master. Then I came under notice.

'Sarah!'

'Yes, sir.'

'Go to my wife, she is in need of you.'

Without further explanation he joined Mr James, and together they walked to the carriage; the little cattleman beside his giant Master looked for all the world like a gnome that had been dropped from the skies.

I climbed down from the dray, and catching up my skirts followed behind them. When I reached the carriage I saw that Mrs Roland was in obvious distress.

'Oh, Sarah, I am indeed glad to see you. I think it must be my stays, I am in great pain. That girl of the Headlams' was nothing but an ignoramus. I don't believe she has ever laced stays before in her life — French trained indeed! I cannot understand how Nora — Mrs Headlam, can tolerate her.'

I made her lean forward as far as was humanly possible and quickly gave her the relief she so needed. Never have I seen such mishandled stays. The flesh of her ample back had been forced into tight little balls. Poor woman, how she had survived hours of being tossed about in that carriage I could not think.

She collapsed back on the seat and I thought would faint.

'Rest a moment, Madam, I believe I have something that may assist you.'

I jumped to the ground and, once again gathering up my skirts, ran back to the dray where I rummaged among my few possessions, at last coming upon the phial of hartshorn from which I had managed never to be parted. When I got back to the carriage Mrs Roland had indeed succumbed to a faint, so slipping my arm under her head I gently passed my precious little phial backwards and forwards beneath her nostrils.

Just as she was regaining consciousness I looked round to find her husband was standing watching us, his arms comfortably crossed on his chest. His calmness would have angered me had I not caught a distinct twinkle in his eye. Could it be that the giant was a more gentle one than had seemed possible?

'You would appear to be resourceful and well-equipped,' he said.

'Thank you, sir.'

'My wife frequently suffers from these little — diversions. She will be quite recovered in a moment.'

As though to prove his words there was a movement on my arm, and looking down I saw that he was right. Presently, with my aid, she managed to sit upright and smile. 'That is a great relief, Sarah. Stays were not made, I think, for travel in Van Diemen's Land.'

'Indeed I should say not, Madam.'

'But we have our pride, even in this country. You have beautiful hands, Sarah. I fear they will suffer here.'

Before I could think of anything to say, her husband changed his voice and movements with such speed I could scarce stop myself from starting.

'Now, that's enough talking, Jessica. Mirabelle is due to drop her calf today and both James and I are here instead of there. James has fixed the wheel and you are sufficiently revived. Back to the dray, my girl.'

With unquestioning compliance we all changed places, and in a matter of minutes the carriage was disappearing out of sight, its driver lashing at the greys. This brought much grumbling from Mr James, and the prophecy that his assistance would be needed yet again before the journey's end. A prophecy which proved incorrect, for next morning we came into view of Ardrossan without again encountering the carriage.

It was with great excitement that I followed the pointing of Mr James's whip as we walked the bullocks up the last hill and came to its crest...'

CHAPTER EIGHT

When they returned to Hobart Sara was sure of one thing—Arna and Richard were sleeping together. So instinctively sure was she that she wished one or the other would be honest enough to tell her, yet at the same time she did not want to hear the final words of confirmation. This attitude of mind was incomprehensible to her. Why should it concern her? Arna was practically of age, Richard well over age. She decided it was because they had so suddenly and of necessity become her close friends that this thing affected her.

It was one thing to discuss sexual relationships, another to have them taking place in one's own circle. She tried to put it out of her mind during these first days of her return, days full of excitement and planning. With the casino at Wrest Point both John and Richard had agreed the girls had hit on a good idea in the setting up of a really modern boutique; on condition that they, the men, held the financial reins. Neither Arna nor Sara was averse to this, although Arna showed such a practical flair underlying her glamorous exterior, that usually it was her suggestions that were followed.

This reaction on both John's and Richard's part amused Sara; she had long since discovered there were two Arnas, but she promised herself it would be she and not Arna who would make decisions in the matter of decor.

The first move was to find accommodation for both girls, and this was more difficult than they expected. However, after spending a whole weekend tramping the streets and visiting agents, they were lucky enough to answer the advertisement of a weary, drab little woman with hopeless eyes, whose daughter had been sent to hospital in Melbourne, leaving three small children to be cared for. She was pathetically grateful for Sara's and Arna's appearance. She followed them about her tiny, clean rooms, extolling the goodness of her daughter and lamenting the shiftlessness of her son-in-law, pointing out that the good Lord must have sent them so that she could go immediately to Melbourne with the children and not leave the poor little lambs to the mercies of their feckless father.

Because of the cleanliness and accessibility to the bus, they took it on the spot, and were told that if they paid a month's rent in advance they could move in the next day. This particularly suited Sara and John; she because she would have him to help her settle in, he because he knew he would return to work with the knowledge that she was well accounted for and on the way to achieving something that would satisfy her. It even occurred to him that if this scheme worked, or even if it didn't, and they merely acquired what she had originally termed a headquarters, he would in time suggest again that they adopt a child. He was pleased with this last piece of cleverness but decided not to say anything yet. Far better to let her amuse herself with being a businesswoman; after all, so long as he and Richard kept a careful check, nothing very much could go wrong.

He had no great qualms about Richard, who was far more shrewd than either of the girls gave him credit for, and John was pretty certain that even for Arna's sake, after investing much of the capital to start the business, he would not run the risk of involving himself in any financial loss. He must be fairly sure of Hobart's reaction to this boutique. A gamble he might think it, but he must have felt it had at least a reasonable chance of success.

On Sunday night before John returned to the dam, Sara said: 'We're going to give the boutique its first publicity tonight when Arna and I go down to *Sunbolt*. We think Rick's crowd will give us a fairly good cross-section of opinion.'

'I'm not so sure.'

'Why?'

He looked at his watch as he lay back on the one modern sofa the room offered. 'I thought you were the one who claimed to understand human nature! You'll have to make public also that this is a foursome investment.'

'Of course.'

'Doesn't it occur to you Rick is something special down there, among the young? One of the most eligible bachelors in Hobart who refuses to be hooked, and you, a married woman, and Arna, an imported piece of glamour, inveigle him into a business venture.'

'Well, you're there to account for me,' she said hastily, and wandered restlessly over to the window.

'Certainly. I'm just preparing you for a possible reaction.'

She swung round, her eyes seeking his. 'Why didn't you say all this before, I mean—'

'My dear, there's no need to get dramatic. I just don't think this particular idea has entered your head and it's as well to be prepared. Stop walking round and come here. I must leave in about ten minutes.'

Lying back in the comfort of his encircling arm, the tweedy smell of his sports jacket about her, she could think of nothing to say. Afterwards she wondered why she hadn't told him she felt certain in her own mind that Arna and Rick were lovers. Could it mean she didn't want to talk about the situation, even to him?

She did, however, tell Arna what he had said when they were changing into thick slacks and jumpers before going down to the quay.

Arna merely shrugged. She was sitting at the dressing table swiftly and expertly applying makeup, but for a moment her eyes sought Sara's in the mirror, and she smiled. 'But of course they will think those things. Your John is right.'

Sara felt the inference that of the four of them she was the least worldly wise. 'Then they will have to see sense,' she said sharply.

Arna returned to her makeup.

'Anyway,' Sara went on, 'if they won't support us, others will.'

'Oh but they *will* support us because of curiosity and because of Rick. They will talk, that is all.'

'There's always talk about something in a small place like this. Are you afraid of the venture now?'

'Afraid! But it gets more exciting day by day. I have not told you—you were too busy with your John—but Rick thinks he may have found just the place for us. Tonight he will tell us more.'

Again that sense of intimacy between these two! Sara looked away and Arna's voice flowed on: 'You look so funny, Sara, when I speak of Rick and me. Do you not like that we are so friendly?'

Sara struggled to be honest. 'Of course not, you are ideal for each other.'

'You say that with—oh, shall I make you see—so much a sense of permanency. We would not like that, either of us.'

'You mean—' Then she stopped, not prepared to commit to words what she was thinking.

'That you think so much of marriage?'

'Is that strange when I am married?'

'No, I suppose not. But it's an *old* way of thinking, Sara. It had to be before contraceptives were so good for us all. We couldn't risk the burden of giving life, but now—' The expressive hands flashed across the mirror and Sara's eyes followed them as though they hypnotised her. 'Now we are free people, making our minds and bodies to work together as they always should have done. Working by the contact with the many, not the one. The one is so narrow, so false.'

Everything that was in Sara was up in arms. She wanted to explain to this beautiful child (strange how old she suddenly felt, so knowledgeable) that what motivates men and women is not just promiscuity, but an inexplicable web, which must be woven from the higher and lower planes of thought and behaviour of two human beings brought together by an indefinable force; that if once that web were broken it was irreplaceable. But it was not possible; she knew of no words which would ring true to Arna. She could imagine her laughing reply: 'Then spin another web, dear Sara!' Could that be? Surely if one discovered a perfect web it was worth fighting for? With relief she heard the sound of the front door bell go jangling through the house.

She reached out and ran a comb through her hair. 'That will be Rick now,' she said.

Arna stood up and was gone. Sara took her place in front of the mirror. Suddenly she felt so tired she did not want to go down to the quay and join with the others. She would far rather have remained and read the journal. But to do so after this conversation would look too pointed, particularly as they had decided to tell everyone their plans.

Out in the passage Richard was alone, turning to meet her as he heard her step. 'Oh, there you are. Arna has just gone out to your next-door neighbour—something about putting out your milk bottles together.'

'Oh.'

'What's wrong, Sara?'

'Nothing.'

'You're not a good actress, my dear.'

She looked at him standing under the cheap light shade, noticed his head not far below its rim. His body was so alive, vital; so fit that it was completely relaxed. She knew him to be an egotist, yet there were times, as now, when he showed an intuitive understanding that was shattering.

He put out a hand and drew her quite naturally towards him; lifted her chin with one finger so that he could look directly down into her face. It was only for a moment that they stayed so; then she managed to push away his finger and laugh. 'I thought it was only women who were supposed to suffer from imagination.'

'Good God, no, just that men, when they have imagination, have a more sensible type.'

'Touché! Help me on with my jacket.'

He helped her into the thick jacket as Arna came lightly through the front door.

'It seems little boys run off with the milk money round here. Mrs Next Door has a box with a lock. We may share half of it.'

'Good heavens! How nice of her! Rick, Arna says she thinks you have found *the* place for our boutique.'

'Well, that's up to you girls. I have found something I believe you could do a lot with. It has a history too, nearly as old as Battery Point itself. I've got the keys. I thought we could go there first.'

So the moment passed, but left her badly disturbed. There was no denying it had been a charged moment.

Richard was right about the house he had found. It stood slightly back from the street, was two-storeyed and had one tall tree at the side which spread it branches like an umbrella over the old slate tiles. There was a waiting quietness about its bald empty windows and Georgian front that reached out to the three young people standing in the street.

'Ah—yes,' Arna said softly, and walked ahead of them through the gate. Sara did not immediately follow. 'What happened?' she asked. 'Why is it empty?'

'Are you superstitious?'

'Not unreasonably so.'

'It was built in 1848 by one of the old whaling captains. He established a family, then never returned. Each generation that followed believed some trace of him would be discovered with an attending fortune. The last member has just died, so—the house is up for sale, reasonably cheaply.'

'And you think I would be afraid of our trying to resuscitate it?'

'Would you?'

She did not answer him for a moment. Then she said quietly: 'No, because if it failed as a boutique I'd love to live in it just as a home.'

As it turned out, when they got to the quay, there was hardly any of their crowd there, and as the excitement of the house was still with them, they decided to call off work on *Sunbolt* for the night and return to discuss plans. The upshot was that Sara was to write to John, while Richard promised to get an option on the house the next morning.

It was late when she got to bed, but even so she settled down on her electric blanket with the journal propped beside her on the pillow.

CHAPTER NINE

So, dear sister, not even you could know how I felt as I looked down at the marshland beneath us. I asked myself: is this the answer? Is this place the end of the road where the good Lord has called me to my future and my destiny? And I knew it was so; here I would stand or fall, and I determined that I should not fall.

Such wild happiness stirred my whole body that I grasped Brutus's chains and drew him on. I watched him take up the traces until they tightened on his soft and supple brisket, so that he had the full weight of the load when he leant forward with all the power and quiet determination that was his birthright. Presently we climbed aboard and the drays turned down into the valley.

It was hot and steamy in the marshland, and where it ended the bush looked even more thick and menacing. It made me think once more of the strange, dark people who lived within it, and the bitterness that so obviously lay between them and us. Surely where there was so much land, His Majesty's government would give protection to those who had lived unmolested in it before we came to bring civilisation. I asked Mr James about this, and his reply was that His Majesty, God bless him, would know little of such as these, a few hundred savages.

'Surely there must be more than that. Have not people been to their villages?'

'They haven't got no villages. They can only live, so I've heard tell, if they roam the countryside — more's the pity. That's how they get into trouble; can't lay your hands on them. They're here one minute and gone the next.'

'But how can they live without some sort of an abode?'

'As I've heard, they get tree bark to make rough shelters as they go from place to place. Myself, I'd not know — keeps out of their way, I does, an' if they get in mine they just have to take what comes to them. If you're wise you'll not be bothering your head.'

I knew it was useless to question him further, but I could not help my feelings for these poor creatures. I knew what it was to be hunted, to ache with desire to hit back and hurt because no one would give you a chance. The hopeless world of being damned without defence.

But soon there were other sights to occupy my interest and my imagination. Before the morning was greatly advanced we were moving beside a clear deep river, and now the bush rose everywhere on high, rolling hills above us, while my nose caught the sharp tingling smell of wet earth and eucalyptus leaves. Mr James pointed with his whip. 'Next turn in the track and you'll be seeing the house.'

Sure enough we came through a clearing, and there ahead, standing on a knoll of raised ground, was indeed a fair and surprising mansion that would not have disgraced the English countryside itself. Built on two floors and in the golden brown stone I have mentioned earlier, with a Georgian façade, it stood facing the sun, a challenge to man and nature alike. Around it the bush was cleared back on all sides to an extent of some hundreds of feet, and on the far side the river glinted through the trees. Even the tree stumps left around, as yet uncleared, could not take away its imposing dignity.

'Master and Mistress's not living there yet. Taken two years it has, to build.'

'But, Mr James, who designed such a house?'

He sucked away at his pipe, a huddled little figure, the whip lying slack in his horny, misshapen fingers. I thought he wasn't going to answer me.

But at last he said: 'The tutor man, name of Haynes. Convict he is. A shame I calls it when an educated man like that goes wrong. Teaches the little 'uns he does, but he wasn't no teacher back in t'old country.'

'You mean he's really an architect.'

'That 'ud be right I guess. Anyway, he drew it all up on paper, and Master had the convicts do the rest.'

'But where would they get all that stone?'

He looked at me sideways. 'You ask a blooming lot of questions, but if you must know, right here on our own property, whole quarry of it. Brutus here, if he could talk, 'ud tell you how many loads he pulled — hundreds of 'em. Come to think of it, that Mr Haynes, he 'as a right easy time of it. Just thinking up ideas and other people doing the work while he sits around, teaching the young 'uns their letters.'

'Of course, there wouldn't be any schools,' I said thoughtfully, and sat quietly awhile, thinking of the tremendous venture it would be to bring a delicately nurtured young family to such a place as this. There were probably no churches or doctors, and out here, in this vast and lonely country, there could be few human contacts, only poor half-crazed savages hiding in the undergrowth waiting their chance to spring on the unsuspecting, struggling whites. But what a world to conquer if one were free. As the Captain had said, a new society to be formed and made to work. My mind went back to my first interview with my Master. He was indeed the man for such an undertaking. I could well realise how he would decide to ship his entire family with their possessions, bring them to this place, and build in the wilds such a mansion as this.

As though sensing my thoughts Mr James said: 'A rare man, the Master, and don't you be forgetting that, young woman. Hard he be, but only a hard man could have brought us safely to this place with all his possessions, even the animals. A regular ark, we was, though I don't reckon as the ark had half such a rough passage as we had, those 275 days we were at sea.'

I laughed. 'Did you count them, Mr James?'

'Aye, and the hours!'

But having just completed a like journey, I was not anxious to hear his travel experiences. It was this family and this place about which I wanted to know.

'How came the Master to choose this place?' I asked.

'He didn't. Government told him to up and come to it, that it were his.'

'How could that be?'

'Master went to the Government while we was unloading the ship and after a long time he came back. When he saw Mistress standing awaiting of him, he waved something in his hand and called out to her: "Do you know what this is?" And when she shook her head, fear written all over her worrit face, he said: "It's a compass, and it'll take us to the finest grant any man could ask for outside his own country." Those were his very words. And so it did! We set off a week later with drays and bullocks we bought in Hobart Town, though none of us knew naught about these here animals then. Loaded to the hubs we were, and a fine sight it was, with Master Matthew on that great black horse of his, a-leading us.'

'You mean he brought his horse from England?'

'He'd not be parted from Oscar, girl. Poor Oscar, devil though he be, he were in bad shape after that trip, but Master Matthew looked after him like a young 'un. We had to hack our way through the bush with axes and knives. There was no track to Ardrossan then, you see.'

Like Mr Haynes, Master Matthew interested me! I could hardly await our arrival. Then another thought struck me.

'Mr James, why did they call the property Ardrossan? That is a Scottish name, and surely the family are English.'

'So they are, leastways Master is. Mistress's family is Scots. Ardrossan were the name of her house in the Highlands, and then when they discovered the town nearby was named Kilmarnock, she begged the Master to call this here place after her old home.'

'So, there is a town nearby?'

'Of sorts — a military post it is.' He pointed with his whip again.

'Now girl, stay your tongue, it looks as though the whole family have come out to take a look at you.'

Sure enough, as he pulled up his team in a swirl of dry, choking dust, I could see the front of a long, log-built house — so it appeared to me — just as though long slender trees, stripped of their branches, had been piled one on top of the other to make walls.

From the house entrance, in the middle of the structure, four young girls and a small boy came slowly down the wooden steps, watching our arrival. I saw at once that their clothes were made of the best material, but were unmodish in the extreme. Madam herself appeared behind them, a smile on her face.

Mrs James climbed down stiffly and gave her stout little figure a shake and a pat. I followed behind her, sadly aware of my dishevelled appearance for this, my first meeting with my Master's family.

The little boy, Bruce, Mr James had called him, left his mother and half came to meet me, staring up at my hair. At last he pointed at it and turned back to the family. 'Red!' he stated emphatically in a loud baby voice, whereupon they all laughed, and his mother said: 'We have been trying to teach him his colours, Sarah. We were afraid he was colour-blind, but that is obviously not so! Come, I will take you to your quarters myself.'

I was aware of Mrs James's sniff behind me as she followed her husband behind the dray, and knew I had made my first enemy, but I was not afraid of the Mrs Jameses of this world.

It was a brief little ceremony, that meeting with my first pioneer family. I curtsied to each member and then followed their mother through to the back of the house, marvelling as I went at the amount of beautiful furnishings and furniture they had managed to bring with them. On the rough-timbered walls there were even tapestries comparable with those at Deerbrook, and what surprised me even more was that they did not look amiss in their strange surroundings.

Mrs Roland asked me if I had noticed the "big" house, and upon my saying that indeed I had, she told me how eagerly she was awaiting the day they would move into it.

'We are so cramped here, Sarah, it is difficult to teach the children the correct manner in which a gentleman's household should live. Many of my possessions are still packed in a shed — there was no room to bring them into the house. I am so afraid they will be ruined with damp and mould after that dreadful journey.'

'And when will the move into the big house take place, Madam?'

She sighed. 'Next month, I hope. Mr Haynes — he is the children's tutor you know, but he's really an architect. All so unfortunate, such a charming qualified man — just one stupid mistake—'

'I know, Madam,' I said, 'Mr James related to me the story coming along.'

'Of course, he would do. Yes, all so awkward... well, he designed the house. It is all being lined with blackwood, you know, and the doors will be solid Huon pine. It will be wonderful to live almost normally again, though I doubt if it would be possible to live quite normally in this country — so bad for the children.'

I felt sorry for her discomfort and her fluttering hands, and I realised what all the problems and fears of the last two years must have meant to one whose concept of living was so obviously based on a conventional society.

We went through to an inadequate-looking kitchen, which no doubt had a certain charm in its bush outlook and pretty cambric curtains, but must be a dreadful place as the centre for running such a large community as Ardrossan. I hoped there would be different arrangements in the "big" house. I was later to learn that all the store-rooms, and what served as a still room and dairy, were apart from the main building and were kept under lock and key, Madam herself carrying the keys on her person.

In this way she made a strict record for the Master of the daily use of all commodities. In addition she supervised the issue, once a month, of rations to all convicts and their families. Some of the more trustworthy convicts had been allowed to have their families sent out from England. In some cases this had proved useful where there were growing daughters only too willing to learn to wash, iron and clean under the happy and well-fed conditions of Ardrossan, after the misery and starvation they had suffered in England when their fathers had been deported.

Thus it would appear the Captain was right in maintaining that Madam required assistance, not only in running such an establishment as this, but also in attending to the happiness and upbringing of her eight children. Maybe I did not have sufficient qualifications for such a position, but I did have the ability to learn and the determination to achieve. Once again I could see the road ahead opening up, and I set down my modest little dress basket on the floor with confidence as Madam began to tell me of my duties.

It took me days, in fact weeks, to get those young ladies' wardrobes in order. I do not think since leaving England their over-and underskirts had been properly starched, their ribbons attended to or their hair dressed. In performing these duties I grew to know much of this family whose inner circle I had entered.

Beginning with the girls — there was Miss Charlotte, who took her duties as the eldest daughter of the house most seriously and who was very afraid that in this bush life she would never meet a man of sufficient position to marry her. She was truly her mother's daughter, kindly, aspiring and virtuous. I saw clearly there was much for her to learn, even though she had a good figure, carried herself with pride, and certainly would take care to be correct at all times.

Miss Patricia, on the other hand, was a born rogue and tomboy, with a lovely little round face sprinkled with freckles (the bane of her mother's existence and the cause of that good lady spending many hours she could ill afford in reading every edition of the Gentlewoman she could find, in the hope of discovering some miraculous cure for her daughter's complexion). She had a laugh that was infectious to the whole community, and a determination to say what she thought and felt at the cost of all good manners and decorum, that was both exciting and embarrassing.

Miss Jessica stood apart from the others, her world one of dreams and imagination. I had the feeling that where she lived did not matter greatly to her personal world of make-believe. All of us around her were her background and necessary to her existence, but she did not really have her being on our plane.

Little plump Miss Dorothy, at the age of eight, cared only for her stomach, her black Shetland pony and books, books, books. 'I am so afraid, Sarah,' her mother would say in a desperate tone of voice, 'that Mr Roland and I have between us produced a bookworm.'

The boys too were outstandingly different. Master Matthew was a replica of his father: tall, broad, determined and arrogant. Next to his father he dominated the family. In a very short time I came to realise he lived for Ardrossan and the knowledge that one day it would be his to rule. This arrogance was easier to understand when I was told he had been destined for a brilliant career in the British army but had sacrificed it when he knew his father had decided to risk everything on this venture to the Colonies.

Master Donald, like Miss Jessica, lived in a world apart from the hard one of toil shared by his father and brothers. What they directed him to do he did with all his physical strength, but his mental strength came from his Bible and his God. Mr James's prophecy that this second son would return to England and the Church, I too believed.

Master Richard was just a young man whose god was his father and whose hero was his brother Matthew. It was his ambition to ride Oscar — a request he knew would never be granted, but which drove him to be his brother's abject slave, in the hope that his reward would be to mount the black stallion just once.

Which leaves the baby, Master Bruce, beloved and spoilt by all.

So there is my family, with, in the background, the figure of Mr Haynes, the tutor-architect, at present in Hobart Town completing a commission for his Master.

My first meeting with that gentleman and Oscar took place on the same day. I had been at great pains to set the frills of Miss Charlotte's muslin frock, which she must wear to a supper party at a neighbouring settler's home, the MacDonalds', who had travelled out on the same ship with the Rolands and had managed to obtain their grant within riding distance. I fear the thoughts engendered by the social gathering, which entailed Miss Charlotte's staying the night at her hostess's homestead, news having come by the mailman that the bushranger, "Gentleman Jim", had been seen in the district, had weakened my concentration sadly during the morning service read by Mr Roland.

I enjoyed the morning routine, during which all members of the family crowded into the dining room, with us servants standing against the back wall, while Mr Roland read a short passage from the Bible followed by a prayer for the day.

I did not always listen to what he said, but rather let his rich, splendid voice roll round me while I watched the bush world stirring outside the window; particularly watched the magpie which most mornings hopped on to the verandah, his head on one side as though listening to the man's voice that filled, uninterrupted, the silent room and its occupants. Sometimes he would add his own spontaneous warble. At such times my eyes would rest on the ever increasing space the men were winning from the encircling bush, or stray to the flock of sheep feeding peacefully in the early morning light.

However, on that particular morning I was worried, for I knew I must ask for more water from the roof tank if Miss Charlotte's rebellious hair was to be dressed, as I had promised her, in the latest fashion when I had left London. Drought having set in, even though the river is so near, the tank water is as precious as mead, and to the men it is sacrilege to use it for the frivolity of hair washing. But the brackish river water makes Miss Charlotte's unruly hair all the more so — oh that she had your beautiful, silken hair!

So after breakfast I was just starting across the yard with my water pail in my hand, when I saw that Oscar was still in his enclosure, a most unusual sight, since Master Matthew rarely went out to the fields without him. I had so often wanted to make friends with the beautiful creature, in spite of his bad reputation. I looked round hastily to see if there was anyone about, but the place seemed deserted, so hurrying back to the pantry I picked an apple off a well-stocked dish. I hoped Madam had not as yet made her store round and counted the apples. Seizing one, I hastily dropped it down the bosom of my dress and flew back across the yard.

Oscar must have sensed something, for he was waiting at the rail, looking across to the house and, to my surprise, instead of snatching the apple and galloping round his enclosure, he took it gently from my outstretched hand, crunched its deliciousness so that the juice ran out through his broad, strong teeth and flecked the soft velvet of his black lips. I felt I must stroke his muzzle, and without thinking laid my fingers on the bony hardness of his nose. So often had I seen him, in the short time I had already been here, rear and strike down at anyone who approached him, that I waited with some trepidation, although the wooden railings were between him and me.

How frequently from behind the curtains of your bedroom, dear sister, had I watched the hunt assembling in the courtyard at Deerbrook: the hounds with their switching tails; the huntsmen in their pink coats; you on Blue Ribbon as though you were a carved piece of ebony. How I envied you, how I too longed to ride over fences on a beautiful horse with the sound of baying hounds and the horn in my ears, the wind in my face. I thought of all this as I felt Oscar tremble, and waited for him to rear up and flail at me with his forelegs.

Instead a hard hand caught my shoulder and spun me round. 'Keep away from my horse! Apart from the fact that he is dangerous, no one touches him but me, do you understand!'

I found myself looking into the angry face of Master Matthew, and was amused at his vulnerability; knew that his anger lay more in the fact that Oscar had not attacked me than in my touching him. However, I curtsied quickly and turned away, but this time I did not run across the yard. Like the Mrs Jameses the Master Matthews didn't frighten me, and while paying him the respect which was his due, this I would have him know.

It was that afternoon Madam asked me if I could climb a ladder and not fall off it. I assured her that I could, whereupon she told me I was to go over to the new house and carefully measure all the windows in the circular entrance hall.

'I was fortunate indeed, when I was in Hobart Town, to procure the most beautiful blue damask. It will be quite outstanding against the blackwood panelling, but I fear there may not be sufficient, although I bought all Mr Henry had of the shipment — four bolts, I believe he said. Truly, Sarah, I cannot contain myself until I know.'

'I shall go at once, Madam,' I said, and taking up my bonnet against the strong sun, I went to find pencil and paper.

So this was to be first sight of the real Ardrossan! My feet flew over the rough ground, and I went so fast my breath was coming unevenly as I approached the heavy, carved entrance door that was standing partly open under the pillared portico. I turned and stood a moment to calm down, while I looked down the valley. I could see the river glinting and, in the two fields below, the wheat standing nearly ripe. From across its waving acres came the ringing sounds of axes, so still was the noon-day. It pleased me to imagine the men working with all their strength to win more of this stubborn land.

Then I pushed back the heavy door and went inside.

I caught my breath, for in all my imaginings I had not thought of this. Slowly my eyes travelled round the spacious, circular hall, with shafts of sunlight from the open door falling across the floor, its walls flanked on either side by recessed windows with deep window seats, the broad passage that led off into the distance, where a white stone staircase twisted gracefully to the upper floor. From the passage, heavy polished Huon pine doors opened into rooms unseen.

'You have an expressive face, Sarah! It is Sarah, isn't it?'

I swung round quickly, to realise a man was sitting in one of the window seats tucked behind the front door.

'I—I am sorry, sir, I did not see you seated there. Yes, my name is Sarah.' Madam has asked me to measure the windows for curtains.'

'I am sure she has, and I can see no good reason why one convict should call another "sir".'

So this was Mr Haynes!

He got up and came towards me. He had one of those lean, rather sallow, but quite devastatingly handsome faces, with dark, deep-set eyes; a face, dear sister, that no woman with any sense would trust.

'So you like it — this house? My name, by the way, is Haynes.'

'I do indeed—'

He waved his hand. 'No, remember what I said, no "sir". Well, you surprise me, 'pon my word you do. The place is an unheard-of mixture, but Madam has been very good to me. I knew she wanted style and pretention. She wishes to entertain the Governor.'

'It will impress him greatly, I feel sure.'

'Maybe, maybe no, but he is an officer and a gentleman, so doubtless he will express himself in terms of pleasure.'

'I think you are wrong, if you will forgive my rudeness and presumption. This has something—'

'That you want!'

'How could you suggest such a thing?'

'I've just told you, your face is expressive.'

'They tell me a cat may look at a king.'

'But you are not that kind of cat!'

'Mr Haynes, I have much work waiting for me. Would you please find me a ladder?'

He sighed, and walked lazily but quite perfectly down the passage and, still without hurrying, managed to return with a ladder in a very short space of time.

'Shall I hold it, or climb and measure?'

'I should prefer to do the measuring myself since I shall doubtless be making the curtains.'

'Independent women always create awkward situations. You're far too beautiful to create awkward situations, Sarah.'

Do not think me conceited in putting down this conversation, dear sister, I merely wish for you to judge for yourself what manner of man he is. I told you in the beginning of this journal it is my idea to record as faithfully as possible what has passed between me and those with whom I have my being.

'Mr Haynes,' I replied, 'you take advantage of my position.'

'How can I take advantage of a position which I feel you yourself do not recognise? Also, you forget, you and I are now of the same status, owing to our misdemeanours.'

I felt the colour race into my face. If only I could take the measurements at another time, but I could give Madam no reason for my returning without them.

'Will you please not make such provoking statements. Madam is waiting for these measurements.'

'And you shall take them to her, but I see no reason why you and I should not talk awhile. I feel sure that you are a good conversationalist, Sarah.'

I saw that I would do no good by arguing, so I took up my measure and climbed the ladder.

He said presently, with amusement in his voice: 'I also feel certain that gossip has given you a picture of my life up to now, so I will not bore you with a further recital of it. On my part I know your story, so we need not waste time on preliminaries. I would merely like to suggest to you that we could gain mutually were we to enjoy a — pleasant relationship. No one would say us nay.'

Still I did not speak, but I fear my silence led him astray, for he rushed into further speech which it became obvious he could carry on unaided for quite some time. At least it left me free to take my measurements, although I cannot honestly say his persuasive voice encouraged my concentration.

'For a man such as myself, Sarah, this is a lonely and singularly uncultured existence. Ah yes, I know what you will say. Our family here is charming and has obviously been brought up in a well-bred society. Indeed I hasten to agree with you, but for a man of artistic and cultured habits, such as myself, there must be a higher plane of thought. One cannot be bounded entirely by this battle for survival which appears to be man's only raison d'être in Van Diemen's Land. There are things in life other than gum trees, burnt earth, pigs and the like. Man requires someone to lift him above such things.'

It was my turn to look at him with amusement. 'I am sure in time you will obtain your wish, Mr Haynes. I understand from Madam there are quite a number of families on their way out from England who plan to settle here.'

He crossed his elegantly trousered legs with a precision that was an art, took out a silver snuff box and surveyed me over the lid.

'Sarah, you are deliberately misconstruing my words. I am sure my meaning is clear to you. We are classed as birds of a feather, you and I. Let us behave as such. Ever since returning from Hobart Town yesterday afternoon, everyone has sought to tell me of your virtues, but they forgot to mention your beauty. I cannot live without beauty. We have much to give each other.'

'Mr Haynes, I fear you try to make fun of me. Will you kindly allow me to carry out Madam's command.'

'Certainly, but I do assure you that I am far more accessible than that arrogant young man who is completely under his father's thumb.'

His self-satisfied complacency would have struck me as ludicrous, had I not suddenly realised that he was putting into words something that must indeed have been lying dormant in the back of my mind. Why not? I would be a fool if I did not know that men were attracted to me. But even as these thoughts struck me I also realised that other men must not merely be attracted to me — this would apply to Mr Matthew as well as others. He would not be above making the same proposition as this man beside me, to keep me at Ardrossan for his pleasure. Further, in his case he could demand, not ask. Refusal would probably lead to dismissal and the end of everything except the grim horror of the Cascades. So many times had I been told coming out on the ship of the misery and degradation of that dreadful place of female correction. But to succeed! The dazzling prospect of such a campaign held me fascinated as Mr Haynes went on talking.

'Don't suppose for a moment I could not read what was in your mind as you walked through that entrance door but a short time ago. Never have I seen the greed of possession more perfectly etched on anyone's face than it was on yours. Had you cried out "This is mine!" you could not have more perfectly expressed your thoughts. And how, pray, could a girl such as you, even beautiful as you are, hope to possess such a place as this, except by laying siege to its rightful owner — the heir?'

I stared at him in excitement. Of course he was right, it was the way, the only way! To lay siege! But with great thought and care, the minimum of emotion; every move would have to be planned.

'But it won't do, Sarah. These things are not for us. We are wanderers on the face of the earth, you and I. The fight will always go against us, but what a delightfully amusing time we could make of it while it lasted. Yes, you would do much better to throw in your lot with mine instead of his. Choose him, and even this hybrid society would seize upon you and literally rend you to pieces.'

With difficulty I pulled myself together and climbed down the ladder.

'Mr Haynes, if you will forgive me, this is a ridiculous conversation. Will you please move the ladder back to the far corner of the hall?'

He sighed.

'A pity you are not sensible. With pleasure I shall move the ladder, and I still think I would have been the better one to measure the curtains.'

CHAPTER TEN

Sara's letter about the house reached John just as he had returned to his office after a meeting with the senior engineer, David Lint, and a Mr McGill, one of the Commission's senior executives. The letter was lying on his desk as he walked into the office, and automatically he picked it up before sitting down in his swivel chair. He leaned back and turned it upside down in his fingers without really seeing it. The only thing that was real to him at that moment was the interview which had just taken place...

David Lint's voice saying: 'We were just having a bit of a recap, John, as things are folding up here. I won't beat about the bush; you remember you and I were discussing the new road project yesterday?'

He had replied: 'Certainly.'

'How would you like to take it over?'

There had been a silence as he had looked from one to the other, his eyes finally resting on the face of McGill. He received a smile in return: 'You've been doing good work, Hilyard.'

He had been conscious they were both watching him as an uprush of excitement had surged over him, then left him almost without feeling of any kind. He had so hoped for this, but now that it had come he seemed to have lost his sense of achievement. Fascinated, he heard his own voice saying that of course he would be delighted. They shook his hand and said the right things, to which he had replied suitably, and now he was back in his office, trying to accept the fact that all this had taken place; that they had even agreed to his having Bill Hurst as his supervisor. Slowly he began to tear open the letter and draw out the pages covered with Sara's neat, even writing. At first the words slipped by without registering.

Then came the phrase: 'I'm sure it's the place we've been looking for ever since we thought about this thing...'

That made him concentrate. It was such a corollary of what had happened to him. The right house, Sara happy and busily settled. He would have to be away so much now—weeks, perhaps even months. What a fortunate thing there had been delays in finding a Commission house for them. Quite apart from the boutique, this would be a home for her to think about and plan; she would not miss him, and when he could get back he would have a home that was really theirs together. Arna of course would be in the background—but not for long, he guessed. Rick was pretty keen; time he went through the hoop and got married; he could more than afford it; or did he think of Arna more in terms of something one tucked away for comfort rather than paraded with a wedding ring? He smiled at the thought, and decided not to let the girls know he was coming up this weekend, but just to arrive and surprise them. He was not a man with insight. He assumed that all that appeared on the surface was all that mattered, or all that anyone felt or lived by. An honest man, he regarded everyone else as honest also. That Sara had any longings apart from those she cared to share with him he did not envisage. Her response to him in bed had increased lately, but that she had any other man in her fantasies did not cross his mind. He was content and looked forward to the future.

When he reached the house and knocked gaily on the door it was Arna who threw it open. 'John!' she said. 'We thought you were not coming home this weekend.'

'Nor did I. Where's Sara?'

She hesitated. 'I think she's gone to do sketches at the house. You did get her letter about the house, didn't you?'

He came in through the front door, shedding jacket and brief case on the hall chair. 'That's one of the reasons I'm here.'

Arna watched him thoughtfully and turned away as she said: 'I don't think she'll be long. I'll get you something to eat.'

He followed her towards the kitchen. 'No, don't bother. It's kind of you but I've—well, I've some special news for her, and I want to take her out to dinner to celebrate.'

Eagerly she turned back to him: 'O-oh, that sounds exciting. I'll be good and not ask you until you tell her.'

As usual, with guilty enjoyment, although somewhat of a puritan, he could not help noticing the way she moved her small round bottom encased in the tightest possible jeans nor the pliant response of her breasts under a long, bulky jumper. She really was almost too much of a good thing.

'What sounds exciting?' Richard's voice asked behind them.

John turned round quickly, in time to catch Richard's amused expression. It annoyed him; but then, in spite of himself, there were times when Richard did annoy him. He said, almost sharply; 'Only a personal matter. I'm looking for Sara to take her to dinner.'

'She's down at the house. I was with her a moment ago. I'll run you down. It's only a few streets away.'

The offer did nothing to remove John's irritation, although he said calmly enough: 'Good heavens, there's no need to do that. Just give me the directions.'

'Less trouble to take you. Besides, I've got some business details to give you.'

Arna watched them drive off with a speculative expression in her eyes. She was well aware of the irritation between the two men, aware too, as they were not, of the reason—Sara. Often she asked herself why she so genuinely liked Sara and missed her if she were not there. She knew that the English girl, if ever she exerted herself, could be a serious rival. Sara, she summed up for herself, was the type of woman men will desert but never forget and will return to in the end. Whereas she felt she herself could lead any man her way for a time—and this was fun, in fact exactly the way she wanted it to be. As she had already told Sara, it was physical fulfilment, not permanency, variety, not the stagnation of marriage. Yet—?

In the meantime John and Richard, after a somewhat silent car ride, found Sara sitting in the empty lower front room of the house at the small portable table littered with sheets of paper. As she saw the car pull up she rose hastily and made a swift effort to gather them all into a heap by the time the two men came through the entrance.

'Darling!' she said as she saw John. 'We didn't expect to see you this weekend. How lovely! There's so much to decide. Did you get my letter? No, don't look, they're only rough—just impressions to get the atmosphere.' This last as he tried to peer round her firmly planted body in front of the table.

'She's incredibly coy about them,' Richard said. 'I've spent the last hour trying to see what she was doing.'

John ignored this and said: 'Come on, pack up. You and I are going out to dinner.'

'What, now?'

'Now.'

'You don't want to see the house?'

'Tomorrow.'

'But I feel an awful mess. My hair needs doing, I—'

'You look all right to me. I'll give you five minutes when we get back. Richard'll give us a lift. Quick, it's special.'

She caught some of his urgency, then searched his face for the answer. 'Darling—'

'No talking. Let's go. Come on, we'll help you with these.'

'Well, no looking.'

'Promise.'

They were as good as their word, and in the space of minutes the papers had been gathered up and they were all in the car heading back. While she rushed off to her room to change and do what beautifying was possible, John and Richard sat down to go over deeds, valuations and prices.

At last, in the car on the way into town, she said: 'I just can't wait another minute. What is it?'

'The best possible, my dear. I've got it.'

'You mean—'

'I'm to be in charge of the new road project!'

'Oh, John! I'm so glad. Will you be able to come home?'

'That's it—one of the things we've got to talk about.'

Over the table of the Italian restaurant to which he took her, he tried to tell her something of this opportunity that had come his way so much sooner than he had dared to hope. 'A man can feel a little god conquering a country like that. Do you know, years ago when they started to open up a similar project it took four men four hours to cut their way a quarter of a mile into the forest? I'll have a team of surveyors, geologists, the latest heavy equipment, workers from practically every country in the world. It's a challenge, Sara; us against Nature and me to devise the means of combat.'

She sat back watching him, caught up in the glow of his satisfaction, grateful that things had gone well for him after all. At that moment she felt more like his mother than his wife. This was not an experience they were sharing; he was purely making her his confidant, perhaps his only real confidant, of an experience only he could know. It was right that it should be so, but it made her feel lonely, even though she was so proud of him.

'Now we come to you.'

'Don't worry about me. Everything is going well.'

'You're sure you're happy?'

'Quite sure.'

'I may not be able to get home now as often as we thought, for a time anyway.'

'If you agree to buying the house, there will be so much for me to do too. What did you think of Rick's report on it?'

At the mention of Richard's name he was again aware of the irritation he had felt earlier in the evening. Without giving it a great deal of thought, he said after a moment: 'You're sure you want to go on with this boutique?'

'Of course.' She watched him, feeling his sudden withdrawal. 'More than ever now.'

They sat in silence for a time, coffee cups in front of them, their minds busy with the change of events.

At last he said: 'What I mean is, I've been thinking about this baby business.' She wished he didn't make babies sound like a new car or dress. 'I think, my dear, we've got to face the fact that it's not for us; but there's no reason, if we bought this house and you didn't go on with the boutique idea, why we shouldn't adopt a girl.'

Sara couldn't help saying: 'Why a girl?'

He looked at her in surprise: 'Surely you'd rather a daughter? She'd be company for you.'

'Of course I would. I just wondered about you.'

'Me? It wouldn't matter to me which it was.'

They looked at each other, and after a moment he picked up a knife and balanced it on one finger. 'Well, I suppose that isn't quite true, but you must be sensible about this, my dear. A boy is a great responsibility. Naturally if he's one's own, his schooling has to be of the best. Then comes university—career.'

'What you're saying, John, is it's a lot of money to invest when a boy is yours in name only.'

'I suppose so.'

'Whereas a girl is a pretty plaything, a toy to—to keep me contented.'

'What's wrong with that?'

'Everything. You're not thinking of the child.'

'Isn't that rather ridiculously dramatic?'

'No, John, it isn't. A girl should feel she is a person in her own right; that she belongs; that she matters as much to her father as if she had been a boy. She must know, without even thinking about it, that our world is her world, and hers ours. It wouldn't work any other way. I could imagine it must be even more so in the case of an adopted child. And anyway, girls these days need just as good an education as boys.'

'You've thought about this quite a bit, haven't you?'

'I suppose I have.'

'You've never mentioned it to me.'

She smiled. 'I was waiting for the right moment. But it isn't now, John. I feel tonight is the start of something you've always wanted. It's your night—ours together, nothing else.'

'Let's go home, you beautiful-legged temptress!'

'Have I nice legs?'

'The only reason I married you.'

Out in the street they walked hand in hand. They were young and in love all over again; nothing else mattered.

But every now and then in the next few weeks, at odd times in the midst of plans, maps, consultations, the engaging of men, John found himself wondering about what she had said. Was it true that he didn't want to give his name to a boy he hadn't sired? Was he really as primitive as that?

Sara too was aware of discontent where there should have been none. As soon as he had seen the house John had been just as excited as she; he'd seen the agent and, subject to checking and valuation, had agreed to buy it. It only remained for an architect to be called in. Arna, for her part, had immediately written to her couturier friend in Italy, telling her of their project, asking her advice on materials and designs and arousing her interest in the venture asking what contacts they could hope to make, and finally suggesting that she come out and join them; pointing out that she could be sponsored for immigration, and housed when she reached Tasmania, but that until they were established wages would be at an absolute minimum.

'Surely anyone as good as you say she is won't accept an offer like that?' Sara asked doubtfully.

Arna smiled. 'But why not? In Europe there are many such as Paulina. Her life is one long affair of competition. She is in her late thirties now, p'raps even forty. Do you not think this competition might become tiring? But here she will be new, exciting—it will be the big challenge. She will understand this, you will see.'

Yes, everything was well under way. Then why this feeling of vague depression—of being unsure of herself? She didn't want to settle to anything, even her beloved journal. Feverishly she flung herself into the business of designing, helped by Arna, an Arna who had no inhibitions, no loyalties, but a firm, intuitive knowledge of what would excite the young and draw them down the quiet, secluded street. Together they planned an underground showroom in the cellars of the old house, with models to be silhouetted in indirectly lit alcoves.

The architect discreetly altered some of their plans, but in the main was intrigued by their ideas, so that he gave their job his particular attention. The upshot was that the old house soon became the centre of men in overalls, ladders and the impedimenta of building. People living near at hand came to stare and ask questions and, as there was no secrecy, the house was a focus of local interest.

As the girls gradually became known, they were waylaid and questioned by many who feared such an innovation, both in their own lives and those of their young. There was a fear that this new boutique would lead to, or at least encourage, so many new happenings of late. Such things as drunken young louts and the increased use of drugs. Also the effects of these things on the roads, with ghastly car accidents involving innocent women and children.

Arna was exceedingly good at dealing with them, much better than Sara. She worked on the old army maxim "Never explain, never apologise" and her exuberance carried them with her, and her childlike, endearing beauty calmed their fears and appeared, except in a few cases, to stir up their own interest and excitement.

But as the alterations progressed there was a period when Sara found herself at a loose end. It was then she got the idea to paint *Sunbolt* and give the picture to Richard for his birthday in a month's time. He's been very good to me, she thought, and all he's got of *Sunbolt* is an enlarged photograph—a very good one, of course—but it would be wonderful if I could just catch the spirit of her, the thing she means to him.

At first she had sincerely believed that all he wanted was the achievement of winning the race, the admiration, the notoriety of being the winner of one of the three greatest yachting races in the world, but since going down to work on the yacht she had known differently—*Sunbolt* was in his very bones. The poor, wretched female who marries him will have to be very understanding, she often used to think as she sat looking up at the yacht, wondering just how to interpret her grace, her speed and hardness, her tough fighting ability.

In all, she made at least a dozen starts and tore them all up. But the more she failed the more determined she became. It grew to be as essential for her to put *Sunbolt* on canvas as it was for Richard to put the yacht over the finishing line of the Sydney-Hobart race.

Then, one night after John had returned to camp, she wandered back into the house, restless and ill at ease. Aimlessly she walked over to the sofa, knelt on it and stared out at the dark river with its reflected lights. She remembered the first time she had sailed on it and they had told her so much of its history that it had ceased to be just a strip of water; had become one of the largest ports in the world. How, astonishingly, the world's greatest navigator Cook had sailed past it and then the next greatest, Bligh, ironically trained by Cook, had done the same. How it was left to Bass and Flinders—again the latter trained by Cook—to discover and explore it. She had learned that the first settlement here had been in the hands of a young inexperienced boy—Bowen, who chose the wrong spot to settle and, unable to control his seamen, sailors and convicts, had carried out the first massacre of the original inhabitants. He was followed shortly by Collins who immediately changed the settlement site to where Hobart stood that day and led it through semi-starvation to prosperity.

It had been the avenue through which countless convict ships had carried their loads of misery—some to degradation, others to a new life of respect.

In the 1840s it had been the world's largest and busiest whaling port, carrying the precious whale oil, equivalent to our day's mineral oil, as far as Europe. The dirty, oily crews rejoiced on entering the town after their months of toil, wearily thinking of the drinking sessions in the numerous taverns—the women to be bought and the stupid, pointless fights born of alcohol and loneliness.

She smiled to herself rather wanly, thinking, 'Judith was right, I do seem to have some kind of kinship with all that past.' Then for no reason *Sunbolt* came into her mind—not the conventional picture of her sailing on fair sea, but rather straining against her moorings, stripped of her sails, her paint peeling, but still in her mast and rigging, the taut determination to live, though everything around her was dying.

She jumped off the sofa and dragged out her paints and brushes from where she kept them. Almost feverishly she went to work with her palette knife, mixing colour she had never thought of before.

'I suppose you know the whole house is open?'

She looked up and saw Richard smiling at her from the doorway. How right it seemed that he should be there at this time, and yet not right. She had wanted this to be a surprise for him.

'I banged quite a few times before coming in. I knew you'd be here. You aren't the one to go out and leave all the lights on.'

'Arna's there.'

'You're wrong. She's with Tony Preston.'

She swung around. 'But—'

'But what?'

It was impossible for her to say that she hadn't the faintest idea who Tony Preston was.

'Sara dear, I despair of you sometimes. Arna and I have an excellent working relationship. Now, what are you up to?'

'You're not supposed to see.' But as she knew he would, he came towards her, lighting a cigarette. 'It's only just started. It won't mean anything to you. I—' Her voice died out. It seemed slightly absurd to go on talking to someone who was not taking the slightest notice. So she knelt on the edge of the stool and sucked the handle of her knife as she watched him.

'Please don't give opinions at the moment, Rick. At this stage it won't look remotely like the finished article. I only started a short time ago.'

'It's going to be "her" of course.'

'Of course. I wish you hadn't seen it.'

He leant lightly on her shoulder, still looking at the canvas. 'What a child you are, Sara, under that calm aloofness. Surprises, wild burst of creativeness—'

'Then you do think it could mean something—I mean to you, as you feel about *Sunbolt?*'

'There you are, you see. You said "no opinions".'

'I did, didn't I? Sorry, it's just—well, this is going to be different. I've never tried anything mildly abstract. Do go, Rick. I'm dying to get at it.'

'You always tell me to go just when you're getting interesting.'

'Best time. You might be disappointed if you stayed.'

'That's trite, Sara. Don't get like that.'

'All right, I promise, but go, Rick, go!'

He allowed himself to be pushed to the door. 'I'll go on one condition—that I'm allowed to see progress from time to time.'

In her eagerness to be rid of him she agreed.

But Richard, going slowly to his car, could not put the scene out of his mind quite so easily. He had no delusion as to what was happening to him where Sara was concerned. Already it had happened to him so many times. It had always been quite delightful, and for a time wholly satisfying; wriggling free when he had had enough had sometimes posed problems, but somehow he had always managed. He sensed this could be different. It had the spice of danger.

He was absolutely sure that John had failed in some way to arouse Sara as a woman. 'Nice fellow. Should have been a bachelor.' He also believed that with a little skill it would be fairly easy to carry on a discreet affair with her; but what kind of a guilt complex was she likely to develop over John? He could not imagine her being indiscreet or hysterical, but the cautious side of his nature warned him that at some stage of the game she would insist on dragging John into the matter; and to be in a conflict with John was the last thing he wanted.

It all came down to the plain and obvious question: How badly did he want Sara? He realised he could not honestly answer that question. She was not beautiful as he thought of a beautiful woman, as Arna for instance was beautiful, but she had a gentle poise which was a complete challenge to his masculinity. He liked the way she walked and wore her clothes. It fascinated him to watch her face break from its quiet composure to sudden, unbridled happiness.

'Let it ride!' he told himself as he drove off. He also realised that her decision to paint *Sunbolt* could pave the way to his decision about her.

CHAPTER ELEVEN

John, meanwhile, had his arrangements well in hand. By the time the last of the winter was over, all plans for the first stages of the road development would be ready for implementation. All equipment had been detailed, most of the labour recruited. Soon, very soon now, the crash of falling timber would be in his ears and the bitter-sweet smell of disturbed virgin bush in his nostrils.

These days, he was learning from Bill more and more of the simple approach to bush life. The approach that had been learned the hard way, from trial and error, until it had almost become an instinct passed from one generation to another, when white men first came to the island with little more than their hands, hearts and heads to see them through; when, if these had failed, then they had failed completely.

He carefully studied one of the biggest road projects under way at the moment and saw how, even with the magnificent equipment of today, the bush still fought back, still presented an almost insuperable task to any but the most highly trained and understanding of men. He marvelled at the main body of workers and decided they were obviously banded together by the love of money. Yet, they could have got the same money in other labouring jobs, jobs that would have kept them among their fellow men. But here they lived for a week, months, in the forward camps, with only helicopters and radios keeping them in touch with the outside world, shut up in a small community.

It was a comfortable community of good food and good beds, but surrounded by the rain forest and mud; working from first to last light; felling trees to the wild crescendo of the chain saws; pushing over others and tearing up the earth with the great D9s, 8s, 7s; fitting in immense drains and bridges to carry away the water oozing like perpetual tears from the ravaged earth; blasting through walls of rock, their ears deafened by the unending roar of the diesel-driven power machines so that speech ceased to exist, and the smallest human thought must be passed on by the language of the deaf and dumb. At night, returning so tired that bed was the only answer, even the ration of beer allowed each man having lost its attraction, their personal lives became a thing apart, lives that existed in periods of oases, to be seized on according to each man's needs. Some would squander a fortnight's pay packet on drink, gambling and sex; some would reorientate themselves with wives and families; others would just sit and stare. Why?

He asked Bill this question one day, when they had gone on a prospecting trip to the place where they would make their first attack on the new road.

'Don't rightly know, John. The easy answer's money—special overtime—but I'll tell you this, by cripes, once you've gone bush, one thing's for sure: you'll always come back.'

'You too, Bill?'

'Guess so. Got a young 'un and a nice little house. Thought she oughta have it, if you get me, even though her mother's gone. I've plenty of savings, but I couldn't stick it. So I up and left her with an aunt on her side.'

'Of course you're right, the money's good,' John said thoughtfully.

But Bill wasn't listening to him. 'Guess too the sound and feel's got something to do with it,' he said. 'Yer haven't sorta got to explain yourself out here. You just get on with things. Haven't you noticed the trees have a sound all of their own when you're among 'em like this? And the smell of that there earth—I dunno. Sounds stupid when you *say* things.'

John smiled at the big man's embarrassment. 'I know what you mean, Bill, but do you really think the poetry of the thing is going to mean anything to the bunch we're going to take out into this primitive country?'

'Guess they feel it but don't think about it, else you'd not get one of those blokes a foot from town. Anyway, I think most men like goin' bush for a bit. Not too long, mind you, for some. Then there's some 'as got themselves hitched up to some pretty nagging sheilas in town!'

John laughed outright, but he remembered the conversation. Thought of the men signed up for this job—his job. Eighty precent of them were Australians, the other twenty per cent a European mixture. He had seen the same variety in those working at the dam, but he couldn't help wondering how it would work when they found themselves thrown together out in the wilds, shut in by wind, rain and forest. Would the spirit then become more national than international?

From a personal viewpoint he knew more strongly than ever it wasn't going to be just the job that was going to test him, but these men also. He asked himself whether he could keep in them that core of content that Bill was so sure existed, thereby making for smooth running in the long months ahead. Himself, he was more inclined to believe they would stick because of the money, and maybe the "nagging sheilas".

This brought his mind back to Sara—Sara and himself. He too was beginning to dislike more and more this weekend existence of theirs, but realised there was more discontent in her now than at any time in their marriage. He knew that, for some reason, a home was no longer sufficient for her. There was no doubt about her loving him. He dismissed the thought the instant it became a question in his mind. Why then wasn't it enough for her to do the things a woman did in a house, the things that satisfied other women?

For a brief moment he allowed himself to think what it would mean if he could come back to her and a small home near the "road". It would mean her giving up the boutique and the whole scheme in which they had become involved, but in spite of what she had said he knew the boutique was not really vital to her, no real bar to their return to their old way of living; rather an excuse to hide the main issue—which was what? He didn't know. The thing he did know was that it existed, and to come back to Sara here, at the end of a day's work, could never be like coming back to Sara in England. In many ways they had both changed since coming to Australia and, much as they were in love, they were no longer so dependent on each other. He tried to argue with himself that this could be a good thing, a sign of maturity, but he knew such an answer was futile. The success of marriage was for two people to *be* dependent on each other.

Even as he argued with himself he feared the answer lay in another question. Could a marriage really founder on children? Anyway, hadn't he offered to adopt a girl? He thought she would have jumped at it. Surely, if she did want children so badly, that was the answer. Were women such egotists that they couldn't accept the care, guidance and successful upbringing of *any* child?

He'd certainly done all any man could be expected to do in the circumstances. It wasn't his fault they couldn't have their own, and he immediately suppressed the thought that it could be.

He was depressed all week but when he got to town late on Friday, she was waiting for him as excited as a child. 'Thank goodness you got home tonight, darling. We're off skiing to National Park. We've managed to get a hut for a night. They're booked from year to year, you know. Someone Rick knows had it, but the whole family has gone down with 'flu, poor things. It'll be our last chance before the snow goes. I've got everything organised. We're off at five in the morning.'

He became as excited as she was. He always referred to skiing as his one extravagance, although it had been more in his mind than in fact since their marriage.

'Terrific! I've been looking at that snow on Wellington and wondering. Some of the fellows told me about National Park.' He disappeared down the passage to the bedroom and tossed his grip on the bed. 'Have much trouble getting the skis out?'

'Don't you remember taking them out? I only had to get the wrappings off.'

'That's right. How are we off for woollies and things?'

'Fine. I told you, I've got everything organised. Rick is picking us up in his car. He's got chains.'

She stood in the doorway, watching him change. He seemed to have dropped ten years in age. *He looks just as he* was when I first knew him, she thought. How different people look when they can do the things they want to do.

'How many of us are going?'

'Oh, three of the crowd, Arna, you, Rick and me. Seven. It'll be a jam at that.'

'Good. I think I'll have a shower now.'

'Don't be long then. The meal's ready and I think we'd better get off to bed early, or we'll never wake up.'

'Suits me!' he grinned wickedly as he made for the shower.

Next morning, tucked in between the two men on the front seat of the Holden, Sara felt happier than she had for a long time. In fact she was experiencing that "everything will come right" feeling, and pitied the few, the very few individuals trundling along the streets, their shoulders huddled down against the bitter wind of that bitter hour before the winter dawn. On the other hand, in contrast, the deserted city lights shone clear and bright as the car sped on to the Brooker highway.

None of them talked. She wriggled her toes under the heater and thought about these two on either side of her. John, his body against hers, not completely relaxed. She knew he did not like other people driving him, and she guessed his thoughts were half on his skiing, probably back in the days when he won the varsity championship in Brücken, the other half assessing Richard's driving ability and the car's performance.

Richard on the other hand was, she felt, amused, and driving with complete relaxation, not giving it much thought; in fact she knew that driving to him was a quite mechanical process, a necessary part of living. When he was driving he was quite free to think about what he liked, and she had the distinct sensation that he was thinking about them at the minute, her in particular. It irritated her, and some of her good feeling evaporated.

The one thing that always affected these two men when together was Richard's adoption of a vaguely superior attitude towards John. She wondered if John noticed it, but if he did he made no sign. What spoilt Richard, she decided, was his infernal egotism; apart from that he was a wonderful person to be with, amusing or serious by turn, always seeming to set his mood to those around him. That of course could be insincerity, part of his scheme to be the one noticed, the athlete, the yachtsman, the one who got around. Yet she knew she was being unkind; he was also understanding, genuinely understanding.

Anyway, she thought, he's going to take a back seat to John on this little venture. And her mind flew back to the day she had stood muffled up to the ears on the icy slopes above Brücken, watching the last ski jump of the day that was to make John the champion. Could see his figure springing up over the great drop; clean-cut, lithe and steady as he swept out into space; the screaming cheers as he made a perfect landing, points ahead of his nearest opponent.

They had been married a week later.

She felt him draw her hand through his arm. 'You're very quiet. Where had you got to?'

She laughed. 'A long way away, Brücken, and the day you won the championship.'

'That was a long way away. Afraid I'm pretty rusty now.'

'That good, eh!' Richard said.

'In the days before marriage hit me. I've hardly been on skis since. What's it like where we're going?'

'Not bad. One or two pretty good runs—not judged by your standard of course—but we have a lot of fun. It's more for kicks. No one gets terribly serious up here.'

'That certainly will be my standard now too.'

Sara could feel Richard stiffen, and knew how he had interpreted John's remark. Funny, she thought, if I'd made a remark like that he'd have teased me and we would have laughed. But she knew there wasn't much laughter between these two, and suddenly she realised John never made much comment about Richard because he didn't even consider him! So that makes him a conceited egotist too, she thought with amusement; in fact there wasn't much difference between these two at all. Perhaps that's why I've got myself involved with the two of them—and knew for the first time she had thought of Richard in the same way as John. It made her uncomfortable, and for the rest of the journey it was mainly she who did the talking, anything to break the silence between these two on either side of her.

Once they arrived the whole situation seemed back to normal, and she wondered if she had imagined that there had been a situation at all.

The other car load had arrived before them, and already breakfast was on the go. The girls rushed her off to see their hut, with all its grimy, primitive appeal. But for Sara the dark interior, with its smell of burnt-out eucalyptus and stale cigarette smoke, its dirty wooden floors and big, grim old open fireplace, had not half the attraction of the little rustic porch outside, where barely two could stand to shelter against the wind. Immediately below it the trail petered out into the sheer drop of one mountain range folding into another, the great white shoulders of snow splashed and dappled with the early morning sunlight. Down in the valley there were curly spirals of smoke from open wood fires, where gaily clad figures were strolling about or toiling off with their skis to the white slopes—no ski-lifts here.

For one breathtaking moment a wave of homesickness swept over her. Could she ever really be one with these happy youngsters who were content with whatever came their way? Who never craved to be different, just wanted to do what everyone else did—for kicks?

'Sara, Sara, come and look at this, it's absolutely beaut!'

She went in to find them in ecstasies over an old black kettle hanging on a weighty hook, equally black, above an open fire that was just beginning to crackle.

'Isn't it just terrific?'

'Wouldn't it be absolutely terrific for a honeymoon?'

Sara took a look at the rusty old mattresses and laughed. They followed her gaze and joined in the laughter just as the four men joined them, their arms full of stores and equipment.

'Come on, slaves, get moving on the breakfast front. We don't want to miss a minute of this, but we're starving.'

Altogether the two days were a wonderful success. John very quickly had everyone's admiration, for it seemed the years had not affected his skill. After about half an hour he had got back his old touch and was executing near perfect crestas, going higher and taking more risks than anyone among them. On Sunday morning he got up early with Richard, and together they made jumps.

Watching him, Sara was filled with pride, and thought: He's not like other people, success doesn't make him difficult, somehow it makes him much more understanding when he's on top.

On top he was. Even Richard gave him unstinted praise, as he and Sara climbed up to watch him try out a speed run from above the Golden Stairs, Arna having refused such exertion. They climbed together higher and higher so that they could get a clear and uninterrupted view of John's curving, swinging body streaming down the run.

'He's good, Sara. I owe you both an apology.'

'Why? You didn't say anything about his not being good.'

'No, but I thought it. That is, I made up my mind before actually seeing him.'

'We can't be accountable for our thoughts.'

'What a delightful fantasy, my English rose. I'm afraid your John gets under my Australian skin at times, and I'm sometimes inclined to be unreasonable.'

'Oh well, your Australianism gets under ours too, but it doesn't seem to matter very much, does it? I expect we'll all sort that out in time. It probably makes our relationship all the more interesting.'

'That's what I love about you: you mix philosophy so wonderfully with nonsense!'

'Come on, Rick, he's well and truly down now. That's about the last run for the day, isn't it? The light's going and we've got to get packed up.'

He didn't answer as they turned to scramble down through the matted button grass buried in its snowy coat, and she was aware as never before of his arm around her, helping her over the rough places; aware of an exhilaration that completely removed the need of words, and sent them skimming through the icy atmosphere locked together.

It was an awareness she had not known with any man other than John, and had thought never to know apart from him.

CHAPTER TWELVE

Back in town, John returned to the Hydro, and Sara fled in relief to the journal. She had never felt less sure of herself and never been more shocked at her inability to control her thoughts or feelings; so she took the ostrich solution of burying her problems in another's.

I have not written in my Journal for some time now, and in consequence, dear sister, there is much to relate. I almost know not how to begin.

I fear that from what you have already read you must think of me as having grown presumptuous, conceited and unfeeling. I do assure you this is not so, but I wish that I might make you understand how very alone I am. Safe all my young life in the protection of Deerbrook, not thinking at all of the future, then of a sudden I find myself torn from you, both my play-mate and mistress, and thrown in very truth across the world to fend for myself. Dear God, I would not wish for you to know what it takes to fend thus for oneself if one is a woman, but I have learnt that success or failure lies in oneself, in the ability to grasp any situation and turn it to one's own advantage.

But I will not ramble on to you of the philosophy I have so hardly learned, rather I will let the facts speak for themselves.

The measuring of the curtains I last mentioned was but the beginning. The big house was nearing its completion; there was no further need for the bullock drays to bring stone from the home quarry; the carpenters were finishing the last of their woodwork, and we of the household spent hour after hour cleaning, polishing and preparing cupboards.

Mr Haynes, that gentleman of dreams and schemes, had much trouble keeping his school-room routine; the younger members of the family would down their books at the slightest excuse and scamper off across the dry fields that separate the big house from the log homestead. Miss Patricia was always the first to lead the defection, her long hair streaming from its ribbons, cotton frock moulding to her legs and ankles. She was gone without a backward glance, her nimble feet making light work of the hard ground. Miss Jessica was generally next, hand in hand with Miss Dorothy, the two of them going at half the pace of their dashing sister, and looking back over their shoulders with half-fearful glances, fully aware they should not leave their studies, but at the same time defiantly determined to share the exciting new world of "the big house", with its echoing rooms and passages, and high-up balconies on to which they could climb to come nearer to their beloved magpies and parrots.

Then last, but not least, would go Master Bruce, a tornado of legs, arms and robust shouts of "Wait for me".

Unless I were bid I did not follow at once. Why should they not have alone their world of make-believe? Even for them it might one day fade. Mr Haynes, I knew, would not follow them. He would make a loud outcry against their wickedness, then settle himself in his own books, particularly as the children always chose the moment when their Mamma was in the storeroom, or busy with some of her many duties.

But presently I would take up my bonnet and go slowly behind them, for if I had one fear it was that Master Bruce would carelessly run across a snake. In truth, dear sister, these vicious, slithering creatures of the bush are my greatest fear so far in this country. No, that is not quite true; there is on thing I fear even more now, but of that disaster I shall bring myself to write in a moment.

I know you will have the greatest interest in the interview related between myself and Mr Haynes. His sudden and ill-considered suggestions regarding myself, I feel, will seem incomprehensible to you. You who, praise be to God, have never known the mind of a convict, which is so controlled and influenced by the social system of this country. Where, in England, could a convict enjoy the position in which Mr Haynes finds himself? Although he is an assigned servant by law, he is sufficiently placed in his Master's confidence to design his home and tutor his children.

Such is a convict's lot in this country that his life can be one long stretch of misery or he can achieve a future undreamed of in England. Much depends on the convict and the position in which he finds himself. In Mr Haynes's case his education and assured manner do much, but in spite of all his privileges he is afraid of the monotony of honest, simple work, with no ambition to turn to good advantage what he has, unless by sly and underhand means. I should say the one good thing he has done is design Ardrossan, which he naturally expects will secure his pardon. But what then? If he remains here he must work in some way. This he has no intention of doing under any circumstances, but I believe in me he senses someone who will fight, and he would like to lean on me. He also thinks of me as an opportunity sent to afford his personal pleasure, and like all of us who bear the mark of convict, he must snatch at opportunity. Particularly in my case because he knows I cannot run away.

He tries daily, in all manner of ways, to break down my resistance, and I am indeed glad that he does not sleep, as do I, in the family house, but has his quarters near the rest of the convicts, so that I have plenty of time each night to secure myself in my room.

He is right. I intend to fight, but not for such as he. He is a man who can give me neither security nor position. He has, however, unwittingly been the means of suggesting a way for me to acquire these two things. About this I am sure you are waiting to hear — the acquisition of Master Matthew!

It is not such a wild fancy as you might imagine. I know already he is not insensible to either me or my person, but I also know that unless I am exceedingly careful he will assume that it would be quite right and proper for a gentleman to acquire me in the same manner as did the Captain.

Any such plan I shall of course frustrate, for once such as he had his way with me, gone would be any chance of my walking through the carved doors of Ardrossan as mistress instead of servant. To this end I am once again well pleased with the arrangements that have been made for me in the big house. At the far end of the big, flagged kitchen, a little circular stairway leads up to a small room above the rafters. Its only access is through a door at the top of those stairs, and its one window is high above the ground, looking out to the bushland and the blue of the mountains that show the grandest pinnacles against the sky. I wish that you might see them in the sunset, or dawn or when the vivid moonlight lies across the bush at night.

Yes, dear sister, that room shall be my castle, its door shall be my defence, past which none shall enter.

The danger, of course, to my plans lies in the fact that other families with marriageable daughters of the right age may come to settle near to us. A further danger would be if he were interested, as are his father and mother, in the Government House circle. I hear his mother deploring the fact that he rides so little to Hobart Town to ingratiate himself with those who are responsible for running the affairs of this Colony. But in this she cannot move him. It would seem he has paid his respects but twice to the Governor since the family has been in the log house.

He strives only to make Ardrossan the greatest property in the district, if not the Colony, and if hard work and determination can make this so he will achieve his object. I myself rise every morning by five o'clock to get through my work, but he is always before me, out in the paddocks, as they call them here, hours before the family is ready for breakfast. Yet I feel it is through no love of hard work that he does this, nor through fear of his father, as Mr Haynes suggested, although I have never yet heard him attempt to run contrary to his father's wishes. Rather it is as though he bears a grudge against someone or something, and this is the only manner in which he can be free of it. But perhaps I am wrong. Perhaps he has become obsessed by a love for this land and has become part of it. Perhaps he is doing all in his power to join with his father in this aim. Perhaps this is why he never actually opposes his father, but rather couches any opposition by the way of suggestions — which I have often noticed his father seriously considers.

Therefore must I bide my time, and find some way in which to convince him that marriage to me would make good sense. Pray to God, dear sister, that some way will be found, for I grow to love this place more and more, but I am in no mind to be its servant for the rest of my days.

But I must hasten to tell you of the tragedy that struck at us all but a few days ago. Even as I write of it, it again fills me with horror.

I mentioned earlier how Mr James told me on that memorable drive from Hobart Town that the Master planned to bring out a number of his old staff in England; also several fine racehorses as well as a pedigreed mare to breed with Oscar, in order that he might, in due course, be the means of starting horse-racing in this country, as he has been already one of the first to be given by the Government Merino rams with which to improve the breed of sheep. Upon hearing news that all had begun their long journey from England, he took four convicts — Marston, Smith, Eltone and Sneaton from their clearing work, and set them to build small wooden cottages and a new stable in the home field. Then he, with his sons and the remaining convicts, set off for the back fields to work at fencing. Fencing is one of the Master's greatest problems, as in Van Diemen's Land there is an increasing roguery called cattle duffing. This means that bushrangers, escaped convicts, and indeed anyone who roams the bush and has a mind to such wickedness, steals and drives off cattle, horses and sheep. This is particularly serious for the Master, as his stock is of such fine quality and must have cost him dearly.

But I digress. The day of which I write was a great one for the rest of us left at the homestead, for that morning after breakfast, when the men had ridden off, we were to start the long-awaited move to the big house. All other work was suspended. Mr James brought round one of the bullock drays, and he and Mrs James, Mr Haynes, Cook, myself and the younger members of the convict families, began the work of loading as much of the household goods and furniture as we could manage, starting with beds and rugs, as that night we were going to move in to sleep.

The children were wildly excited, and rushed round getting in everyone's way, pushing in toys and personal possessions in all the wrong places; the dogs which had remained with us all barked and the cats fled. There was a scorching north wind blowing, and with rushing round so much the girls could not possibly hope to keep on their bonnets, so that I feared they would be sadly burnt, and could foresee a tearful, exhausted end to this exciting day. How tearful it was to be I mercifully was not aware.

We worked steadily all the morning, and by lunch I began to feel faint with the unaccustomed physical work added to the heat, the latter being far greater that day than anything I had yet known. We had already put Madam to bed in a hastily arranged bedroom, with Miss Jessica and Miss Dorothy taking it in turns to bathe her head and face with tank water.

I had just sat down, with my back against the smooth white trunk of a nearby gum tree, to eat some lunch I had cut earlier, when I saw Master Matthew and Oscar break from the bush on the far side of the log house, and come galloping towards us like a black streak. I had seen Oscar gallop before, but never like this! I sat watching them, the food halfway to my mouth; I knew throughout my entire body that they came to us at this pace with bad news.

In a moment they were upon us, and I struggled to my feet as Master Matthew pulled up the great horse almost on top of me, so that I was aware of its hot belching breath, distended nostrils, staring eyes with bloodshot whites, and the long black neck sheeted with white foam.

'Where's everyone? Where's my mother?'

'Madam is lying down—'

'Never mind, leave her there. Get everyone. Get every available bucket and utensil of any size and fill it with water. James—James, where are you?'

'Here, Master Matthew. What's to do?'

I had a quick glimpse of Mr James getting himself out of the bullock dray, where he had gone to have a few minutes rest, as well as Mrs James's anxious face peeping over the side.

'Fire, that's what's to do. Do you know how to make a flail?'

'Yes, sir, I think so, sir.'

'Start making them as quickly as you can; the whole bush is alight! Unless the wind changes we haven't a hope. Haynes, where are you? Oh, there you are. You'd better get down to the river and get as much water as you can. Use the dray. I'll get the rest of the men, we'll fight as long as we can before dropping back.' And wheeling Oscar he was gone again.

There was a petrified silence, then the children came running out of the house. As I write I can see them in that dry, brilliant sunshine.

'What's wrong, Sarah?'

'Why's Matthew riding Oscar so fast?'

'Didn't Oscar look funny with all that white stuff on his neck. What is it, Sarah?'

I found it hard to speak, but I caught them by the shoulders just as Miss Charlotte came running to join them. I thought how merciful it was the Madam could not have heard Oscar's arrival.

'Quickly,' I said to Miss Charlotte. 'You and the girls run to the kitchen where we have piled all the pails and preserving pans, bring everything you can find and put them in the dray for Mr Haynes.'

'Why, Sarah? What has happened?'

'There's a big fire, and your father wants all the water he can get to put it out. Hurry now!'

They ran off chattering and I turned to Mr Haynes. He was standing with his hands in his pockets, looking at the distant bush where only a moment ago we had seen Oscar come bursting out with Master Matthew.

'Please, Mr Haynes, don't just stand there. If you go back to the loghouse there are those old baths and half a tank by the kitchen door. You could be back with them while the girls are collecting the pails and pans. At least the house is of stone. I'll help Mrs James make the flails while you are gone.'

I hardly knew what I was saying, I was so afraid, thinking of every dreadful possibility. Mr James had already run to the dray and, pulling out an axe, begun to lay about all the young saplings he could see, then lopping off their thin branches.

'Now look,' he said, 'this is what you does.'

With a beating heart I watched him twist the slender branches he had left along the stem.

'But what are you going to bind them with?' I cried.

'In the dray there's some wire.'

I picked up my skirts and ran as I had never run before. Ardrossan must be saved. Must be saved — must be saved. The words were beating over and over as I found the wire and rushed back. I watched his old gnarled fingers twisting it round, back and through and round again, and even in my panic I marvelled.

'Got the idea?'

I nodded. 'Yes, go please, go quickly. Here are the girls with the pails, and Mr Haynes has got the old tin baths.'

As they drove off, lashing the oxen, I told the girls to make more piles, then Mrs James and I set about making the flails.

In no time at all my hands were skinned and my body was soaked with perspiration so that I could feel my clothes sticking to it, but by the time the dray was back we had made two apiece and the girls had found yet another pile of odd-shaped utensils. The two men and the children threw them in and were off again while Mrs James and I toiled on. The minutes seemed hours — then we could smell the burning eucalyptus; it came to us in a wave, and up in the sky above the bush a curling cloud rolled as though by sudden magic. The smell of burning eucalyptus trees is one not forgotten and, combined with the hot smoke and black ash, always brings terror to everyone who has ever experienced it. I pray that it will never happen to me again.

'May the good Lord 'ave mercy on us!' the old woman muttered, and I echoed her prayer as I worked on feverishly.

It seemed an eternity before they got back from the river again, then we dropped our flails and rushed to help them unload, staggering under our spilling burdens. When we spaced them out along the side of the house, some fifty feet away, they looked so pathetic as a means of defence that I felt quite sick.

Hardly knowing what I was doing I rushed to Brutus and dragged him forwards.

'Sarah, what are you going to do?'

'I'm going to see what else I can save. It will break Madam's heart. We must save some of the furniture. Miss Charlotte, please go to your mother and tell her what has happened. Keep the children with you.'

The two men joined me and Mrs James stood staring from us to the disappearing children. Then we left her to carry on with the flails. In a frenzy I rushed into the log house and pushed and heaved with the men at tables, chairs, anything on which I could lay hands. I tore down pictures and tapestries; all the things that were going to be brought over in a more leisurely manner during the next few days.

I had lost all feeling in my muscles, and when the dray was loaded to capacity we returned to empty it pell-mell into the entrance hall which had so captured my imagination, but which was rapidly acquiring the appearance of a nightmare place. I would have gone back for another load had I not looked out through the windows and seen, on the edge of the bush, a tongue of flame lick out into the clearing through a black cloud of smoke in such an obscene manner that I was rooted to the spot.

At the same moment I heard Madam's voice say behind me: 'Where are my sons and husband?'

I realised I had not given them a thought!

I turned and stared at her in horror. Helplessly I looked back to the bush, and at that moment we saw four horsemen break out into the clearing; then, as though the appearance were a signal, the whole of the bush behind them broke into a wall of flame, and for one dreadful moment we could see clearly the trunks of the tall trees outlined before they were submerged by rolling smoke and a curtain of fire.

We rushed to the door and watched in silence as the men galloped towards us. The air was now filled with flying particles and we could all taste the smoke on our tongues.

The master somehow reached us first. Oscar, magnificent as he was, was showing signs that even he had come to an end of his endurance, and I realised how relentlessly Master Matthew must have used him. That alone was more frightening than anything else.

The Master flung himself from his horse.

'James, get the horses down to the river. Jessica and Dorothy, you take Bruce and go with him. The rest of you women form yourselves into a bucket chain between here and the river. When I give the word keep filling and passing up buckets. If the worst happens and the wind doesn't change, when I give the word, wade into the river up to your necks. Do you all understand?'

We all managed to say "yes", whereupon he shouted to us to get into position while he, his sons, Mr Haynes and the men picked up flails and walked back towards the fire line. Madam rushed after him and caught his arm.

'How long before it will come?'

He gave her hand a quick grip and then pushed her back.

'Go back, Jessica, and pray. Only God can answer.'

He was gone, striding over the grass so soon to be blackened, and in our ears now was the steady crackling of the all-consuming flames.

I could not stand there and wait and watch. Quickly I bent, picked up a spare flail, and ran wildly after the men, and as I ran I saw a small band of people running towards us — pathetic, stumbling figures; some fell and struggled to pick themselves up again. I guessed they would be the Macdonald family, and wondered why they would be coming to our aid when their plight must be as desperate as our own. Once again I felt bad tidings were being brought to us, but still I ran on boldly, my breath coming in gasps, the heat from the flames already scorching and searing my face. I took a place in the line of beaters and began as savagely as any to beat at the burning grass. Half-blind with the acrid, choking smoke, I hit down at the wicked red tongues which seemed to spring up round me as fast as I could wield my flail to destroy them. My eyes stung and tears rolled down my face, but I hit and hit in a futile rhythm.

'Why are you not back with the women?' the man beside me shouted. I half turned my head, and through the tangled mass of my hair saw the smoke-grimed face of Master Matthew.

'I could not stand and watch; let me be, Master Matthew.'

'Then if you must stay, do the thing properly. With those frenzied strokes you will exhaust yourself. We have not time for fainting women.'

I saw that he was not looking at me as he used his flail with long, hard sweeps.

'I shall not faint, Master Matthew,' I answered.

'See to it that you don't. Watch now.'

I knew then that he would not send me back, so taking a deep breath I made myself do as he did. How long he and I laboured, falling back step by step, I know not. It seemed that we had entered into an eternity of blazing heat and agony, endured only by a determination greater than both. I forgot even his presence. Ardrossan must and should be saved. I lost all sense of time and place, knew only that I must go on and on, beating — beating. If I did not beat, did not force my weary arms to make one more stroke, one more stroke, Ardrossan must die, I would die. This great blasting all-absorbing heat would bury us, me and my plans for the future, in a useless, endless void. I would not have it so, I would not—

'Sarah, stop, do you hear me, stop I say, the wind has changed. Do you hear me? We are going home now.'

But I could not stop; his voice was part of this blackness; it was mocking me. Then I felt my wrists gripped and held, but I could not see, my eyelids were too swollen, and my eyes too full of tears from the smoke. I was forced to stand there.

'It is time you learned discipline, Sarah,' the voice said, and this time I recognised it and realised the fight must indeed be over. 'This is the second time I have had recourse to give you an order which you do not obey.'

'The second time, Master Matthew?'

'You know quite well that you still feed Oscar when you imagine my back is turned!'

'He is most partial to apples, and you have not the time to pick out the ones past ripeness.'

'If you have that much spare time I must acquaint my mother of your need for employment.'

I thought it better to remain silent, and fumbled for the handkerchief I had pushed down the bosom of my dress. Somehow I must stop this moisture pouring from my burning eyes. It was agony and I was much concerned how I would find my way back to the house. There would be much to be done, and doubtless Madam would be looking for me.

He did not speak again as I still tried in vain to wipe away the flood of tears that seemed to have no end, but at last I managed to make out a blurred picture of the house in the distance, and stumbled towards it. I assumed Master Matthew had left me, after warning me that he would report me to Madam.

I was not afraid of his reports. I more than filled the requirements expected of me, being the first, except himself and the men, to rise of a morning, and the last to my bed. Madam knew this and I believed she would be just. Unlike many of the settlers, she and Master were able to control their convict labour without having recourse to physical chastisement by the local police magistrate. Strict the Master might be, but no man appeared unhappy under his rule. As for Oscar — yes, Master Matthew was right there, I had risked his displeasure and its consequences to make friends with the temperamental stallion. I could not resist him, and already knew there was a bond between us.

So, fighting my bitterness, I stumbled on in the general direction of the house, only to be aware a short time later that a figure was blocking my way, a tall broad one. It was my tormentor again.

'Stand still.'

'If you please, sir, Madam will be looking for me. I must return.'

'You must do as I say, Sarah. Stand still.'

I knew determined resistance would not aid me, so I stood before him, chafing sadly at the command he had of me.

To my surprise I felt something cold, wet and soothing placed across my eyes. Hastily I put up my hand and felt what must be some kind of bandage.

'Yes, you must hold it. Now come, I will lead you to my mother. By the time we reach her you should be able to open your eyes. On the way you shall entertain me with the reason for your noble and self-sacrificing act of fire-fighting today!'

I imagined sarcasm in his voice and thought it better once again to give no answer.

'When I ask a question, Sarah, I expect an answer.'

I felt it was with him much as it was with the Captain all those months ago.

'I do not think, sir, that you are prepared to accept my answer.'

'That is not for you to judge.'

The exhaustion of my body now weighed me down like a chain, it became an effort to walk forward. Because of my physical weakness, for a moment my spirit quailed. What was the use of fighting this man who had everything on his side — money, position, the law?

'There was no pretence, sir. I have come to love your home. I could not bear that it should die before it really lived.'

His laugh rang out on the smoke-laden atmosphere. 'A thief who thinks! Of a truth there is nothing that cannot take place on this island.'

'I said, sir, you would not accept my answer.'

'So, you can read my mind also. Or is it perhaps that there is no trick or artifice to which you would not stoop to curry favour in our sight, in order to gain your freedom? One cannot of course blame you. But what would you do with your freedom, Sarah? Flaunt that hair of yours in Hobart Town, in order to join the line of fancy ladies being set up with carriages and accommodation?'

Rage and exhaustion so combined in my body as to render me almost beside myself. I longed to strike him but dreaded the result; also, something warned me that he was deliberately baiting me. Gritting my teeth and closing my throbbing eyes under the bandage, I so controlled myself as to allow him to lead me on, and not so much as a word did

I give him back. Let him have his masterful triumph. One day I would have mine.

Thus we arrived before his mother. A sorry sight indeed I must have looked, for she cried out: 'Sarah, my poor girl! Your dress is quite ruined, your face — and your eyes! What is wrong with your eyes?'

'It is nothing, Madam. The smoke has made them sting a little. They are much better now.'

And indeed they were. I removed the bandage which had dried hot from the congestion of my face, and found that I could open my lids almost normally, and although the stinging was there it had greatly abated. At my benefactor I did not look.

'With your permission, Madam, I will get some water from the river.'

'There is no need to go so far as the river, Sarah. Praise be to God we did not have need of all those utensils. The wind changed in time so that the house was never in danger.'

'Was much damage done, Madam?'

'Not as much as we feared. My husband said one wheat field went, two of the men's cottages have been burned out, half the log house and one shed of furniture, but much has been saved. You have helped us greatly today, Sarah, and you will not find us lacking in gratitude. I fear the story for the Macdonald family is not so good. They have been completely burnt out and have come to us for shelter.'

'I will hurry, Madam, and clean myself.'

I picked up the first pail of water I saw, and took myself to the kitchen sink. I remembered a piece of mirror glass we had taken from the log house, and found it among the piled-up things on the floor. Although the afternoon was well advanced, and there had been no time to find or light the lamps and candles, I could see well enough what a dreadful picture I presented. The face that looked back at me was swollen and streaked with black; the eyes buried in puffed and roasted flesh; the hair wild and matted.

But my plight was as nothing to that of our neighbours. Convict I might be, without rights, money or position, but at least I had food, clothing, a roof over my head. Imagine a family of twelve suddenly without so much as a basin in which to wash themselves! Everything they owned burned to ashes. Even the farm implements twisted and ruined, their crops burned to the ground, their animals fled.

As quickly as I could I removed the worst of the grime from my person, and managed to find and trim a lamp before returning to the entrance hall. Everyone had collected round the pathetic figure of Mrs Macdonald with her sobbing family clinging to her skirts, while her menfolk stared despondently through the windows at the darkening, smouldering bush. My heart turned over for them. There was no comfort to be given in words, for what words could be found in such a situation? Out of the corner of my eye I caught sight of Master Donald, one hand over his face and I knew that he was praying.

I too silently prayed that his prayers would be answered, while I led away the younger children to wash and comfort them as best I could, while Cook busied herself to find food for her greatly enlarged family.

But I will not dwell on this sadness, my dear sister. These happenings, it would seem, are part of life here, and in an extraordinary way they become the personal concern of the community. Since there are no governmental rights or privileges to speak of as yet in Van Diemen's Land, all settlers band together to help each other when tragedy strikes, as it appears to do with unfortunate regularity.

So it was on this occasion. The Macdonalds were installed in what was left of the log house, and half of our men joined with theirs to rebuild their house and replough their ravaged fields.

With us the busy days flew by. Ardrossan must come into its own. To mark the occasion it was decided to have a Ball, and at the same time celebrate Miss Charlotte's twenty-first birthday.

There is another event also causing great excitement and expectation. The township of Kilmarnock, some six miles up the gully, is to be the first in the area to have its own church, the minister for which, also one of the first in the island, has been appointed and is due to arrive at any time. According to the mailman, many of the well-to-do townspeople and settlers have offered money and assistance for the building of the church, but there are great arguments about its denomination, as the churches of England,

Scotland and Rome are all represented hereabouts. I can see much trouble arising out of this unless all agree to worship in the one church, which would surely make world history.

I must tell you about the mailman. His way lies through the bush, over the mountains and rivers. He knows everyone and they know him. In addition to his official mail, he carries all kinds of notes and personal communications. He is the world's greatest gossip. He knows everybody's business, from their love affairs to their burials, but wherever he goes he meets with hospitality. Even the bushrangers respect him, and no settler would dare to provoke him for fear of what tale he would spread.

So, all being well, we shall be celebrating Miss Charlotte's birthday a month hence with the Ball on the Saturday night, and then the first service with our own minister on the Sunday morning in Ardrossan's red barn. Everyone here is in a flutter; there are plans and counter-plans, as well as unending work from early morning into almost the early hours of the next morning.

Myself, I hope all this chatter will not tempt the bushrangers to plunder the neighbourhood while so many will be away from their homes. There is talk of starvation in Hobart Town and among the prisoners at Port Arthur, even in the so-called model prison. They even say prisoners will be encouraged to escape, so desperate is the food situation, and Governor Arthur has warned all military posts throughout the island. It is even suggested that he will *be in Kilmarnock, personally inspecting the post there, at the time of the Ball, and may even grace it with his presence. As you can guess, all this has put Madam in a rare to-do. But if things are really as serious as rumour makes them, I doubt if she will be able to count on the young military officers being present.*

Master Donald is expecting great things from the arrival of this minister, the Reverend John McKirtle by name. He is more than ever anxious to leave this country and enter the Ministry ...'

Sara put down the journal. She felt one with it, felt she too had a part in those days, when life had been uncomfortable but was packed with living drama that no longer existed.

CHAPTER THIRTEEN

Everything was organised. The last of the snow had gone from the mountains. In the rainforest the tall gums stood tight-packed, their incredibly smooth straight trunks reaching hundreds of feet towards the sky, so that their burnished branch tips might find light and the sun. At their base, in darkness, the mighty boles had thrown out finger roots like giant hands, to grab tenaciously at the earth. There was the damp, pungent smell of moss, tree ferns and wet leaves; about all an abiding stillness. One heard the fall of a leaf, could hear it the whole way as it spiralled down through the mat of branches—but not the note of a bird. In the winter there were no birds. The rainforest was so vast, so possessive, so bereft of food, that it had no place for the bright sweep of wings.

On that day of the beginning of the road John got out of his bunk before first light and, walking through the camp, finally stopped by a mighty swamp gum, leant against its silver trunk and felt for pipe and tobacco, only realising after a moment of fruitless searching that both had been left on his bunk in accordance with the strict rule of no smoking in the forest. A rule so enforced that the men carried a thermos with their packed lunches, and no man was allowed a packet of matches on his person.

He folded his arms on his chest and stayed still that he might listen to these last unmolested moments of a forest which had known peace such as this for thousands of years. He let his mind travel back over the past months: the steady, methodical work that had brought him to this moment; the aerial surveys which had determined the shape of the road that would lie before him, from its beginning to its end. He thought of Hurst, the project engineer who, in a quiet and efficient way, had taught him so much about this vast forest he was about to enter; not only taught, but filled him with an impatient excitement to come to grips with it. A man who knew so well the way to combat the years of the forest's undisputed control; a man who was patient where nature was concerned, but most critical of human ideas and problems.

John knew as he stood there listening to the unsuspecting forest gradually awakening that his own problems of the road held no real fears for him. He was not conceited but he had confidence. He had been given the men and the machinery and, above all, Bill. Yes, Bill was more than his answer, a natural man of science though he had not been given the chance to learn academic theory, a man who could handle men. John smiled and counted himself lucky, relaxed in this hour of anticipation, and watched the first spiral of smoke from Cookie's kitchen stove pipe, as the men came straggling out to ablutions, towels thrown over their bare, hard shoulders.

An hour later four of them went in through light horizontal bush, Hurst pointing out the peculiarity of the growth, hung down in sprawling arms, from which other thin trunks would grow straight, until they in turn bowed over, making a network of tenacious screens, layer upon layer—a house of tough intermingling floors, so that the bottom of the gully could not be seen, and men could walk on the top of it, in some places at a height of twenty feet, and utterly treacherous.

He found himself stirring to the challenge with an excitement that swept everything from his mind; found himself recalling Bill's voice when he had asked the big man what kept him in the bush: 'Don't rightly know, John. The easy answer's money—special overtime—but I'll tell you this, by cripes, once you've gone bush, one thing's for sure: you'll always come back.'

He wasn't sure that he had "gone bush", but as the hours passed while they crept and crawled in the all-pervading silence he knew a satisfaction he hadn't known for years. It was unmitigated, even by the real discomfort he was suffering. Heat and sweat built up beneath their rain clothes, branches tore and scratched them, their feet slipped on the wet wood, and always the great trees stood tall and contemptuous. The trail in was blazed by the two bushmen following them. The thud of their marking slashers cutting into the bark of the trees to be felled became a challenge that echoed and was lost, as though the forest heard and rejected it. Indeed, after half a day they had only pushed in a quarter of a mile.

'There are a lot of natural shelves in the hillside. You've got luck,' Hurst said.

'I'll need it. Hope that "7" driver knows his job.'

'He does, one of our best. Besides, he'll get danger money for this.'

'Money certainly rules the position in Australia.'

'In most places.'

Later, after "tea" as John was learning to call it, they settled down to a beer before turning in, and Hurst returned to the subject of money: 'You can't afford to get cynical about money, Hilyard. It's taken the place of "class" in a country's potential, particularly in Australia. Her potential is almost unlimited, and her only worry is to find the cash to exploit it. To get anywhere in big business abroad you've got to talk big, act big; maybe our expense account can't stand up to that sort of thing but our potential can. Any minute now someone's going to wake up to that. We've got to get in before they do. On a smaller scale these men feel the same about their jobs—cash in while they can. We pay pretty well, as you know, and they're not a bad bunch. They do a good job.'

'If they're handled in the right way.'

'You couldn't have a better supervisor when you're fully manned.'

'I know.'

They smoked in silence for a while, and John gave way to the peace and relaxation of the place. He looked at Hurst lying back in an old chair, his eyes half-closed. A quiet man who didn't air his knowledge but could impart it. It had been a revelation to watch and listen to him assessing and explaining the nature of the bush they would have to conquer. Fascinating to watch him combine science and the almost sixth sense of the bushman. At a glance he calculated the dangers, the impenetrability and problems of the bush and scrub about them; its history, how and where it would give way to men and machines; yet at the same time he would find the thick moss and examine it with the touch of a woman.

He looked a lonely type of man, one who would prefer his own company to that of others. Did this sort of life make one like that? For the first time John wondered if the bush could take too strong a grip of a man—make him impatient of the ordinary give and take of human society. He had heard that Hurst had been married but was separated from his wife. Already he knew that this kind of life had no place for any woman other than the patient, waiting kind. Admittedly, ninety per cent of men in ordinary city jobs and professions left their wives in the morning and came back at night, having put them out of their consciousness if not their subconsciousness, for the space of a day; but when a man went to the bush he left his wife to go to his mistress, and when he returned at night there was little he could share of a day's experiences.

Was this what had happened to him and Sara? They were still, and always would be, husband and wife—he had no doubt of that, but the bond which had existed in the unspoken word, the silence where two minds could drift and touch without notice or effort, had gone. They no longer stood on a common ground. Something was happening to their lives together, something vital, and he had a feeling there was nothing either could do to stop or fight it. It was too intangible for either words or action.

He sat up and knocked out his pipe. 'Takes a lot of understanding, this bush life of yours,' he said.

'It does that.'

'To begin with it seemed simple, new, a challenge— whatever you like—particularly to someone like me. In fact, a new job and a new approach.'

Hurst waited, watching the ash drop off the end of his cigarette.

'Now I'm finding it could develop into a way of life.'

Hurst smiled but made no comment.

'I've been wondering where it will lead and whether I want to go the whole way.'

'Meaning?'

'I left England because I was tied completely to an office and the concepts of other men. It was never "I", always, "they".'

'If you don't mind my saying so, you sound ambitious.'

'In a sense, yes, but not completely in the way you are thinking. I believed that if I had experience I could prove my ability to think along practical lines as well as on paper. I could not get those above to listen.'

'The mind that designs and the mind that does don't always mix.'

'So I'm discovering. I'm beginning to say to myself: When I finish this job, providing all goes well, I will probably be given another like it, and so on.'

'Probably.'

'In other words I could become an educated workman, in my particular rut.'

Again Hurst smiled.

'And by the time I have completed five such projects, ten-odd years of my life could be gone. Will I want a drawing board again after that time? This could become my life. I could go on and on, deeper into the bush. On and on, playing the little god in my own sphere—'

'Hold it! Maybe we're coming to the crux of the thing now.'

'In what way?'

'Being a little god in your own sphere! Isn't that really what you want?'

It was John's turn to smile. 'Maybe.'

'It hasn't occurred to you you could be a better-sized god in the designing world?'

'With so many white-collar gods there, fishing for position, one would lose the sense of being a god at all. I'd rather be a little god completely in charge of a little world.'

'Then what's the problem? Domestic?' Hurst fished out a packet of cigarettes from a wrinkled packet in his jacket, and resettled in his chair.

'Partly, but not altogether. I expect I've changed my view of life too quickly to judge yet.'

'Your wife not exactly bending over with excitement when you introduced her to one of our "villages"?'

'Well, you see, we haven't any children—'

'This part of your problem's a common one. There aren't too many of the wives who like the villages.'

'I don't think it's so much the villages as their men going to the bush. When a man goes to an office he's doing what the majority of men do. He's taped. But when he does a job like this he does something about which she knows nothing. If nothing else, she becomes lonely, disorientated.'

'You could be right at that. So?'

'Either he accepts a job like this, decides it's a project to be completed, carries his wife with him, or—' John stopped and looked at Hurst, watched him exhale a long spiral of smoke, 'he thinks again before he is seized with bush fever.'

The other man got out of his chair and stood a moment with his hands in his pockets.

'My advice, Hilyard, for what it's worth, is finish your project before you think too deeply. Let the end of the road give you its answer, and let your wife into some of your thoughts on the way. Fifteen years ago I took your rough-shod solution, because at some stage of the game we all think like you, and I made a great mistake. Goodnight. Camp ruling is early to bed. See you at six.'

When he had gone, closing the door surprisingly quietly behind him, John found he was thinking more of the other man's problems than his own. Hurst provided, in fact, one answer to the problem. Clever and all as the man was, to finish up like him, in the same kind of rut, was far from John's calculations.

Back in Hobart the boutique was taking shape. The alterations to the house in Battery Point were nearly finished; Paulina was on her way from Italy, and Sara had completed some designs which found great favour with Arna. So much so, she suggested that as soon as Paulina arrived she should set to work to make them. 'You know,' she said to Sara as she watched her putting the final touches to a sketch, 'I like so much what you are doing that if Paulina agrees, has the right material and can get them finished in time, we should open the boutique with a fashion parade.'

Wearily Sara pushed the hair back from her forehead. 'D'you really think we are good enough for that?'

'But of course. If we do not think we are good, the people will not think so. You see what I mean?'

'I suppose so,' Sara said. She had been grateful for the work entailed in the designs, but she wondered what Arna would say if she knew the work meant more than the design itself. Work kept her from thinking too much about that day on the mountain top at National Park.

She knew she was up against the first major problem of her life, the first one she couldn't take to John. She found herself examining minutely the code with which she had been brought up, the behaviour pattern which fell into two departments—the things one did, the things one didn't do. The belief that if one belonged to a normal, ordinary, happily set-up family with more or less adequate means, one did not go round wearing black leather, try out erotic sexual experiments, take drugs for kicks, beat up old people, or demand the type of individualistic life that spelled trouble for others. Lastly of course came the matter of loyalty in marriage—*that* definitely was one of the "things one did".

Yet she could not get out of her mind those moments on the top of the mountain when, with Richard, she had experienced sensations that should belong only to herself and John. They always had until now. She knew too that Richard had felt as she had felt. It had come suddenly, unexpectedly. She had not wanted it nor done anything to bring it about. Or had she? Had she taken him for granted? Always so used to a man around, had she, with John away at work all week, allowed someone else to take the role of "a man to lean on"? Surely not! Yet she and Arna had turned to him for advice, for entertainment. She had even returned to painting to make his beloved yacht come alive on canvas. He perhaps had every right to think she meant more than she did. Appalled, her first reaction was to have this thing out in a sane and civilised fashion, but what would she say? Above all, did she want to say it?

'Sara,' Arna said close beside her, 'I have talked to you at least twice and you do not answer. I do not think Rick is good for you really.'

Startled, Sara turned sharply to Arna's mischievous, smiling face. 'What do you mean by that?'

'You know quite well what I mean. You have a bad conscience and you don't know what to do with it!'

It was such a relief to lose her temper that Sara lost it completely. 'How dare you say that!'

Arna shrugged. 'You see, you are not a person of bad temper, yet you are ready to abuse me without finding out what I mean.'

Sara could not trust herself to answer, and Arna went on smoothly: 'Let me tell you something about us Europeans and see if it does not fit what is worrying you. Like you, many of us believe in this marriage idea; it keeps a family name, it is a haven for children, but unlike you, because we know it is natural to love in many ways, we agree to have those other loves behind closed doors, so long as the marriage itself is not publicly harmed. Would you not say this is also a marriage of loyalty?'

'A marriage of convenience!' Sara snapped.

'If you wish, but what is wrong with that?'

'The complete removal of trust from the person round whom you build your life.'

'But,' Arna said patiently, 'if you believe in it, it is marriage round which you build your life, not one person. As you know, I do not believe in marriage.'

'What you don't believe in,' Sara said quickly, 'is the absolute communion between two people. You're content to flit from one pleasure to the next. But what happens when you get tired of flitting but must go on living?'

Arna laughed outright. 'Ah, there you have a point, Sara dear. I promise I will give it my greatest consideration, but by the time I am tired of flitting I do not think I shall mind!'

Sara joined in her laughter and felt better, relieved in spite of herself that Arna had guessed at some of the thoughts which had been worrying her, although she was not prepared to discuss them. However, before she needed to say anything more the phone rang.

She looked across at Arna. Intuitively they both knew who was ringing, and it was quite a few seconds before she reached out to lift the receiver. It would have to be Richard—and it was.

'Sara! Are you going out?'
'No.'
'Good. I'll come round.'
'No.'
'What?'
'I said, "No", Rick.'
'What's up?'
'Nothing's up.'
'All right, come to dinner with me.'
'No.'
'Can't you find another word to say the same thing?'

As always with Richard, she found herself smiling regardless. 'I just want to work at the picture.'

'That all? Remember the bargain. Anyway, it's *my* picture.'

'All right, Rick. If we went out tonight you'd feel I was annoyingly English, and I'd feel you—'

'Were annoyingly Australian?'
'Exactly.'
'Sounds interesting.'
'It wouldn't be. Thanks for ringing. Goodnight.'

She sat looking at the phone. How easy it made things. You just cut off an awkward conversation whenever you liked. She also found she was wondering if Richard would ignore her flat refusal and come round, or even ring up again. He did neither, and somehow that made her more afraid than if he had come.

Sarah, she thought, it's you tonight. You'll just have to keep me going, and don't for heaven's sake let me down.

CHAPTER FOURTEEN

For weeks now the work has seemed without end. Our only remaining acres of wheat have been harvested, the Macdonald family is well advanced with the rebuilding of their homestead, our own burnt-out cottages are on the way to being replaced and the grounds round Ardrossan itself have been finally cleared, awaiting only Mr James's plough.

On the last ship to arrive in Hobart Town were two of Master's grooms from his old estate in England, as well as several brood mares, and a pony and trap for the girls; also various seeds, plants and trees. How the latter have survived the journey I cannot imagine. So once Mr James has ploughed up a goodly portion of ground round the house, and harrowed it, it will be the duty of the girls and myself to plant out the garden as best we can, under the direction of Madam.

The men are too busy on the rest of the property to assist us, and can only spare enough time to burn out the sawn-off tree stumps and grub them up out of the way of the plough. I love the smell of the burning eucalyptus, when it is not out of control, to say nothing of the glow of the burning stumps after dark. They look so pretty round the big stone house.

I am looking forward to the laying out of the garden. It will be most rewarding and a new experience. Madam is most knowledgeable about plants and shrubs, and has many interesting books on the subject. I understand the family's old home in Warwickshire was quite a sight. I am very strong, praise be to God, and do most truly love being out in the warm sunshine with the beautiful hills and valley around me, to say nothing of the sound of the birds whose song is so different here — there is one called a Wattlebird, a large bird, active and playful, but has a raucous cry. And can you imagine — the magpies here sing!

In addition to this I have had to make all my ladies new dresses for the Ball, which is only a short time off and causing much discussion among the neighbouring families as the time comes nearer. The mailman brings us most amusing accounts of the general comments. It appears now that the Governor will not be in the neighbourhood for the event. Madam is bitterly disappointed, having spent so much time planning for his presence.

Master Matthew has been much more watchful where I am concerned, since the fire. I feel he is puzzled at my attitude to Ardrossan and does not trust me. Why? There is no harm I can do, and why should I not love this beautiful place, demanding though it is on our time and strength? I find great pleasure in using my physical energy, which I do not believe I should ever have found in England.

However, I have no wish, as yet, to cause Master Matthew's interest in me to be too great. As I have already said, he must learn to think of me other than in terms of his rightful possession — I do not go with the kitchen. At the same time I must not over-play my hand. It is a difficult balance to keep, my dear sister; also one's position is hard to establish. As yet there is no clear division of society such as in England; everyone depends so much on the other. Though gossip does say that the Government House circle and the Military vie equally with the wealthy settlers for precedence, we convicts of course are the servants of all. But as far as I can see, when our time is finished, Governor Arthur is only too anxious for us to become ordinary citizens of the community. How else can this colony be fully inhabited and made to prosper? It is for this time I must plan and wait.

Now my candle is burning low up in my little room, which I have made pretty with curtains and a bed-cover of material that Madam found in her trunks. I wish you could see it. I even have the likeness of you, mounted on Blue Ribbon. It is the only small picture I have on my four walls but it is all I want, and was not easy to keep by me during those dreadful months of my imprisonment. Goodnight, my dear sister. Never a day passes but my thoughts are with you.

Two weeks later:—

I fear since my last entry there has been no time at all for the writing of this Journal. The hours of daylight have been full beyond measure.

Madam has been anxious for me to assist Cook make wine for the still room. Her great friend, the Commandant's wife at Kilmarnock, sent word that all her fruits and berries were at their best, her garden being well stocked and established these five years; so nothing must do, in spite of the fact that the Ball is now so near at hand, but Miss Charlotte, myself, Mr James and Mr Haynes (the men to bring their guns in case of bushrangers and blacks) must drive over at once in the new pony cart.

Mr Haynes rode beside us. Of late there has been much talk of bushrangers, and in particular of the one whom I mentioned earlier, who goes by the name of Gentleman Jim. He has been playing most audacious tricks on any settler who has openly criticised him. For instance, some two weeks ago a Captain who had boasted that if Gentleman Jim so much as put his nose over the bounds of his property he would settle him once and for all, was sitting at his Sunday dinner, when the bushranger rode up in the most leisurely fashion, and before the startled Captain could so much as move, came into the dining-room and, playfully flicking a gun at him, ordered him to sit in a chair other than the one at the head of the table. That chair he proceeded to occupy himself, and also to eat the handsome meal which had been set upon the table. Having finished and declared himself well satisfied, he then took every gun in the house and rode off in as leisurely a fashion as he had come, having first thanked his "host" most courteously for his hospitality. A few days later a note was delivered saying that if the owner of the guns looked by a particular gate in one of his fields, he would find his weapons.

The manner in which this Gentleman Jim has such knowledge of all the settlers' movements and remarks makes me think he has an accomplice conveniently placed in someone's house. It is an unnerving thought, and gave me cause to watch Mr Haynes with great speculation that day as he rode so gracefully beside us. His horsemanship is as easy and controlled as everything else about him. I could well imagine him to be capable of any trick, and it would be quite in keeping for him to be in league with a bushranger.

It amazes me how everyone is so amused by him. But then, his manners are perfect, and he is so truly the picture of the charming gentleman who has gone wrong through really no fault of his own, that he manages to engender pity in every person he meets, especially if that person be a woman.

He never misses a chance to pester me when the opportunity arises, and sometimes I wonder how I can abide the situation. If it does not end soon, and this I cannot foresee until he receives his pardon, I feel I shall be forced into taking steps of some kind, though what they could be I have no idea. I only wish I knew how he intends to use his freedom (to no good I feel certain) but so long as it takes him from this place I care not. Therefore I was unprepared for Miss Charlotte's whispered confidence, while we were stooping over the redcurrant bushes, that she thought her tutor so wonderfully romantic!

I looked at her in great consternation. 'Miss Charlotte,' I said, 'if you mean what I think you mean, please disabuse yourself of such thoughts.'

'Oh, Sarah, how can you say such a thing.'

I made a sudden resolution: 'Very easily, Miss Charlotte. He is, like myself, a convict, no matter how charming you may think him. Also, he is a very selfish man. He would bring you no happiness.'

Whereupon she leant her arms on the bough of a young apple tree, and her pretty young face under its fresh pink bonnet looked at me roguishly.

'I never think of you as a convict, Sarah, and I never think of him as one either.'

'Then you should,' I said sharply.

But I did not deter her. 'Tell me, Sarah,' she said, 'I've wanted to ask you for a long time, were you really guilty?'

I did not answer for a moment but went on picking the berries, trying to make up my mind whether or not I could turn this conversation to good effect. But finally I decided on discretion.

'Miss Charlotte, your Mamma would not like to hear you ask such a question.'

'Oh, come Sarah, this is a different world. If I said, or did not say, everything Mamma wanted I would not get far. Also, if one waited to keep up standards here, with about two eligible settler families coming to our district in years, one would never marry.'

I could see she was safely back on the track of marriage again, but was sadly upset by her way of thinking, which had greatly altered in the last few months — a circumstance I laid at Mr Haynes's door.

'It is far better to wait for the right man to marry, Miss Charlotte. I understand from your Mamma you are going to Hobart Town to stay with Captain and Mrs Dalton in the autumn. You will be going to all the balls and parties at Government House.'

'But I don't like those stiff-necked young officers, and I'm sure there aren't many young settlers with prospects of keeping me in a home comparable to Ardrossan.'

'And how, pray,' I said with great asperity, 'could Mr Haynes hope to keep you in such style? He is not even a free man as yet.'

'Oh, but he soon will be. Papa will see to that!' she said dreamily, not even looking at me, while I was shocked to realise she had given me the answer to my previous wonderings as to what Mr Haynes intended to do with his future! And with my position and his charm he would soon be accepted here,' she continued. 'It is not like England. There are no real social barriers here. Anyway, none we couldn't surmount.'

'That is where you are wrong, Miss Charlotte. It is families such as yours which will make society here and set the standards. I am sure your brothers will one day go into politics and help to shape the — the whole political and social structure of this country. You must be a credit to them.'

She looked at me, her mouth dropping open rather prettily, and her eyes widening.

'What a strange thing for you to say, Sarah. There, I just knew you're not a convict, not really, I mean!'

I decided this conversation had gone far enough.

'Whatever you think, Miss Charlotte, we must hurry now. We cannot risk being on the track after dark.'

So we all climbed into the pony cart with our baskets, while Mr Haynes mounted and rode beside us in his inimitable style. I tried to see him through Miss Charlotte's eyes, the fascinating man of the world. As I watched them, the way in which he played up to her, and she young, pretty, the daughter of one of the foremost settlers in Van Diemen's Land, everything to offer any man, and herself at the mercy of such a man as Haynes, I shuddered.

Yes indeed, the plan was obvious now. Ardrossan would win him his freedom, and Miss Charlotte pave his way to the social world with easy money. I, or so he thought, would help him pass away the intervening time. 'No, Mr Haynes,' I promised myself. 'If it lies in my power, you shall have none of these things!'

Yet wasn't I planning to do just the same where her brother was concerned? How could I preach one thing to her and carry out the opposite myself — was I really such a hypocrite? Almost immediately I decided I was, and only consoled myself by arguing that in her case she must marry her equal; she had never known my side of life, could not stand up to it. Married to a man like Mr Haynes, in a country like this, she would not last a year; whereas I had everything to gain and nothing to lose. I would make life pay me back for what it had already taken from me.

That night, long after Cook had gone to her quarters, I stood in front of the kitchen stove. Although the night was warm, it was pleasant standing there on the flags, looking into the flames from the logs. Round me were the dim shadows in the corners of the big kitchen, the firelight flickering on the scrub-top table in the centre of the room, and on the sides of bacon hanging from the rafters.

Yes, I loved this place, so different from anything I had ever known; so lonely yet so satisfying. Outside, across the yard, the warm night wind brought the bush noises and the singing of the crickets.

I turned away with a sigh, and was just about to light a candle to take up to my room (I must not be too late to bed for Cook had set her bread and I was to be up by five to help her make and bake it) when the door into the kitchen opened and Master Matthew came in.

'No light! All by yourself in the dying firelight — most romantic. Beneath all that red hair and wilfulness are you romantic, Sarah?'

I looked at his big form approaching through the shadows. In the gloom he seemed of even greater stature.

'I was about to retire, Master Matthew. I must be early astir in the morning.'

'As I have remarked before, you have a most annoying habit of not answering questions, Sarah. If you wish to do well in this household you must correct it. I will ask you once again, are you a romantic?'

I saw that I must give him an answer.

'I beg your pardon, Master Matthew, but it did not seem to me that you could possibly want a convict girl to answer such a question. Romance is hardly part of our lives.'

'Ah, the philosopher again! No, do not light your candle for a moment. It really is a pity you are a convict.' He threw one leg over the end of the table and folded his arms. 'Tell me, how is it that a girl like you is so conversant with the English language, when most of your kind can hardly read their letters?'

Alas, dear sister, you know how prone I am to lose my temper, for even you have often gently chided me for this, but at that moment rage, temper and humiliation nearly overcame me. Always Master Matthew's cold choice of words, and the hardness in his voice, cut into my very being with the power to hurt more than any of the rough physical usage of the Captain. Yet I was determined he should not have the better of me.

'Sir,' I said very quietly, to control the rage that was shaking me, 'I think you know my story.'

'I know one version of it — the Captain's. It pleases me to hear it from you.'

I looked him straight in the eyes (we must have made a most strange pair as we stood there in the now almost dark room) and said as briefly as I could: 'I am the illegitimate daughter of the Earl of Bede. To pay for my mother's silence he arranged for me to have an adequate education in writing, letters and arithmetic. All of which, though convict I be, does not give any man the right to my mind or person. Have I your permission to retire, sir?'

'Begad you have not! I—'

'Matthew, Matthew, where are you?'

It was Miss Patricia's voice, and he looked at me and smiled. I couldn't help noticing that when he did he looked unexpectedly charming. Just as his voice could intimidate, so his smile could endear. He dropped his leg from the table.

'No doubt you think well-timed! There will be other times. Kindly remember to answer questions in future; I am somewhat tired of reminding you. Well, Sister Pat, why are you so put about? Shouting, I must say, in a most unladylike fashion. We did not expect colonial living to make such a hoyden of you.' And placing his arm round her shoulders he led her back to the main part of the house.

When the door had closed behind them, I lighted my candle in its stick on the table and climbed to my room. Next day I asked Sneaton to put two bolts on the inside of my door, having first told Madam I was nervous of being right at the back of the house at night.

I feel you will smile at this encounter, but there again you do not, and never will, thank God, know the agony of being in a position which both humiliates and enrages you, and having absolutely no power to avoid it, except by the use of your wits.

A week later:-

I shall now hasten to tell you of the Ball. I wish that you might have seen it, and above all felt it. You who are so used to the glittering, fashionable Balls of London. For it is these people's spirit that made it such an entrancing affair. As well as the need to maintain the dignity of the occasion, there was an unrestrained enjoyment in the air that carried everyone with it. There was no hint of fashionable boredom as you have so often described to me. These people came, not only to be seen in their glory of silks, satins and jewels drawn and resuscitated from old trunks, but also to meet each other, to keep alive in the face of adversity the art of gentle society.

As I have already told you, for weeks now we have been sorting all the best silver and china, fine damask cloths and napkins. Many of the chests were opened for the first time since the family's arrival, and there was much excitement and many exclamations over almost forgotten treasures. I indeed felt and shared their joy as we knelt round the chests, everybody's skirts mingled over upturned posteriors, as we delved up to our elbows in paper and packing. Alas, much was broken, particularly some of Madam's best crystal and china, and she was quite worn out by the tinkle of broken glass that greeted so much of our unpacking.

However, much has been saved, plenty indeed to make a goodly showing. Praise be, the magnificent crystal chandelier, of which Madam has so frequently spoken, was saved. It took me one whole day to clean it. I could not bear that any of the young, untrained girls should do so. Now it hangs, a sparkling centre-piece for the entrance hall, and with its many candles, lights softly and elegantly the long, sweeping folds of my blue damask curtains.

So, to that entrance hall, with its carved doors, came the surrounding neighbourhood, in carriages of polished woods drawn by fine horses; so also came gigs and jinkers, as well as many of the gentlemen riding on horseback, the younger ones racing each other up the track regardless of their fine clothes.

As I waited upon Madam where she stood with the Master and Miss Charlotte to receive their guests, I had a wonderful view of this, one of the greatest social occasions in the neighbourhood. The men had purposely left a line of tree stumps leading from the house down the track. In these they had built flare fires, with cunningly hidden buckets of water should an emergency arise. They had been lit after dark so that the whole façade and portico of the house was lighted, and stood out like a golden carving against the blackness of the bush behind. So bright were the flames that they caught the shimmer of the river as it twisted around us.

While the men were not in spectacular livery, they all wore clean white shirts and their polished faces made a brave and competent showing as they held the excited horses and helped down the ladies from the carriages and conveyances. Meantime, in the background, at the base of the staircase, which had been decorated by the girls with posies of flowers found in the bush, the orchestra, composed of all the available local talent, was filling the air with the lilting swing of a waltz.

Care-worn hands were hidden in long kid gloves — gloved hands which had lost none of their cunning in sweeping aside full, brocaded skirts; and for the first time in what must have been many months, creamy white shoulders rose from silks and satins. Gentlemen wore their velvet jackets and ruffled shirts and buckled shoes. Manners and social procedure were as carefully displayed as in the most exclusive salon in London society.

For this night the problems of pioneering a new and remote country were put aside — the gay and gracious scene was indeed good to watch, and it chagrined me not a little to notice how well Master Matthew took his place among them. For this night he was the perfect host. For all the days he toiled on the property, where he could outwork any of his father's men, he now appeared so at ease both in manners and clothes that he seemed to me another man. I should have so liked to criticise him, but in fairness could not do so. Even you, dear sister, with your fastidious taste in men, would, I am sure, have found him charming. There was a great sadness in me that I should never know him in such a role, for I saw only too well that were I to find some way in which to trap him into my schemes I would never know him as he really was; he would never forgive a wrong done to him. Just for the moment I asked myself if this house, and all that went with it, was really worth his enmity, but I hardened my heart. There was no other way to remove the slur that had been put upon me. No other country where such a reprieve could be obtained.

Then came one of those incidents which makes life so unpredictable in this country.

In the kitchen quarters we were all occupied with the last arrangements for the supper, when we heard a great commotion coming from the front of the house. It made itself obvious through the music, which presently stopped, its place being taken by the ladies' screams.

After one startled moment of listening, Cook threw her apron over her head and rushed for a large cupboard at the end of the kitchen.

'Glory be to God!' I heard her whisper as she slammed the door on herself. 'It'll be those bushrangers, for sure.'

Of course! I had always been afraid of bushrangers since the first mention of the Ball, but surely they would not dare to come here on a night like this when nearly the whole district was assembled? To properties left unguarded, yes, but not here!

I crept cautiously to a door leading on to the back passage connecting the main entrance hall. What a sight met my eyes as I peered down the passage! There was the tall figure of a man dressed in a fine snuff-coloured nankin suit, with white ruffles at his throat and sleeves. He was wearing a small mask and leaning with great nonchalance against the entrance doors, pointing a pistol at the company in a most conceited manner. I realised there must be other armed men whom I could not see for the bend in the hall, otherwise this man could not surely have stood there so at ease with all the gentlemen guests about him.

Everyone seemed paralysed; the ladies that I could see were clutched to their escorts, who appeared at a loss. Yet another finely dressed gentleman crossed my vision, also carrying a pistol, and I began to realise how the raid had been planned. After the reception it would be a simple matter for any man dressed as one of the gentry to mingle with the guests until a given signal.

I began to wonder what I could do, as it appeared I was the only free person, when I felt my wrists seized and my arms were twisted around behind my back.

'Doubtless, my pretty one, you had ideas of interfering.'

'Doubtless, I had,' I replied. It was useless to struggle.

'Come, then, you shall join the gentry. Redheads are not good ones to be left to their own devices. Don't fight and you won't get hurt.'

So I was pushed down the passage and thrust rudely in among the guests.

I quickly looked for Madam, and saw her in a chair by the Master, a look of horror on her face. I also saw that there were four armed men in complete charge of the crying women and angry-faced men. Opposition was useless.

'Now then,' said the gentleman in the nankin suit, 'let's be quick about this. Everybody line the walls, and as my friend here passes round the hat, all jewels, rings and money into it, please. Ladies, you may keep your wedding rings, we must not interfere with the sanctity of marriage! Madam, what are you doing standing there? Join the circle if you don't want to be harmed.'

I all but smiled. The lady to whom he referred had the meanest reputation between here and Hobart Town. She had been widowed a twelvemonth before I came to Ardrossan, but had insisted on carrying on her husband's farm, undeterred by the atrocities of the blacks and the raids of the bushrangers. As it was such a prosperous holding she had been granted special permission to keep it. She had been more than successful over the last year, especially as the bushfire had missed her property, but no one had seen her with any money, nor had she been known to give so much as a penny to anyone.

Even though tonight she was dressed as well as any of the company present, I could not believe that the bushrangers would get much from her, although it was rumoured she never went anywhere without her sovereign belt strapped round her person.

As I watched, the languid gentleman who was obviously conducting affairs stepped up to her and told her to turn round with her hands in the air before joining the other ladies against the wall. He then proceeded to run his hands quite effectively but impersonally down the plump lines of her person. I detected quite a few ill-suppressed smiles on the otherwise anxious faces of the company, and it crossed my mind: 'Is this Gentleman Jim?'

Instinctively I looked for Mr Haynes, but he was there against the wall, calm and poised, even managing to look somewhat bored by the proceedings.

'This, sir, is an outrage!'

'Business is business, Madam, and where better to find it than here tonight? Rumour has it you are a passing successful farmer.'

'And would I be likely to attend a ball with my pockets full of money?'

'Madam, I have little knowledge of the workings of a lady's mind.'

'So I should think,' she snapped as he motioned her to move away and join the other ladies.

Fascinated, I watched the collection of jewels and money pouring into the hands of the masked collector as he stood patiently while frenzied hands pulled at rings that fitted over-tight on work-worn fingers which had once been soft and slim.

One young officer from the barracks turned around and shook his fist at his elegant tormentor.

'You'll pay for this! We'll make this country too hot to hold you.'

'But not yet, my young friend! And until now it has not been very difficult to hoodwink you. Even the blacks have you beaten!'

Whereupon, young and all as he was, our gallant would-be protector looked as though he might at any time break a blood vessel.

In an incredibly short time the collection was over, and once again my wrists were seized.

'And now, my Redhead, supper! We are hungry and thirsty.'

I caught sight of Master Matthew's face as he stood by the dining room entrance. His mouth was such a straight line as to be almost indistinguishable, and his eyes were so cold they made me shudder as I was marched away. How could a man look so charming one minute and such a devil the next?

We reached the kitchen just as Cook must have decided it was safe to come out of hiding. I found it hard not to laugh at the expression on her horrified face as she realised she too was caught.

'Well, now,' said my captor from somewhere above my head, 'with two of you to wait on us, time will indeed be saved. Off you go and join our companion.'

Whereupon he gave me such a push that I could not keep my feet on the flags, and went flying in a stumbling rush on to Cook's ample bosom, so that he let out a great bellow of laughter. However, when I recovered my balance I found his humour had not disturbed his vigilance, for my eyes, as I raised them, were looking straight down the barrel of his pistol.

'Now, the fun's over. Pile up plenty of that stuff over there, and take it in. Fowls, eh! I understood tonight's little entertainment was to be quite a feast.'

Cook spluttered with indignation. Though her life was in danger, her culinary powers must never be questioned.

'Fowls indeed! They be the Master's finest turkeys and ducks, I'd have you be a-knowing of.'

'Is that so!' he grinned. 'All the better; we can do with a good feed. Wouldn't mind a little rape either, save for the fact we're in a hurry tonight.'

Even Cook was speechless, and made no further protest about filling up trays of food. In a short space of time we were marched off to carry them to the other men still holding the guests at gun point.

I have never seen food so quickly demolished, and what they could not eat they stuffed wholesale into their pockets, before the shocked gaze of all who stood there. Then their leader, fastidiously wiping the greasy morsels of meat from his fingers, looked around the room.

'Thank you for a most entertaining and profitable evening. My companions and I have found your hospitality charming. Any man trying to follow us will be regrettably deterred with this.' He waved his pistol at them and without so much as turning his head, snapped at his followers: 'Get the horses!'

With almost bated breath we listened to the clatter of horses' hooves at the entrance.

'Mount!' he called, 'and hand me my reins through the door.'

Then, before any man in the room could move, he sprang backwards, vaulted into his saddle and was gone.

Pandemonium broke loose, but through it all I saw two things. The lady farmer bent swiftly, pushed back the end of the sofa on which she had been sitting when the bushranger had made her rise to be searched, and dragged out her famous sovereign belt from under it. Obviously she had somehow managed to loosen it, and when it fell beneath her petticoats, kicked it under the sofa. The other thing was the quick movement of Master Matthew, as quick indeed as the bushranger himself, and I guessed he would run for Oscar.

My heart went cold at the thought of that magnificent animal being ambushed in the dark and being shot. Without hesitation I picked up my skirts and ran to one of the side doors, sped across the newly turned earth at the back of the house, and raced for Oscar's stable, just as Master Matthew led him out and sprang on to him bare-back.

'Master Matthew, you can't do it, you mustn't — let them go. They'll kill him in the dark and you will never catch them with him unsaddled.'

'Your concern for my horse is most touching, Sarah! Out of my way if you don't want to finish up under his hooves.'

I had indeed to spring back, as together, in one black shadow, they thundered down the track, past the smouldering tree stumps and into the bush. There was nothing for me to do but hurry back to attend to the ladies.

Well, dear, sister, after such a night — and I assure you it was decided the Ball should continue, a great number even staying to breakfast — you would not think many would be ready to attend that first divine service on the morrow, but this they did. It was a truly wonderful sight on that summer Sunday morning to see all the carriages drawn up in the shade of the gum trees round the barn which had been painted for the occasion, and filled with posies gathered by the children.

As I walked behind Madam, carrying her prayer book and Bible, I looked across the burnt and dazzling fields to the blue haze on the mountains, and strangely felt much at peace with the world. If one could survive long enough in this country to achieve one's ambitions, it was as good a place as any in the world to live.

The barn was packed to its creaking doors, and all of us servants stood outside to follow the service. I wondered if Mr Haynes had managed to get himself included in the company within, but presently I saw he was making his way towards me, and in a moment took his place by my side.

'You look very fresh this morning, Sarah, particularly after such an exhausting night.'

'Thank you, Mr Haynes. Fortunately I am still young enough to deal with physical discomfort. Unfortunately my mind is not so at ease.'

He looked at me gravely. 'I am indeed sorry to hear you say so. Would you care to share my hymn book? I imagine we are about to sing.'

But even though the scene around me was a fine one, I could not wholly concentrate on it. During the third verse I whispered: 'Mr Haynes, those men must have had someone helping them last night.'

He raised his eyebrows and whispered back: 'You could be right.'

'They knew exactly when supper would be served.'

'It does seem strange.'

He continued to sing, and I noticed that he had a fine voice to add to his presence and manners. However, during the last verse he appeared to have come to a decision.

'Sarah!'

'Yes, Mr Haynes.'

'You weren't suspicious of me — were you?'

'I see that in some things, Mr Haynes, you read me aright. And,' taking a deep breath, 'there are other matters.'

'Such as?'

'Miss Charlotte!'

It was said now and I waited, almost holding my breath. I had never interfered with any plan of his before, apart from his intentions where I myself was concerned. I believed, if my reading of him was correct, I would now have to face a different man from the one he presented to the Roland family.

I was not disappointed. Inclining his head over his hymn book, he said with a coldness that made me aware for the first time he was not only sly but venomous: 'I would advise you not to concern yourself with my affairs.'

'I happen to be very fond of Miss Charlotte.'

'You mean you are fond of the thought of what your protection of Charlotte could bring you!'

The way in which he used her name, with such easy familiarity, confirmed my worst fears.

'You are misreading my ambitions.'

'Rather shall we say that your ambitions set me on the path of an ambition of my own.'

'Yours is an unworthy one and you know it. A girl reared as Miss Charlotte has would never be able to live your kind of life when you get your freedom.'

'That is for her to decide.'

'You would never give her the chance to decide. She is romantic and knows nothing of the world outside her family. With no other men around you have mesmerised her. And with every moment that passes I believe more strongly you are in league with those poor devils of bushrangers.'

'And I am warning you, any interference with my plans means the total destruction of your own. I know exactly how to handle this family. I have devoted the three years of my assignment to them both in their interests and in my own. It will be a simple thing on my part to make them believe your intentions with regard to their eldest son. So, when you think of fighting me, think about the inside of the Cascades, and the dirty trolls who inhabit the place; then think of this place. Do you really think it is worth while to keep alive your pathetic little flame of loyalty?'

I hated the way in which he spat the words at me above the pages of his holy book — the mockery of it all. Above all I hated the fact that he was right. I wanted nothing but time to find a way to win the confidence of this family as he had done. But Miss Charlotte — how could I leave such a romantic child to her fate?

I knew he was watching me, reading me. Then he smiled, and gracefully closing his hymn book walked elegantly away. I remained where I was, murder in my heart.

'You make quite an amusing picture when you are angry! But surely there is a language among convicts? How is it that Haynes can possibly make you so angry?'

I lifted my head to see Master Matthew standing with Oscar's bridle over his arm. He had not yet replaced his hat after coming from the barn; the wind was lifting his thick brown hair and the white linen ruffles at his throat. He made a splendid picture standing by his great black horse. I would not have been a woman had I not wished these to be different circumstances — any other than master and convict servant.

'I regret the quickness of my temper, Master Matthew. It has always been so in spite of my striving to the contrary. May I please stroke Oscar's neck before I collect Madam's books?'

'You may if he permits. But there, I do not have to warn you that he too has a temper. I believe you use your feminine prerogative to appeal to his stomach. I'll swear you have a sugar lump concealed somewhere on your person!'

I had not seen him in such a genial mood, at least when he was in my vicinity. Almost happily I reached up my hand to the shining, arched neck of the horse I so loved, and he, knowing in his own way that I would have something for him, inclined his head towards me, his nostrils wrinkling in anticipation.

'He is truly beautiful, Master Matthew. Thanks be to God they were not able to harm him last night. They must have thought only of getting away.'

'An understandable way of reasoning since they had stolen some thousands of pounds worth of jewels and money!'

Once again there was the sarcastic flick to his tongue that put us so far apart. I turned away from Oscar as he chewed delicately on the sugar I had given him, savouring each grain caught on his lips.

'Madam will be waiting, I must hurry.'

'You've not told me why Haynes made you so angry.'

'I would rather you did not ask me that, sir. Please, I can see Madam looking for me.' And gathering my skirts I ran hastily through the trees.

CHAPTER FIFTEEN

As usual Sara put down the journal because of an interruption—this time it was Sally, one of *Sunbolt*'s devoted slaves, thus also Richard's. She stood there on the doorstep, dressed in jeans and a delightful pale, striped skivvy that showed off to perfection the young rounded line of her breasts.

Sara thought she looked adorable, tried to think of her as a man would think and realised she was just one of the many adorable jean-skivvy-clad youngsters who roamed the streets and beaches, boy and romance hungry. They were all so determined to do the same things, wear the same clothes, keep their figures to the same proportions, that they became a regiment of indistinguishable young robots. It must be hard for any young man to know what he wanted for his own when he could turn so many ways and find always the same pattern.

Sally strolled into the room. 'What's happened to you lately, Sara? You've hardly been around.'

Sara closed the door. 'Oh, I don't know. Arna and I have been very busy getting organised for our opening next week. You know we're having a fashion parade to start the ball rolling? As it's "Invitation Only" Arna was going to take cards to everyone on *Sunbolt*. You got them, didn't you?'

Sally nodded. 'Thanks, Sara, we're all coming to do you proud. It's causing a lot of talk, you know.' She wandered over to the canvas of *Sunbolt* in one corner of the room and knelt on the stool in front of it. 'It's coming on—the picture, I mean,' she said, but somehow Sara had the feeling that although Sally was looking at the picture, she wasn't really seeing it.

'Yes.'

'Do you really see *Sunbolt* like that?'

'It's not necessarily how I *see* her, but how she could be.'

'Oh! Do you think that's how Rick sees her?'

There was a silence which had somehow become electric.

'I wouldn't know,' Sara said at last, 'but I hope so,' and decided she must get Sally out of the room. All of these last weeks she had so determinedly tried to shut Richard out of her mind, refusing to see him except where business demanded, pleading that there was far too much to do before moving into the house and boutique, and that at night she was too tired to enjoy going out. She had not even gone down to *Sunbolt* to work, letting Arna set off without her.

But with this visit of Sally's, Sara wondered if keeping away had been the best decision. Obviously they had all been talking about her absence, although Richard himself had made no comment. Suddenly she realised just how much she had missed him.

Sally was talking about the picture again: 'But haven't you discussed it with him?'

'Why would I? It's up to the artist to decide how he or she is going to represent an idea or subject.'

'But *Sunbolt* is his, and you are painting her for him, aren't you?'

'Yes, of course. What's unusual in that? His birthday is soon.'

'Nothing, at least—oh, I don't know. Oh, Sara, I love him so much!'

The girl's misery was so pathetic that to her horror Sara found it almost comical, but as quickly took herself to task. Love like this, even in passing, was not comical. To see it so nakedly in the girl's eyes made her embarrassed as she faced her own thoughts where Richard was concerned. Sally had the right to such feelings. She had no such right.

'I know you do,' she answered quietly.

'Oh—is it as obvious as that, truly?'

'I'm afraid so, and it isn't the way to go about things with anyone like Richard; he's too spoilt.'

She listened to her own voice with satisfaction. It had just the right amount of sympathy. Her conscience would be salved a little if she could advise this child; it would make her feel virtuous, and apart from the situation. But Sally's next remark spoiled her role completely. The girl had gripped slender fingers round her knees and was looking directly up at Sara, as her words came out with a rush.

'That's why I had to come. You see, you have so much more experience with men, there isn't much chance for any one like me with you and Arna around. It's not that I mean you would really do anything wrong—I—oh, I'm putting this so badly—it's just that you must be much more interesting to him.'

She came to a painful stop, while Sara got up and walked to the window. She did not really see what lay in front of her. Her heart was beating uncomfortably fast. At last she said, her back still turned to the girl: 'Aren't you forgetting that I am married?'

'Oh, I know it's simply dreadful of me, but I just had to say it, had to know why you haven't been down to us lately, because you see I know he's missed you; it makes him—different.'

Sara was aware of yet another lurch of her heart. This was absurd, ignominious—but exciting. But it was an excitement which made her feel guilty. She was not a teenager, she was a responsible married woman in her mid-twenties. How to deal with it? How? Moralising wouldn't do; she had already gone over that. So he missed her, it made him different, but he hadn't come to tell her so.

'Sara, I'm sorry, please don't be angry. I had to come. I couldn't bear it.'

A sense of the ridiculous made Sara turn and manage a smile. 'Sally, you're making too much of this. I really have been too busy to come down to *Sunbolt* lately, and as far as the picture is concerned, at this stage I would rather paint away from the yacht.'

'You mean—you've quarrelled.'

All of a sudden Sara was tired of the whole thing.

'Sally, will you stop being so ridiculous? I'm sorry to say this, but you really are behaving like a love-sick teenager. No man of Rick's age can be bothered with such behaviour, and that's about as good advice as I can give you.'

To her disgust Sally bowed her head on her hands and began to cry quietly but uncontrollably. Sara looked round in desperation and saw a packet of tissues on a small side table. She walked across and pulled a fragile scrap of paper viciously from the packet, then came back and put it in the girl's damp fingers.

Sally took it and stood up.

'I—I don't know what to say.'

'Don't say anything. As far as I'm concerned the matter's finished, but if you want to attract an older man, for heaven's sake learn to control yourself.'

'You've—been very good—th–thank you, Sara. We can still be friends, can't we?'

'Of course.'

Sara once again felt nauseated by the young, tear-flooded eyes looking into hers; also uncomfortably aware that she was so ashamed as to feel physically sick. All she wanted, most desperately, was for Sally to go and leave her.

When she had gone and Sara was alone with the picture again, she told herself it was all horribly like a cheap little paperback, the last thing she would have imagined happening to her. In the same instant she knew that what hurt most was the plain, stark fact that she was not, after all, apart from any other woman in this matter. Never again could she be critical or impatient of the failing of others; she had allowed her body to overcome her mind.

She sat very still, thinking of herself and John; looking back over the years as though she were watching two strange figures acting out a drama; how they had met, he at London University, she at Art School. Until that time she had never had much to do with boys. Then somebody had taken her one evening to John's room in college where about a dozen of them had sat on the floor drinking beer or coffee, arguing about everything under the sun until the early hours of the morning. At least, they had argued and she had listened. She'd never been much good at that sort of thing. Then she had met him again accidentally in Kensington Gardens, and they had stayed to wander down to the Serpentine. He had said he had often thought about her since their meeting; he remembered her because she had sat so silently, but he realised she was not bored. Women did not do that sort of thing nowadays. She had replied she would rather watch and listen to people than talk to them. He had said that made a man feel good.

They had taken to meeting quite often. It had all become completely satisfying, and she had known almost at once that he would want to marry her; knew they were both mysteriously wrapped in a sudden and emotional world that was quite apart from their ordinary daily lives; knew too that it would end thrillingly in marriage, with a life ahead for them to mould. They had been so eager, confident, sure. The years had passed and they had been even more sure, until this strange upheaval.

Sitting there, dry in the throat, so still that the clock ticked audibly on the mantelpiece and a mouse scuttled under the edge of the sofa, she knew she was still sure. Yet, somehow Richard had stepped into their world and she could not banish him.

A busy week followed. Summer had gripped Hobart. The gardens were full of flowers and the gossip columns full of party notices, charitable functions, pictures of posed women at parties, at teas, at dances, and above all, sport. The whole island shook under the attack of tennis, golf, swimming, surfing and yachting. Shopkeepers, office workers, business and professional men and women alike, got through their week to reach the weekend and literally throw themselves and children into sportsclothes, to say nothing of cutting their lawns and washing their cars.

For Arna and Sara it seemed even more hectic than for anyone else. The move into the old house, now a boutique in the basement with living quarters above, at last stood waiting for the new life they were about to impose on it. Paulina had arrived two weeks previously, managing to bring some exciting designs to give a real start to the opening, and had also professed herself delighted with most of Sara's sketches and had begun work immediately.

The furnishing and arrangement of the boutique itself, to say nothing about the more domestic floor, had kept the two girls on the run from morning till night, a state of affairs which had taken its toll of Sara, so that the day before the fashion parade she was aware of an exhaustion which brought her near to panic. Both she and Arna, with the help of two young models under training, were doing the entire modelling for the show.

The afternoon before, she wandered down the black-carpeted stairs to the underground showroom, switched on the gold lights above the dress racks, so that they lit up the overhead mirrors suspended on steel chains above the catwalk, and caught the dim outline of the draped red hessian curtains leading to the changing rooms. Saw too the idea that had been Arna's, the arrangement of cube structures covered with black felt for the guests to sit on, and remembered Arna's remark that afterwards they could be used as display equipment. Always Arna was practical.

She sat down on one and wished that John could have got away for the opening, and been with her on Friday evening for the celebration dinner Richard was giving. It was to be a double celebration: the opening of the boutique and *Sunbolt's* first appearance in the real racing world the following week—a race round Maria Island—one of the many preliminary races before the yachts went to Sydney.

She heard a sound on the stairs and looked up to see Arna, in sienna-yellow pants coming down the black-carpeted stairs. Each colour was so dramatically right for the other.

'There you are! I have looked in all places for you. Leave it now. It will be all right, you'll see. Come with me for some fresh air; we haven't seen *Sunbolt* for a long time.'

It made Sara think of what Sally had said last week. Why not? And the fresh air would be good, it was probably what she was missing. The mere thought of it brought her to her feet. Quickly she changed into a pair of flat casuals, a light skirt and bright jumper, and set off with Arna along the front to the Yacht Club. Out in the sunshine, with the traffic rushing past on one side and the blue water stretching still and deep on the other, it was hard to feel awkward or worried. The whole thing had assumed an importance that was laughable.

As they cut down the private road leading to the Yacht Club, she could see *Sunbolt* in the distance, men and women working on her. Again she thought of Sally's visit. Was it true they had all wondered why she had not come for so long? They knew of course about the boutique. She slowed her walk, dropping back behind Arna, feeling embarrassed, but still she moved and found herself on the wooden jetty with *Sunbolt* tied up alongside. With every step she dreaded their looking up and seeing her. Finally it was Sally, a smiling, happy Sally who looked up from coiling a length of rope on the deck and saw her. 'Hi!' she called, and as Sara returned her wave she could not help feeling a pang. Why was Sally so happy, so different from her emotions at their last meeting?

They were all there, all pleased to see her, and *Sunbolt* looked as she had never looked before. She had been completely repainted; the decking was scrubbed white; the brass plates on the rails were polished; the ropes were humming in the wind, and when Sara climbed aboard she could see that the woodwork in the galley and cabin had all been polished until it shone against the bunks. Coils of ropes were ready, slung along the sides; and forward of the cabin, the sail locker was full.

She stood a moment looking at the navigation table and radio and visualised Richard here, immersed completely in this world of navigation, wind and water, quite literally sovereign of all he surveyed.

But she was not alone for long. They followed her down, all talking at once.

'She had her first run today. Only a few hours, though. Next Wednesday's the big day.'

'We were going to come and tell you, Sara.'

'Have you finished the painting yet?'

'You haven't been down for ages.'

'I know, I'm sorry; we've been so busy with the boutique.'

'Feeling nervous about tomorrow?'

'More than a little.'

Sally came up. 'What do you think of her? Doesn't she look glorious?'

'You make me feel awful that I did nothing at the end.'

'Oh, we know it's different for you.'

What did they mean by that? And where was Richard?

They accepted her so quickly. The little whirlpool of excitement her arrival had caused rippled out and she was back in the groove, part of the light-hearted badinage. She felt her spirits rising to meet theirs. She had been stupid to stay away. She must make John come; it would do him a world of good.

She felt a hand on her shoulder.

'You're back, Sara!'

Just that, but she felt her heart would burst with happiness. She was home—with her man. Nothing else mattered for those few seconds. Then she came back to earth. Words were impossible. And he was clearly the same.

'I knew you'd come,' he said.

'Why?'

'Maybe I'll answer that in two nights' time when I've had plenty to eat and drink. Come and see what we've done while you've forgotten us. She's in pretty good shape now, although I'm still not perfectly satisfied. Next week's run will settle a few problems.'

'When will you be back?'

'The Friday after.'

'What are the chances of her winning?'

He shrugged his shoulders. 'Who's to know? Pretty good I'd say. There're four yachts from here in our class, but we've got strong overseas opposition.'

She knew they were talking because it was easier, and because everyone had come crowding round Richard. However, she and Arna didn't stay long, making the opening of the boutique next day their excuse.

And on the next day it was an awe-inspiring sight to Sara, as she peeped through the changing-room curtains, to see that the felt-covered cubes were packed with people and already others were lining the walls. Could she, she asked herself, walk along that catwalk and try to impress a critical and fashion-conscious audience with a different and daring way of dressing? People who had their own very definite ideas were not easy to persuade. To them, the world in general had not a great deal more to offer in the way of living and achieving than had this, their island.

She knew too that to them as yet she would be "unplaced"; could imagine them saying: 'Who's she, I wonder? Where does she come from?' She was not at all annoyed at this game of "placing", as she called it. In fact she thought that if she were a Tasmanian it would be rather pleasant to be so accounted for; one of a fold, known and positioned. Yet of course it could work the other way if the fold were indignant, threw one out for some reason or another—then the outside world could be a lonely, threatening place. On the whole, she decided, it was better that she did not belong. It was more comfortable to be *with* than *of* a small community like this; free to make one's own decisions without being accountable to anyone. Yet this "belonging" in Tasmania had clearly come about through those settlers and convicts of the other Sarah's days who had to cling together in the face of hard living, whose children had intermarried and struggled on from generation to generation, until representatives of their families sat here, in this room in the most modern of surroundings.

As though to complete the sudden switch of her thoughts to those old days of Tasmania, her eye caught sight of a familiar figure at the top of the stairs. Richard was standing there, a quizzical expression on his face as he looked down into the room full of excitedly talking women.

Suddenly he saw her, and in a moment his face changed. Across the crowd they shared the noise, the eagerness, the humour at the overdressed, the pleasure of the well-dressed; the fact that she herself could be looking rather delightful. She wondered if he was surprised by the effect she created, dressed for the occasion; and knew that he was, and that the knowledge was dangerous.

She deliberately walked down off the catwalk, passing through a cluster of Arna's black cubes, encouraging the guests to examine the suit she was wearing. When she could no longer avoid facing the stairs, she saw that he was no longer there. A sense of desolation caught at her as the compere said: 'Sara is followed by Arna in an adaptable day-night casual.'

She passed out into the changing rooms, wishing either that he had not come or that she had not seen him; dreading the empty night ahead with no husband to put her back into perspective, for even Arna was going out to yet another dinner date.

In the morning, however, things seemed better. The paper was full of praise for the opening of the boutique, had commented that it could herald the "wind of change" in a new look and modern Hobart. In spite of herself she was excited, exhilarated, almost convinced for the moment that she could foresee a future which would take the place of anything she had known. So it was in this mood she went upstairs when the doors were closed on the boutique's first day of business, and decided to relax for a while before she got dressed to accompany Richard and Arna to the celebration dinner.

Curling up in a comfortable chair in what had once been the drawing room of the old house, she turned the leaves of the journal until she found the place where she had last left it.

CHAPTER SIXTEEN

The more I thought of Mr Haynes, the more certain I became that he was not to be trusted and that he was in league with a set of bushrangers. Indeed, dear sister, the more I thought upon him the more afraid I became.

Due to her innocent and romantic nature, Miss Charlotte had inspired him to ambitious thinking. As plain as though he himself had written it before me, I knew what he was about. In fact, during the times he still pestered me with his presence, he kept me in a state of misery by using veiled hints of the entirely satisfactory future which he felt now lay ahead of him; at the same time making it just as obvious that, should I confide in any other than himself, the Cascades lay just as surely ahead of me.

It was common knowledge that any time now the Master would procure Mr Haynes's freedom. He would undoubtedly then, with all his charm, sue for Miss Charlotte's hand. Not that he would have any intention of remaining to work at Ardrossan or even set up on a nearby grant, which, as a free man with backing he would undoubtedly get; but banking on the fact that the Master would immediately refuse such a request, he would persuade her to enter into a runaway marriage with him, when, far from marrying her, he would merely hold her as a hostage.

With all this in mind, it came to me that I too was in great danger. I was the one person who knew him for what he was, the one person who could interfere with his plans. I began to fear that in some way he would try to get rid of me, either by taking my life, or by keeping his word and in some clever fashion rendering me in such a light that the Master and Mistress would send me to the Cascades. The more I thought of this monster, the more I knew I was right, but the more desperate one's situation becomes, the more determination one is given.

Day by day summer slipped into autumn, and I saw how wrapped up in her dreams Miss Charlotte was becoming. I also noticed that she no longer confided in me, and knew once again that I had been right about that evil man. First Miss Charlotte against me — who next? Master Matthew? No, Mr Haynes would want to prove that I was carrying on with Master Matthew. That would be part of his evidence. He would hope to catch us together; and this of all things worried me most, for of late Master Matthew, when he comes from the fields of an afternoon, has formed a habit of removing the first dust and dirt from his person under the water pump in the yard, before coming into the kitchen on the way to his room.

I have come to look on those moments as the happiest of my day, and whatever duties I have to perform, be they in the still room, sewing room or garden (which is now beginning to take shape, as many of the seeds from England have sprouted) I always manage to keep my kitchen tasks for that hour. Sometimes he doesn't even speak. At others, if he does so it is mainly to make one of his sarcastic remarks; by now they have become almost a language between us. They satisfy his pride and give him a sense of superiority, while I know that he notices me in spite of himself. I have been content with this, knowing that I may only move near to him with the slowest and most careful of steps; but now I fear even this meeting must cease. Simple and all as it is, Mr Haynes knows of it, has gone out of his way to remark it would seem I am moving nearer to my goal. I had better take care.

Oh, dear God, that there might be a way to rid myself of my fears and suspicions, as with every day Miss Charlotte is becoming more and more within his toils. I grow almost afraid to eat my food or to leave the kitchen door after dark. I believe I would do anything to rid myself and Miss Charlotte of this man!

It is four weeks since I wrote those words, and as I sit here in my room looking at them, what horror they strike to my soul. Would that I had never thought nor written them! I have been exceeding ill, indeed almost out of my mind, but since I made a resolution when I began this journal that I would write nothing but the truth in it, as God is my witness, the truth as far as I know it, you shall have.

For some time now, Madam has made me more and more responsible for running the house, except of course for apportioning the daily rations. That is something worked out between herself and Cook, Madam being entirely responsible to the Master for the needs of all souls on Ardrossan. It is a responsibility I should not like, as food in this country is of greater importance than money, and everything, as I've already told you, must be kept under lock and key, the keys being worn at all times by Madam.

However, on this particular morning of which I am about to write, Madam was busy in the store room, and Mr Haynes had set lessons for Miss Patricia, Miss Dorothy and Miss Jessica, while Miss Charlotte practised the harpsichord most diligently. She is to give a solo at the Literary Society's first meeting next Thursday, in Kilmarnock. Mr James is to drive her over in the afternoon to stay with the Commandant's lady; she will return the next day.

So, having set the girls to work, Mr Haynes announced his intention of taking Master Bruce for a nature walk. The river was in flood from the first autumn rains, and the little boy was just reaching an age to be stirred by such a sight. He was wildly excited, and I could see he was paying absolutely no heed to his mother's remarks that if she were to let him go he must not go near the water, but must keep a tight hold of Mr Haynes's hand.

Watching that gentleman's confident handling of the child's mother, it crossed my mind that he was the last person to have charge of such a highly excitable child in the circumstances, but as usual he won his way and Madam gave her consent. It was with a strangely heavy heart that I watched the two set out; the one so small, dancing at every step; the other as elegantly positive in all his movements that he seemed to me like a wound-up doll.

However, the matter was not in my hands. There was a great deal to do that day, as on the morrow, it being Miss Jessica's birthday. I had gained permission from the Master to take the four young ladies, as well as four children of the same age from the Macdonald family, on the bullock dray which was to carry wheat to Kilmarnock mill, and while the dray was being unloaded, and reloaded with flour, we would have a picnic by the mill itself. Possibly the last of such outings, with winter being so near.

The mill is a favourite picnic place. It is so warm on the banks of the gently flowing water, such a happy place with the fields about us and the birds singing. The children love climbing the willows, whose long, lacy branches trail over the swirling mill-race. Just lately we have all helped to build a rustic bridge that spans this mill-race, and are very proud of ourselves.

So the morning flew by, until Madam disturbed us by saying: 'I cannot understand why Mr Haynes is keeping

Master Bruce out so long. The child will be too tired to eat his lunch.'

As she spoke, the old grandfather clock in the hall chimed one o'clock, and I realised with a shock that they had been out since ten o'clock.

I went out through the kitchen and, climbing up a bank by the pump, looked down the track to the valley, but there was no sign of the two figures. However, I did see another child running towards the house, and after a moment recognised it as that of little Jimmy Blight, the head shepherd's son. Fear made me run to meet him. When I reached him he was gasping for breath. 'Sarah—' he mouthed at me. 'Quick — they'll be drownded!'

I felt quite sick as I caught hold of him. 'What do you mean, Jimmy — is it Master Bruce and Mr Haynes? Are they in trouble?'

He nodded, his mouth open and his breath still coming painfully.

'Where?'

He pointed back along the track. 'All of a mile — I—'

But I did not wait to hear. My mind was suddenly made up. Oscar was in his stable, Master Matthew having taken the bullock team that morning for logging. I had never been on a horse in my life, as you well know, dear sister, but I knew that somehow I must get on Oscar's back! It was the only way to get there in time, if indeed I would be in time.

I rushed across the yard and pulled down his rope halter that always hung on a nail outside the stable door. I did not even stop to think what Master Matthew would do to me when he knew that I had dared to try to ride his horse. I had no idea how to saddle or bridle, but surely even I could slip a rope halter over his head and tie the long piece of attached rope to the head piece the other side to make a single rein. If only he would let me do it!

I opened the stable door — his body seemed immense in the darkness of the building — and I could see his big eyes shining as he turned his head to look at me.

'Please, Oscar,' I whispered, 'you must help me, we are in such trouble,' and without more ado I scrambled up on the manger in front of him. He sprang back, and for one dreadful moment I thought he would kick open the door I had left swinging in my anxiety, and be gone. But as I held out my hands to him he gave a great snorting sigh and came forward again. With shaking hands I pulled the head piece over his ears and tied a knot on the far side. Then, taking a firm hold of his mane I climbed on his back.

'Please, Oscar,' I whispered again, 'we're the only ones, you and I, we've got to do it.' Firmly I pulled him round and we went out of the stable doors. I was terrified lest he should rear and plunge as he did when Master Matthew mounted him of a morning. If I slipped off now I had no idea how I would ever get on him again. But as though he knew, the big horse went down the track in a fast, easy gait which enabled me to hang on to him — for how long I wasn't sure, but at least with every yard we must be drawing near to whatever had happened to Mr Haynes and Master Bruce.

The wind in my face was cold and strong, and the noise of the rushing water as we approached the river made me realise how swollen it had become. I was more and more afraid.

Then I saw him — out on a log in the middle of the river! Master Bruce's little figure was huddled in the centre of the log, and I could just see Mr Haynes's hands holding him there. He himself was half across the log, half in the water. He looked as though he had no strength to drag himself farther.

I pulled and tugged on the halter and called to Oscar to stop, and once again the wonderful animal seemed to understand, and came to a halt as I slithered from his back. In a flash it came to me what to do. I pulled him round until he faced Ardrossan then I tugged wildly at the halter until I pulled it over his ears, and as it came free and he plunged back I brought it down on his flank. 'Good boy,' I cried, 'go home, go, Oscar.'

I knew that if anyone saw him galloping loose round the place they would guess something was wrong, and please God, that, added to what Jimmy would tell them, would do the rest.

As he felt the rope, Oscar reared to his full height; then, bucking as he went, raced for home.

I rushed down the slippery bank, or what was left of it. Already the river was practically to the top. At the same time I remembered having heard Mr Haynes say that he had never learnt to swim. He disliked cold water far too much! I could see them clearly now, the log eddying, with a maddening swirl, to the pace of the river. The dreadful sight of the little huddled body lying face down along the wet, shining wood horrified me. Was he already dead? And the hate in me for the man whose frozen hands and body clung desperately to the child and the log grew to a frenzy. It was his fault. How had he come to let the child get into the water at all? He cared for nothing and no one but his own wants. I was filled with a blind unreasoning rage, but at the same time fear left me. I must think — think.

The log was going down stream and farther on, only a little way, the river narrowed. If only I could wade in at that narrow part and throw the halter over the end of the log where I could see some torn branches, I could perhaps hold on long enough to pull it towards me. I could not hope to hold it with its load against the current, but if I could only deflect it at least a little from its course, it might of itself head for the bank.

Before God, it was my only thought at that moment to save the child we all loved so much. I hurried along the bank to the place where I had planned, and cautiously entered the water, clinging as long as I could to overhanging trees and branches. The icy cold made me gasp. In a matter of seconds I was up to my waist; my skirts were tangling round my legs, and I knew that at any minute I too might fall and be swept away; but gasping and shouting to them I struggled out towards mid-stream as the log came swinging towards me.

Very quickly, from the intense cold, I began to lose feeling in my limbs. My teeth were chattering, and in no time I could no longer shout. Then the log was level with me, and I raised my arm and threw out the halter with all the strength that was in my hands — the halter must have caught on something — and immediately I too was dragged out into mid-stream.

Then began a battle that seems like a nightmare now, but I must write of it in the hope that my actions will become clear both to you and myself. Hand over hand I dragged myself along the rope, sometimes going completely under the water, but always I managed to advance a little, until one of my hands reached the wet, treacherous log. Shaking the water out of my eyes, I managed to see the jagged broken branches at its end, also saw that they offered some kind of grip where the log itself offered none.

Bit by bit I dragged myself across it, and there, in front of me was Haynes's hand! So dead was the circulation that all colour had gone from the flesh. That hand, and one leg half across the log, were all he had to save himself from death. Seeing the starved expression on his face I knew that the cold had paralysed his muscles, and that he had no strength left to pull himself up alongside the child. Nor could he speak, but his eyes mocked me, dared me to come within reach of his grasping fingers and he would make the supreme effort to pull me under with him. Yet, if I were to get to the child I must go past the man!

I knew my whole future was at stake, and realised that he knew it too, and desperate though his position was, he had clearly decided that if he couldn't use me to save himself he would deliberately pull me under with him. He cared naught for the boy — let him drown — he, Haynes came first. I had never hated him more! But I must do something quickly for I too was becoming paralysed by the cold. Unless a miracle happened we would all be swept away.

With what feeling was left me I pulled myself astride the log and squeezed my legs as tightly as I could on either side of it, while with both hands I tried to edge myself forward, even though it meant getting nearer to that foot and hand. I watched, as an animal watches, the last convulsive effort he made to kick at me, and at that minute I heard a whimper from the little sodden bundle ahead of me and my heart turned with joy — he was not dead! I must find a way to get past this vicious, clinging parasite. Wildly and weakly I struck again and again at that white hand and the ineffectual leg, until I felt the log roll under us. I tried to *scream, and could have laughed at the stupid sound I made, although I watched panic-stricken as the little boy rolled sideways. I made a super-human effort to reach him, and suddenly realised there was no hand in front of me — no leg!*

At the same instant my fingers gripped the child's clothing as he slipped face down under the water. I hung on as the log rolled over and away from us, but Master Bruce was in my arms, even though I too went under the water with him, and my last conscious thought was that there were other arms about us both, whose, I neither knew nor cared...

The bell rang sharply, and Sara started so violently she nearly dropped the journal. She glanced at her watch; she had been so absorbed that she had forgotten the time. She jumped to her feet and hurried to the door, to find Richard already half-way up the stairs.

'You're half an hour early,' she said.

'And you look as though you'll be half an hour late. You haven't even begun to change.'

'Come in, I won't be long. I thought I had time to do some reading of the journal—I must tell you about this some time. The trouble is I get so interested I forget the time. Get yourself a drink.'

'Thanks.'

'Why did you come so early, anyway? Anything wrong?'

'Always looking for trouble. No, nothing's wrong, and why I came will have to keep if you're going to be worth looking at.'

She smiled as she left him. He was always so at ease, knew what he wanted to say and said it. It was probably one of his greatest charms, she decided, as she heard the record player start up and visualised him lying on the sofa, smoking and listening to it, a drink in his hand. She thought of John in like circumstances; the dear old sausage would almost certainly look for the daily paper and sit reading it in a most correct manner. That's the trouble with us English, she said to herself as she headed for the shower, we look one way and feel another. This must be awfully misleading for others; no wonder they think we are peculiar. I wonder if Arna is ready.

But presently she discovered the other girl had not as yet come up from the showroom. How like her! She is so single-minded that I sometimes think this boutique means more to her than any man. She turned back to her room, wishing that she could be like Arna, wholly satisfied with what she was doing at the moment, whether playing with a man or organising the boutique.

No more than a quarter of an hour later she went back to the lounge to find Richard just as she had imagined. He glanced up as she came in and swung his legs to the floor.

'That's better!'

'You approve?'

She had put on a simply cut apricot chiffon frock with a black stole about her shoulders. The soft femininity of the delicate apricot was striking against her dark hair, dark eyes and clear flushed skin.

As he silently took in the effect she made, he could cheerfully have wished John Hilyard under the sea!

He stood up, put down his glass on a small side table and, taking her hand in his, drew her over to the window.

'What are we going to do, you and I?'

Trembling in spite of herself—she had meant to be so casual when she returned to the lounge—she wondered if she should try to ignore the meaning of his words. Instead she heard herself stuttering a miserable: 'I don't know.'

He held her even more tightly as they stood side by side locking down into the darkness of the garden.

'You realise of course that something has to be done?'

'I—suppose so.'

'It would help if you had a more modern approach.'

'Meaning—'

'What's happening to us is as old as the hills. Writers couldn't do without it. But we needn't really make it a problem.'

She turned in his grip to look at the side of his face nearest to her, and feeling her gaze he also turned, and after a moment kissed her deliberately, intensely.

When at last he held her a little apart so that he could look at her, her heart was hammering so fast it was impossible to speak. So he kissed her again, until she stood weakly against him.

It was then that for the first time he was afraid for his own glorious independence, and turned away to search clumsily for a cigarette in her little inlaid box. 'We'd better go, it's no good talking now.'

'Or ever, Rick.'

'Yes, we must talk, but not now.'

'You're right, I'm not modern enough to play with fire.'

'You could have that child you've always wanted—he'd never know.'

'So, you've guessed that too? But it wouldn't be in the way I wanted it. Oh, God, I wish we didn't have to go to this dinner.' She leant her head against the glass and closed her eyes, and as he saw the dejected lines of her body he knew another emotion; the unexpected desire to be strong enough to solve the problem for her; at all costs bring back into her face that glow which had lit it only a few moments before when she had walked into the room.

'Go on, off you go, collect Arna. Do whatever it is a woman does to put on a mask. There'll be a way—I promise.'

CHAPTER SEVENTEEN

The days passed and a gap was torn in the wet, dark forest. The crude yellow of the D7 with its mud-clogged tracks showed up obscenely against the mass of hewn-down timber and slowly drying piles of undergrowth. The dark atmosphere was filled with the smell of petrol fumes and the whine of chainsaws. Man was winning, but the forest brooded.

Already they were taking advantage of every moment of daylight—every moment when the steady curtain of rain lifted. Never, not even in England, had John known such rain. Quietly, endlessly it fell from the thick, matted foliage, creating a moist heat inside the rain clothes that was depressing in itself. Yet still the men worked doggedly on, ploughing through the piles of torn-up soil in their mud-caked gum boots; brushing away the ceaseless tree drippings with routine movements of the back of their hands, like automatons.

This was the moment for which John had been waiting, when the love of a pay packet, or Bill's "core of content", or a mixture of both, would either win or lose for the men; for, looked at from most angles, this life was mere existence for them (it would be even worse when the forward camps were set up, when men would be dropped by helicopters into enclosed areas of rock and forest for weeks at a time, their only communication with the outside world by radio). Admittedly they returned at night to their aluminium caravans to more comfort and good food than they would have found in their own homes, but many of them, he knew, were too tired to do anything but sleep.

But as the long days wore on he could not but admit the majority worked well and with a certain amount of pride. Already he could pick out the minority, the troublemakers, the ones who lived to whinge for whingeing's sake; even the few who found a peculiar satisfaction in this wet scrambling in the silent, dark resentful atmosphere of unending tree pride, this humbling of the "big ones", as they were brought crashing down through the undergrowth to lie majestic in their downfall. These were the small souls, the ones to be watched whom he did not find among the Australians, but rather among the displaced Europeans, who obviously treated their work as a project leading to greater gains; who found pleasure in conquering these tree giants as a means to conquering their own terrors of poverty and the loss of belonging.

He discovered too that Hurst was right; he was unquestionably pleased with himself for fighting nature in the raw and using the men he directed to do it. But would Hurst be right in his suggestion that the end of the road would give the clue to whether he, John, would want to turn round and do it all over again? This was the question always somewhere in the back of his mind as he walked in the forest and came back to pore over his plans and work out the daily problems of this untamed country.

There was something else he had to face. With every weekend that he returned to Hobart, he saw that this work life and his domestic life were not matching; that what he gained in the one he lost in the other. What worried him most was that he did not know why they needed to match; they were two different worlds, to each of which he gave, in different ways, all he had. Yet match they must if he were to be at peace.

On each return he had felt it almost impossible to get near to Sara in the real sense; their old peaceful togetherness seemed to have been swept into the vortex of the boutique, and was lost. He was more than thankful the venture had proved such an immediate success, and was the first to admit that now was the time to push it in case its very newness was its main attraction. Its normal routine was demanding enough, but the social commitments it brought in its train were what he found debilitating after the physical exhaustion of work. There were always people doing things, going somewhere. Sara too appeared to have changed. Probably for the first time in her life she had been caught up into a social life. John did not feel it suited her. She was always on the go from one event to another—gone were the weekends which meant so much to him, when after a fatiguing week's work he could spend time quietly and happily with her, both of them emerging emotionally renewed to face another bout of work. He did not enjoy the new Sara and he doubted whether she enjoyed it herself.

'There's one thing about Australians,' she had said only the previous weekend, 'they don't stagnate, they *do* things. They enjoy art, music and all the things we also take for granted. But unlike us, they want to know more. They don't just talk about it, they get on with it; they're so much more alive.'

The old Sara would never have spoken like that, nor had such thoughts. He wasn't sure that he knew how to handle this new woman, but she had to be handled if their life together was to carry on in a sane and understandable way.

They hardly spoke together any more, and never in the old way. She didn't seem to have any interest in his problems and when he was honest with himself he realised that it went both ways. The marvellous boutique frankly bored him. He couldn't understand Richard's interest in it. To John the whole thing was women's work—how could a real man get caught up in it so intensely? Then he laughed to himself—perhaps that was Rick's real interest; Arna would get any man in if she wanted to.

It struck him, as it always did when he thought of himself and Sara, that she was still not pregnant—perhaps he'd better do something that he'd been putting off for some time.

On Sara's part she was getting more and more desperate. The affair with Richard was getting out of hand. He thrilled and excited her but he gave her no peace. John always did— she still ached for the days and nights when they were together, warm and comforting each other; other problems either solved or forgotten. With Rick this just did not happen—with him excitement, vivid and intense, was followed by emotional and physical exhaustion.

She knew the situation could not last, John was certain to find out sooner or later. It was a wonder he hadn't realised it already! Not that any mutual friends would be likely to tell him. Arna naturally knew about it, but true to her nature she was neither vindictive nor jealous. On the contrary it gave her a bit of a kick. Her main comment was typical: 'Now you are starting to live, Sara—keep it up, girl, as they say, you'll be "with it" in no time.' It left Sara in despair. They would never understand each other as long as they lived. She didn't know whether to laugh or cry.

Guiltily she began to search for legitimate and plausible excuses to stop John coming down from the camp. She wanted time to think, to sort out exactly what she felt about Richard. For instance, did his attraction lie in the fact that before marriage she had not had many male friends, certainly no one like Richard? Was this what Arna took for granted every day of her life? Without John around she must somehow get herself out of the tangle. Then she remembered she could use the pretext of going up to see their Launceston agent, who was arranging northern publicity for the boutique. In fact it was not only a pretext; he had worked hard on their behalf and had already sent down some good customers. Only the week before he had written saying he had found an excellent travelling salesman for materials.

So she set about convincing herself that a trip up north was nothing but good business. It was impossible for her to leave during the week. In the first flush of success Paulina had her hands full of orders, and it would be out of the question to leave Arna alone to cope with the rest. Whereas, if she left on Friday afternoon (and it would be quite easy to find someone to give her a lift) she could be back on Sunday.

From her own point of view it would be a great relief to be out of Hobart and on her own for a couple of days; a relief to be able to think without anyone influencing her. So, before she could change her mind she sat down and wrote to John, but to make the argument even more convincing to him, she told him that Mr Lister had particularly asked her to go. It made the whole thing sound right.

When it was finished she rang the Commission and asked if anyone was going up to "the road" the next day. On being told there was, she put down the phone with such relief as to be almost light-hearted, and went in search of Arna to discuss the trip. She was immediately successful. Arna clapped her hands. 'What a good idea. Paulina has only just now said if things go on like this we shall not have enough material for our spring casuals. But this Mr Lister, are you sure you will be able to see him at the weekend? Had you not better go earlier? Besides—'

'Of course I can,' Sara stopped her hastily. 'I couldn't possibly leave you both during the week. I've written to John, and I'll ring Mr Lister now.'

Once again things went her way. Mr Lister said he would be delighted to see her on Saturday morning, and he felt sure she would like the samples he had collected for her. It was almost too good to be true, and when the boutique closed she made herself a drink and picked up the journal. Now was not the time to give way to the thoughts that were beginning to race round her mind.

CHAPTER EIGHTEEN

'...I thought I should never know what it was to be warm again. I believe I must have lost consciousness when they took me from the water, for I do not remember how I got back to Ardrossan. I came to, shaking uncontrollably all over and I found myself on a sofa that had been pushed in front of the kitchen stove. The door of the stove had been left open, and from where I lay I could look into the heart of the flames. But their brightness hurt my eyes and I closed them again while I strove to control my icy, shaking body.

'Sarah, you must drink this!' It was Madam's voice and I reopened my eyes to see her pale, distraught face near mine. I could see too, that the pins had come out of her thick hair, which was beginning to straggle down her neck. The Master would be cross if he saw it. He did not like untidy women. I often overheard him say: 'We may live in the wilds, but they must be tamed by us, not us by them.'

'Master Bruce, Madam—' I managed to force my lips to say — of the other I did not dare speak, '— is — he—'

She nodded, her eyes filling with tears. 'He will be all right, Sarah,' she whispered, 'he will be all right, thanks to the good Lord and you.'

'Now, Jessica, stop being sentimental and see the girl swallows that brandy.'

I had not realised the Master was also in the kitchen, and I tried to twist my head that I might see his face and know by it if he had seen — if he would be likely to accuse me of that other.

'Lie still, girl, do as you are told.'

'Come, Sarah, I will hold the cup for you.'

The raw spirit nearly choked me as I obediently tried to swallow some of it, but after a moment or two what I did swallow seemed to start a flame spreading about my whole body so that soon I ceased to tremble and could take better stock of what had happened. I saw at once that my wet clothes had been removed and replaced with dry ones, and blankets wrapped about me.

I wondered how long I had been there, and struggled to sit up. I felt embarrassed by my position, and with every moment of my returning memory, began to relive those dreadful happenings in the river. But I felt Madam's hand on my shoulders: 'No, Sarah, you must stay until you are quite warmed or you will be ill. I must go to Master Bruce, I have left the girls with him. We have sent for Doctor Mortimer; I do hope he will not be inebriated, he is so very partial to Mr Walker's beer.'

'Your hope, my dear Jessica, is destined not to reach fulfilment. Mortimer grows more unreliable daily. The boy is only shocked and chilled. We can do as much for him ourselves as that old soak.'

'You don't know, Matthew, the dear little chap could have suffered internal damage of which we know nothing. Remember we don't even know what happened to cause them both to be in the river at all. They must have had some kind of accident. Besides, there is — Haynes.'

'Even a drunken old fool like Mortimer can't do anything for him, except sign his death certificate. Can't think why they let fellows like Mortimer immigrate. Obviously he was a failure at home and came here to drink himself into the ground.'

I listened as one in a trance. The Master's calm acceptance of Mr Haynes's death made me realise afresh the enormity of what had happened. Clearly now, before my eyes came the picture of the hand on the log, his hand! I knew I must steady myself, must not show the fear that was beginning to swamp my efforts at control. These people must never know, never.

Without realising, I dropped my head, and above me came Madam's voice in a shocked whisper: 'Matthew, you should not say things so bluntly. I'm sure Sarah could not have known.'

'Sarah is not a stuffed doll, Jessica. She must know sometime, the sooner the better. I believe, my dear, you were going to see how Bruce is faring.'

As the rustling of her skirts faded from the kitchen I felt I could not be left there with the Master. Also, my thoughts switched to Miss Charlotte. No one could know what she must be going through: I must get to her. But the moment I once again made an effort to get to my feet the Master's voice said sharply: 'Will you do as you're told, girl! I'll tell you when to move.'

He was standing watching me, legs astride, hands behind his back, and I felt convinced he was going to question me now that we were alone, but that was the one thing I knew I could not do, answer questions — not yet. First I must discover how much I was expected to remember; must rehearse the part I was to play. So, pretending that I was overcome with the attempt to move, I lay back and closed my eyes, feigning sleep, and presently I heard him go. But almost immediately there was the sound of other footsteps on the flags and a voice said: 'Well, Sarah, once again we find you at the centre of a most interesting situation! No, don't rise. I hear you are to be treated with the greatest care — undoubtedly we have to thank you for my young brother's life.'

I struggled to a sitting position, pushing away the blankets.

'I assure you, Master Matthew, I am greatly recovered and am very sensible I owe you an apology. You see—'

He nodded. 'I know. Young Phillip told you they were drowning downriver, and you believed Oscar was the only way to get you to the rescue.'

'Indeed, sir, that is the truth.'

'And you, who have never ridden a horse in your life, secured and rode mine bare-back, a horse no one but myself dares to approach.'

'Master Matthew, it was his life or mine.'

'Truly courageous, truly noble!' he said quietly, and strangely I felt he meant it!

But then came the question, 'And what of Haynes?' thrust at me in such a way when it was already the greatest fear in my mind, caught me so unawares as to make me gasp: 'What indeed of — Mr Haynes, sir?'

I stared at him, fascinated. I believed that when he answered I should know whether he suspected that I was in any way responsible for that man's death.

He walked across to the stove and stood with his hands behind his back, looking remarkably like his father. Then he shook his head, his gaze solemnly on mine. 'Poor fellow, they are drawing in his body at this moment.'

A feeling of both triumph and revulsion swept over me so that I lowered my gaze from his and gripped the sofa either side of my knees. I allowed myself to accept the fact that at last I was free of that dreadful man's threats and his nagging attentions. Yet, could I live with my conscience? Could I ever truly convince myself that, had I not even so much as touched his hands, he would have slipped in any case and been lost? Would I ever be free of the vivid picture in my mind of myself striking, striking with all my might at that ineffectual white hand on the log? Yet I knew, had I to go through it all again I would do no differently.

'You talked a great deal, Sarah, when I carried you back in front of me on Oscar's back.'

So it was he who had brought me back. Perhaps I was not free after all if I had said too much? Would he tell me or would he keep to himself whatever he knew, to produce it in his own good time. My mouth felt dry.

'I — talked, Master Matthew?'

'Indeed, Sarah, you did. A most interesting monologue.'

'You were — very kind, sir, to — to rescue me.'

I do not think he heard my reply, or else he was not to be diverted from his subject.

'I was most interested in your concern for Haynes's person! I believe he must have meant more to you than any of us realised.'

I hung my head, afraid of being drawn into committing myself. I had learned to be wary, when as now, everything he said was half-serious, half-sarcastic. I knew too, that under the guise of talking he was watching me intently. So we remained in silence — each keenly aware of the other, until I could bear it no longer, and forcing myself to look straight into his eyes I got to my feet and said: 'Please Master Matthew, I am greatly recovered and would like to go to Miss Charlotte.'

'Charlotte, eh! What has she got to do with this little drama?'

Too late I saw how foolish I had been.

'There is a matter I must discuss with her. She will expect it.'

'Haynes, I'll be bound. I'd not be surprised if my romantic little sister were somewhat fetched by the bounder's charm.'

My astonishment made me turn to look at him. 'You did not like him? But I—'

'Certainly I did not like anything about him. He had too much liberty in this household. But you women are all the same, a man with pretty manners can make a fool of the best of you. However, you went through a bad time in that river — he is not worth your regrets, Sarah.'

It was one of the few times I had ever heard him say a genuinely kind thing to me, and I realised in my present upset state, kindness from him was the last thing I must have. I wanted to tell him that man had meant nothing to me, that I was, in fact, his murderess. Was I?

So I stood there, knowing that by my silence he believed my thoughts to be with the man whose body they were at that very moment bringing to this house. If only he knew, if only I could take him into my confidence, but such weakness would merely spell the undoing of all I had planned for the future. Plans that would be far far simpler now that Mr Haynes was gone.

I thanked him and turned away as the Master came through the house door.

'Oh, there you are, Matthew, I've been looking for you. We need your help.'

And as I passed through the door I heard him go on to say: 'She's recovered pretty quickly!' and Master Matthew's level answer: 'She's a strong young woman, Father, and a brave one.'

I closed the door quietly behind me and went up the stairs. If only things had been different, what that conversation would have meant to me!

The funeral was a sad one under grey skies. Everyone from around came, funerals ranking as occasions. It was the first Mr McKirtle had taken, and I could not help feeling this first should have been that of some brave settler who had met his death in an upright manner. They buried him in a plot of ground near to where Ardrossan's little private chapel was to be started in a week's time — the chapel whose plans he himself had drawn — but I could feel no pity for him as his coffin was lowered into its clay resting place before a handful of soil was cast upon its lid.

I hope you are not shocked, dear sister, but as we all stood there with bowed heads, in a bleak wind that made the gum leaves rattle around us, I had no regrets, no remorse for what I had done.

In the days that followed Miss Charlotte was deeply unhappy, and as her only confidant I had to suffer long sessions of the release of her pent-up feelings. But time soon made her glory in the thought of her short love affair and its tragic end. She began to feel a woman with a woman's experience of life. And from spending hours at her tapestry and needlework, she began once again to be her mother's right hand in the life of the neighbourhood.

She has also been to many riding parties and even daring moonlight picnics — near to homesteads, of course, for fear the blacks — given in return for the hospitality of the Ball, and within the next month or six weeks she is due to go to Hobart Town for the winter festivities. Almost a "coming out" visit.

Many new settlers have arrived of late and need advice and the little comforts Madam is so insistent be given to all newcomers to our district. So it has become a common sight to see Miss Charlotte and Miss Jessica, accompanied now by Mr James happily driving the little pony cart down the track. Also, the day after Mr Haynes's funeral, Mrs Macdonald gave birth to yet another little girl, which caused great excitement among the young people. Fortunately her husband is as good a midwife as a farmer, for, as we all expected, the funeral proved too much for Doctor Mortimer who, when it was over, returned to his cottage in Kilmarnock to drown his unmedical sensitivity in alcohol.

Two months later:-

Once again there has been no time to relate daily the events and happenings in this, my little world. At first, being so isolated, I believed time would lie heavily on my hands, but this bush life is a busy one, with so many tasks there is never time to be lonely, for which I am most thankful. Also, once again I am come to a great crisis in my affairs, in fact, dear sister, the greatest of all, and I find that in writing to you of events as they occur, I am helped to see things clearly.

We have now come to winter in real earnest, and the last of the picnics to the hill and up the glen. It's over a year since I came to Ardrossan. I can hardly believe this, so much seems to have happened to me in that time. The big event lately has been the arrival of Oscar's first foal. If you remember, I told you that the Master has brought out some fine horses for racing purposes, and among them the most beautiful Irish mare for Oscar. He hopes great things from this foal, and the children have hardly been able to await its arrival. For the last week before the event no one settled to breakfast before first going on a pilgrimage to see if Diana, the Mare's name, had obliged. And when the great morning arrived, that was the end of work for the day!

I do not think there is any more beautiful sight than a newly born foal and its mother. As for Oscar, he does not share at all in the excitement. He feels, and rightly I fear, that he is no longer the centre of attraction. Still, however, I take him his early morning tit-bit, a procedure which I am now allowed to carry out without pretence. Although I have not been given actual permission, Master Matthew comes and stands beside me while I cut up apples or carrots, whichever we have at the moment, and makes no comment. How I love that horse and that short period of time while he munches his small offering and his master and I stand together.

But on looking back I see that this daily routine was observed by the Master, and while he too made no comment you will see from the development of events that he could not have approved.

You will be surprised to hear that only one tree of all the seeds, shrubs and trees sent from England has died. I am proud of my gardening attempts, and in the hours I spend on my knees weeding I try to put from my mind Mr Haynes's dreadful death. No member of the family has discussed the matter at all with me, and as far as I know no one associates me in any way with the event, other than that I jumped into the water in an attempt to save Master Bruce's life. I have never believed in the Roman Catholic faith, but strangely I often feel that I would give much to be able to discuss that shocking happening with a priest to whom I could unburden myself, but who would not divulge my secret. Indeed, if I could not write of these things in this Journal I believe I should go out of my mind.

Or would I? Sometimes I feel I am a person born to be driven through life whether I will or not. That I must do things whether I want or not, and in very truth I wonder where it will all end.

However, I have to relate one pleasant outcome of events. A delightful settler family has not long taken up their grant on our westerly boundary. We were returning from taking comforts to old Mrs Cauley in Kilmarnock, when we encountered their bullock drays coming up the gully.

Being inexperienced, they had over-loaded the drays as well as packed them badly, with the result their bullocks had been unable to make the pull. Mr James and I helped them to unload, while their young people and ours quickly made friends, delighted to find we would all be such comparatively close neighbours. I was not slow to notice that their eldest son must only be a few years older than Miss Charlotte, and of a most pleasant and open countenance; and that in between helping his father, Mr James and myself, he was most sensibly aware of Miss Charlotte! She, for her part was careful to include in her helpful remarks on pioneering life that there were various social activities among the neighbouring families, including the newly begun literary society in Kilmarnock.

I also noticed that after we had got them up the gully and sent them on their way with much more tidily packed drays, she was of a much happier disposition than she had been for many weeks, and was not so desirous of leaving for Hobart Town the next week. I could not but be pleased for her, but wished my own affairs could be as easily settled.

It was about this time that Master Donald finally took his courage in both hands and informed his father that he wished to return to England and enter the Ministry — a decision received much more equably than I would have imagined. His mother of course had known for some time that this moment would be reached, although she also confided in me that with the passage of time she had hoped he would change. She was not a woman to part easily with her possessions, and her children she counted definitely as possessions. As for the Master, it had always been obvious he had looked on Master Donald as one apart; just as he depended on Master Matthew and after him Master Richard, to support him on the estate. Therefore he made no demur when Master Donald asked his permission to go.

I wondered what Master Matthew thought of his brother's return to England, not that it would lay any greater burden on his shoulders, for Master Donald had played but a small part in the running of Ardrossan, as little in fact as his father would allow. Books and solitude were his life, and I had a strong feeling that much of his father's acquiescence in his departure was due to the fact that as a worker on the station they were all better off without him.

So no comment passed Master Matthew's lips when I was anywhere near, until the day came when we all assembled by the front door to bid the traveller God's speed. It was almost an English day, the sun being hidden by rolling banks of grey clouds, and a bitter wind coming off the snow-capped mountains as we stood uncomfortably bunched in the misery of farewells. There is always such a loneliness in the act of departure. How well I knew it! And since I did, it drew me near to these people in this lonely land: Cook, with her tear-reddened eyes, hands twisting, without her knowledge, at the big apron round her ample hips; Mrs James, as always, standing in the background; the cowmen and the shepherds with their families clinging wide-eyed about them. Even the rest of the convicts in the home fields had left their work to watch their master's son leave his fine home in order to return to the country they had left for ever. It was interesting to see the incredulity of their faces.

Then there was the family itself, all drawn together much as I had seen them on that first day, only now they were going to be one fewer, as they were experiencing that first time of break-up that must come to all families.

The younger members were whispering among themselves, underneath enjoying the drama of this departure, albeit they kissed Master Donald very prettily and with a great show of feeling when he bid each of them farewell. Madam looked very pale and composed. Later, in the privacy of her room, I would be called upon to tend and comfort her. The Master looked impatient; he wanted to be done with this uncomfortable performance.

Then Master Donald came last of all to his mother and, putting his arms around her, kissed her gently, more as a woman would kiss a child.

'Come back to us, Donald,' she said; 'it will be a wonderful place one day.'

'I will, Mother, if God wills it.' And with that he climbed up beside Mr James, and the last we saw of him was a pale-handed wave as the gig departed at a smart trot down the track.

It was then that Master Matthew, who was quite close to me, said: 'Strange it was he who had the courage to do what he wanted!'

I realised then what I had always suspected: he did have a grudge. I wished at that moment I could have gone to him and talked to him as a friend; could have made him understand that I knew what it was to fight for and against oneself. I felt too we could understand each other if only the chance could be given, but I also knew it would never be given unless in some way I could make it possible.

However, since that day strange things have taken place. But before I write of these you must know that little Master Bruce recovered at great speed, and seems to recall little of what happened that day, except that he was "awful cold and wet". His mother had told him that Mr Haynes was sent away, so there is little to mark the passing of that man. Strangely, like most things that take place here, there is little discussion once the event is over. There is a general acceptance that what must be must be. Only the two younger girls occasionally pick wild flowers in the bush, and make a pilgrimage to arrange them on his grave; then stand awhile to look silently, with a child's questioning wonder in their eyes, at the raised mound of clay with its solitary wooden cross.

I have told you the Master is most interested in the rearing of sheep. He believes this country, when cleared of its forest, will prove excellent land on which to raise great flocks. To this end he is spending everything he has in adding to the Merino sheep originally granted to him. At the time I write many of the ewes have begun to lamb; it would appear they mainly do this by night, keeping the men late from their beds.

It is for me to wait on them with hot drinks when they come in cold, wet and tired from their ministrations. I do not mind this, for there is a warm and social atmosphere in the big flagged kitchen. While I wait for them to come I stoke the fire, and as often as not do not light the candles. I love the red flames and the dancing shadows on the walls. And when the men come to stand in front of the built-up fire, their clothes steaming from the warmth, I am happy to hear them talk of earthy things and the animals they tend while I pour out the burning hot brew they demand. Often they draw me into conversation, and for that short period there are no barriers, no fears. I wish that it could always be so.

On the night of the great event of which I am going to tell you, Master Matthew came roughly through the yard into the kitchen, kicking the door as he came. I could see he carried a little white bundle in his arms.

'Quick, Sarah, an old piece of soft blanket or such like — a box!'

I hurried to do his bidding as he knelt down carefully in front of the stove, shielding the little thing in his arms from the greater heat, but ensuring it got all the necessary warmth. He handled it so expertly, yet so gently.

'Have you always done this kind of thing, Master Matthew?' I could not resist asking as I placed a box beside him.

He looked up and said: 'Warm some milk — just a little, not too hot.'

I wondered if he had deliberately not answered my question. When I came back he dipped his fingers in the milk and placed them quickly in the lamb's mouth. This he kept repeating until the little creature made some effort at fastening its lips to his fingers. Very slowly he trickled a little of the milk into the side of its mouth, then wrapped it in the piece of blanket I had found and warmed. It lay inert, and I could not believe that it would live, but he seemed satisfied and presently rose to stand looking down at it.

There was a great stillness as we stood there, the tiny scrap of an animal between us. At last he looked at me closely and said: 'No, I did not always do this.'

'I'm sorry, sir, I — did not—'

'Yes, you did. You're a bad liar, Sarah, but no matter; it was a simple question as far as I understand it. Did you have a meaning for it that was not so simple, since it appears to worry your conscience?'

'Indeed no, Master Matthew. I — just wondered how you came to know so much about animals.'

'Just treat them like humans, as simple as that, Sarah. However, that wasn't quite what you wanted to know. I was never a farmer, never wanted to be one, nor expected to be one. Does that answer your question?'

'Yes, of course, I mean—'

'You mean you would like to know what I wanted to be?'

I realised that for some strange reason he wanted to talk about the past; that it had been worrying him ever since Master Donald's departure; above all he wanted to tell me about it. A great delight stirred me, but at the same time I knew I must be careful, not too eager, but — yes I must take a chance, I must.

'Yes,' I said, 'I would like very much to know, if you don't mind telling me.'

'You look ridiculously like a child about to receive a sweet! In fact, Sarah, you are quite out of character. Come here and don't step on the lamb.'

I walked around the end of the table and stopped. There was nothing I could do or say.

'If you were anyone else, Sarah, I would say you were afraid of me. But you don't give way to fear, not even when you see a man's hands grasping a log, the only thing between him and death!'

So, he did know! The knowledge made my heart jump sickeningly.

'Don't look like that, Sarah. I might find occasion to kiss you, and then you would think the worst. Would you fight me like you fought in that river? Come here, Sarah!'

Fascinated, I walked slowly forward, my eyes on his. He was not going to make me afraid!

'Was it wrong to fight, Master Matthew, when my life and Master Bruce's were at stake?'

'How innocently you put it, Sarah. Unfortunately it did not look quite like that.'

All the elation, all the happiness of a moment ago left me. I was a fool ever to think I could meet him on equal terms. He had only led me on, using his promised confidence as a bait to trap me. Now he could blackmail me into anything he wished. I searched in my mind for any topic that had nothing to do with the last comment, and said presently:

'Perhaps before you go you will tell me what I'm to do with the lamb?'

'But I am not going.'

He suddenly reached out, caught my wrists and drew me near to him; far too near, so that I could smell the earth on his hands, the bush scent in his hair; could see, as I had never seen so closely before, the expression in his eyes.

'It grows late, Master Matthew.'

'It does, indeed, Sarah, but you remember you wanted to know what I wanted to do with my life.'

I did not answer. I could not. All I could do was strive to hide from him the weakness that was sweeping over me in waves.

Then a thing happened for which there is no accounting. In his attempt to draw me still closer and my determination to hold my ground as long as possible, for I was certain he was going to kiss me, he slipped! Maybe his foot was on some of the spilt milk that had been dropped when he had been trying to make the lamb suck, or maybe something was stuck on the sole of his boot. I do not know, but he slipped, with his feet going from under him, and since he had me firmly by the wrists he pulled me with him, and I was powerless to save myself.

For one agonisingly perfect moment his body was wrapped round mine, the taunting sarcasm was gone, and we were both swept into an embrace where there was no time for us to calculate our actions or behaviour. As we lay there, the door was pushed open and the Master strode into the room! The expression on his face I shall never forget. In absolute horror I struggled to my feet, and stood trying to smooth my clothes into place. I wondered how I could go on living; panic so gripped my mind that it became blank. I could only wait.

'Dear God!'

The two words sounded like doom itself.

'In my house, sir — how dare you!'

'Father—'

'Don't use the word. Go and get your brother.'

'Please allow me to explain.'

'There can be no explanation. That I should live to see the day when my son has the insolence to go whoring in my home! Go and get your brother.'

'Father—'

'Go!'

Master Matthew strode from the kitchen, and now his face was a match for his father's. I stared at his retreating back. To me no word was said.

When Master Richard came, looking from one to the other of us, the Master turned on him. 'Saddle your horse and ride for McKirtle.'

'At this hour, Father?'

'Do as I say. Wake James and tell him to ride with you. Take a shot gun.'

When in silence his brother went through the yard door, Master Matthew again tried to speak.

'Father, will you listen.'

'Silence!'

'Sir, I will not be silent. Why are you sending for the parson?'

But his father did not deign to answer; nothing disturbed his measured pacing up and down the flags. I did not dare to look at Master Matthew. The anger of these two men made me very afraid. What the outcome was to be I had no conception.

I was greatly relieved when Madam came into the kitchen, her hair in disarray, her hands fluttering. As she came through the door her eyes fastened on the pacing figure of her husband. She stood staring at him as one who was watching an apparition.

'Matthew!'

But even of her he took no notice. It was as though she had not called his name. I could see this made her even more afraid, so that she hurried to him and took his arm. 'Matthew, something has happened, you must tell me. What is wrong?'

He shook off her grasp as if she were some insect. Then at last, seeing her worried face, he said: 'Go to bed, Jessica. This is no matter for you.'

Then as I had seen her do before, she put aside her timorous nature. 'Matthew, you are wrong. Whatever is to do with this family is to do with me.'

'My dear, you can have no part in this. I have sent Richard for McKirtle.'

'Mr McKirtle! What can possibly warrant your bringing the poor man through the bush at this hour of night?'

He took her arm and guided her from the kitchen, leaving me and Master Matthew standing like graven images. There were so many things I wanted to say to him, but my lips would not voice them. A mixture of fear and shock held me powerless, and I believe it was so with him. We remained there, waiting — for what? It did not occur to either of us that we were free to go.

Then, after what seemed an eternity, Master and Madam returned. She came to me with tears in her eyes. At Master Matthew she did not look at all. 'My poor child,' she said, 'my poor child!'

Master Matthew did move then. 'Mother,' he said, 'this is absurd. If only Father will listen to me there is a very simple explanation.'

'Dear, I am sure your Father is the one to judge.'

As I watched the Master pacing, pacing, a new and dreadful fear seized me. Was he sending for Mr McKirtle as a means to have me removed to the Cascades? Was the reverend gentleman being called to witness the wickedness of my character yet again, so that the Master could, with a clear conscience, consign me to that unspeakable place?

I thought of the poor wretched convicts and understood why they would risk facing starvation and thirst in the unchartered bush, rather than go on trying to live in those conditions. For the first time I understood too why Mr Haynes had spent years plotting and planning his freedom and the rewards it would give him. Until this moment I had never really looked on myself as a convict, knowing myself to be innocent of any crime, until that dreadful day in the river. Now, as an individual I didn't exist, I was merely the pawn of people such as these. How then could I judge Mr Haynes for trying to take his freedom in the way he wanted? Indeed, I had helped him to lose it, and the dreadful predicament in which I now found myself could be my punishment.

I looked from one to the other and knew there was no mercy. The Master had resumed his pacing up and down; Master Matthew was staring at the fire, his hands behind his back, which was turned to us, and Madam did nothing but stand wringing her hands.

It seemed hours before we heard the horses outside, and the sounds of people dismounting, then the hurried, dishevelled entrance of the reverend gentleman, bringing a draught of cold night air with him. He adjusted his spectacles, looked at us all in turn, then went across to the Master, who had at last stopped his unnerving pacing.

'Sir, what in heaven's name has happened that you send for me at this hour of night? Your son—'

'Knows nothing. Richard, kindly go to your room.'

I felt sorry for the boy as he stared from one to the other of us all, obviously so agog that he would have given much to remain. But no one gave him so much as a glance, and he knew his father too well even to make a request that he remain. After a slight hesitation he turned and walked to the door into the main part of the house, merely staying to give a quick glance to his brother, who had made no move from his position in front of the stove. I knew he would not so much as dare to listen at the other side of the door.

Whatever was to happen would not be known outside this kitchen.

As soon as we five were alone, the Master looked down on the small square figure of the parson. He, poor man, sadly at a loss, had removed his spectacles and was polishing them vigorously.

'And now, Parson McKirtle, I can explain to you that I have sent for you on a very delicate mission. I regret the hour, but the work of God does not count the hours.'

'Indubitably, sir.'

'Very well. Then I call upon you to marry these two young people with all speed! My wife and I will then be delighted to offer you hospitality for the night.'

Marriage! Dear sister I thought of a truth my heart would stop its beating. Then I was filled with rage. The blundering old fool, he had spoiled all my plans. Did he know so little of his son as to think he would accept such treatment?

Even as the thought entered my head, Master Matthew swung round from in front of the fire, and I knew he too was stunned by such a proposition. He stared at his father as though he were a stranger.

'Sir — how dare you!'

'Young man, you forget yourself. Parson, I rely on you as a man of God, that what I am about to say to you will never go beyond these walls. My son, God forgive me, has seen fit within the precincts of his own home to take advantage of a convict girl who has but lately risked her life to save that of his child brother. With my own eyes I came upon them—'

This was too much for me. 'Sir,' I cried, 'before God and this company, I can explain.'

He turned upon me with all his over-bearing presence. 'Young woman,' he said, 'can you stand there, and, since you are so free with the Almighty, tell me in His name that you are a virgin?'

I know I should have lied, at once and with no hesitation, but to be asked to do so at once, and in the name of the Lord, made me try to think quickly, but thought at such a time is fatal. I was confused and the Master seized upon such confusion.

'You see, Parson, she cannot, dare not deny it.'

I looked to Madam for help, but she had sunk on to the kitchen chair, her face buried in her hands.

Sick with a misery that defies all description, I turned back to the two older men watching me. At Master Matthew I dared not look. My hands gripping the sides of my skirt, I gave the others back their stares. At that moment I had nothing but contempt for all men.

'Sir,' I said, addressing the Master, 'I am not a virgin, it is true, but he — it was not your son. This you must indeed believe.'

At this Mr McKirtle made a determined but hopeless effort to control the situation.

'Sir, if I may suggest, it is late, and a night's rest may bring us all to a calmer way of thinking. In the morning we can go more deeply into the matter.'

'I require no rest to know right from wrong. My son shall not play fast and loose with my reputation. Fool that I was, I should have known what would happen when I saw them frequently together. If she is good enough to cohabit with under my roof, she is good enough to marry!'

Master Matthew looked straight at his father. 'And if I refuse, sir? I am of age.'

'Then you will leave this place tonight and for good.'

His mother cried out: 'Oh, Matthew, please, I cannot bear it. Your father means it, you know he does. First Donald and then you. What am I to do in this God-forsaken country? I beseech you.'

Once again Mr McKirtle made an attempt to control the situation.

'Sir,' he said, 'I cannot marry two people over age against their will. In the eyes of the Church—'

'Then perhaps this will change your ideas!'

I stared at the Master as did everyone else. There, on the other side of the kitchen table, he stood facing us with the gun that Master Richard had laid down when he left the room. Madam screamed and slipped from the chair in a faint. Instinctively I moved towards her, but he ordered me back, and I began to wonder, looking at his white, tight-lipped face and angry eyes, if he had taken leave of his senses. Almost immediately, though keeping an eye on his wife's prostrate form, he addressed himself to Master Matthew.

'If you think I'm having your unwanted bastards running around my home, making of me a laughing stock when I have striven greatly for so much, you have made a mistake, young man. I am well aware I have the right to send this young woman to the Cascades, where she would receive the treatment meted out to those in her condition. No questions would be asked, nothing would be known — unfortunately such affairs are common. But before God I hold myself a just man. Lately she risked her life to save my young son from drowning. She shall not be turned away from my home to the unmerciful treatment of those stinking cells because of your weakness.'

I felt so ashamed of my previous thoughts as I listened to him, that I could have wept. I realised that he too was suffering; his love and need of Master Matthew were great, though he would never admit to either, for his principles came first. He would sacrifice everyone of his family for them, and I knew it as surely as I knew I was responsible for this scene of misunderstanding.

The awful truth struck me that while I had been standing there, pitying myself, condemning those around me, I was being given my due for saving the life of a child, albeit I had caused the death of a man; and unless something be done quickly I would cost another man his heritage. Certainly I had wanted my freedom, had schemed to get this man who was being thrust upon me whether I would or no, but this way freedom would cost me my self-respect for the rest of my life. It was too great a burden, and I wanted none of it — but what could I do? No one would listen to me; the more I tried to protest Master Matthew's innocence, the more the Master believed I was trying to shield him.

Then Master Matthew's voice, cold and clipped, cut across the chaos in my mind: 'Very well, Father, since you point a gun at me, I assure you I have neither wish nor intention to trade my life for any woman. Also, since you will not listen to reason, and are determined to acquire a daughter-in-law from a convict ship, there is nothing I can do about it. But when this farce of a marriage has taken place, I leave this house tonight, and shall not return to it until the law has made me a free man again! Now, Parson McKirtle, I shall be glad if you perform this ceremony with all despatch.'

I stared fascinated at the two men watching each other across the kitchen table. They were so alike, both so determined, yet I sensed in the elder a moment of surrender, but only a moment. I saw by the still tighter grip of his jaw that he believed he had gone too far to alter his course of parental discipline.

So, in the big, flagged kitchen, by the light of two candles guttering in their holders, I became Matthew Roland's wife!

I feel you will be glad to know, dear sister, that since the entire matter was now out of my hands, I proceeded to comport myself with the dignity belonging to the family name I must never bear, while I received, no matter how temporarily, the name of my husband (how absurd that title seems) — a name I am sure you will realise from the foregoing, held with as much pride as ours holds lineage!'

CHAPTER NINETEEN

Sara put down the journal and stretched her arms over her head. What a wedding! A wedding that could not be the end of Sarah's story—only the beginning. She felt so close to them all, even Donald, who went out of their lives with a "a pale-handed wave as the gig departed at a smart trot down the track" to become a bishop.

How strange it was that, although they lived in two different worlds, both she and Sarah were always pushed from one set of circumstances to another while striving so hard to work out their own destiny; the earlier Sarah hemmed round by the Law and almost unbreakable conventions; she, the modern Sara, free of all such problems, except perhaps the latter, still unable to break free.

'The only difference between us,' she thought, 'is that she tried to be honest, tried to work out every step she took, pleasant or unpleasant, whereas I drift and feel sorry for myself when I've really nothing to be sorry for. I've just allowed myself to slip from married security to a muddled state of emotion that is dangerous. John and I are "getting through" life; we don't "live" it any more.'

Looking back on their old life in England, she was appalled to realise how they had both changed. John had developed an ambitious side of his nature that she had never known existed. She had gone from a life of narrow bovine contentment to excitement, achievement of a sort; a love affair of which she was not proud but could not banish. 'I've got a bachelor girl's life without any of its privileges, yet I'm starting to take them because I need a man to love. It's all right for John; he's got what he wants—the bush all week with himself the big white chief, and me at the weekends. What have I got? So I didn't want to live in a country camp, looking at beautiful hills, watching other people with children I can't have—just waiting for him to come home at night. What's wrong with that? Nothing. I've made a busy, interesting life here, then why doesn't it have meaning? Why don't I know what I want, where I'm going? Why do I feel depressed, positively ill sometimes?'

She got off the sofa, letting the journal fall to the floor, and began to pace up and down the room. Thank goodness Mr Lister was only too pleased to see her on Saturday. John too had got a note back to her in answer to her letter, saying that the trip to Launceston was a good thing; that he had a lot on his plate at the moment, so it would be better if he stayed on at the camp this weekend. As always, she could count on him for a sensible and balanced outlook, but there again she didn't really want him to be sensible and balanced. She wanted him to say why the hell did she have to go away this weekend.

She hadn't even told Richard she was going; anyway, she wouldn't be seeing him. At that particular moment for instance, with the great race coming up, he wouldn't be giving her a thought. The momentum was increasing and rebellious thoughts kept coming into her mind. Why, for instance, was it always the woman who had to give way? Why were her interests given last place? She was so angry that she threw down her palette and swore never to touch the picture of the yacht again. There was something else to be tested on yet another trial run—and always this came first.

She tried to imagine what it must be like to have a life's ambition to win the Sydney-Hobart race, one of the three great classic yacht races in the world—to save for it, live for it, train for it. She could see him as a little boy round the waterfront; in and out of boats that would get progressively larger; listening to sailors' stories while his toes curled in the water, and his eyes watching intently the weather-beaten faces of the men of the sea. Then would come his first navigation course, working in his father's office to save every penny, still saving when he came into the family business, his one thought to put more and more aside for the *Sunbolt* of his dreams.

What he must have felt when she became a reality!

But if he won the race, what then? He'd have to face ordinary life. What did it feel like to gain the one thing you really wanted? To know that the need to fight for it, plan for it was gone—that it was yours—it could be a dreadful anti-climax. She thought of the old saying: "Beware what you wish for—you might get it."

She wondered if John really had what he wanted, or if he just had an overweening ambition which never came to an end with one thing, but carried him onwards to the gaining of something still greater. 'Maybe he's the only adjusted one among us,' she thought; 'never stop, always continue on, no matter what.'

Sarah had wanted nothing more than Ardrossan, had been ready to wrap her whole life round it; she, the Sara of today, wanted a child.

Beaten by the feeling of tiredness that of late seemed always with her, she bent down and picked up the journal and decided she would pack her suitcase tonight; then she needn't get up so early in the morning.

She put out the lights and stood in front of the plate-glass doors; looked down at the moonlight in the garden, on the harbour, at the thousands of twinkling, coloured lights of the town and foreshore. They represented people—people living, dying, being born, or just sitting in front of their television sets. Suddenly she felt a great need to go out and be among them—to leave the packing of her suitcase after all. It would be a good thing to walk along by the water, feel the wind in her face. She slipped on a coat and let herself out of the house. As she started to walk along the pavement towards St Stephen's church, her attention was caught by a child on the other side of the road. He was crying in the desperate way a child cries when he is lost, the knuckles of his podgy little hands rolling in his eyes, his feet shuffling on the pavement without taking him anywhere in particular.

Wondering what he was doing on his own at this time of night, she stopped; then turned back and ran across the road to him.

Where the car came from she did not know. She was only aware of a high-revving engine, the sudden confusion of headlights and screaming brakes, a woman running frantically for her child, her own body being tossed sideways; her head cracking down on the black, hard road.

Bill received the message for John. He had just got himself a bottle of beer from the canteen; had decided to drink it while he read the paper before turning in—already half the camp was in darkness. Stevens, the admin clerk, came and tapped him on the shoulder. 'Seen the boss around?'

Bill shook his head. 'Thought he was in the office.'

'He was before this message came through for him on the radio.'

'At this hour?'

'His wife's been in an accident.'

'Bad?'

'Must be; they want him urgently.'

Bill threw down his paper and got up. 'I'll come and help you find him. Did it say what happened?'

'Car hit her. They've taken her to the Royal.'

They found him in the dark by the generator. They listened to its "thump thump" as they approached. Bill kept wondering what he was going to say. How did you say to an unsuspecting man that his wife might be dying?

John saw their figures coming out of the darkness of the night and smiled at them. 'Exercise at this hour?'

Bill did not return the smile. He felt so uncomfortable he thought the words would never come out at all. 'Sorry, John, your wife's had an accident. They've taken her to the Royal. Just came through on the radio.'

John looked from one to the other, the noise of the generator seeming suddenly to be beating in his head. 'You mean—'

'No, John, not that, but they want you at once.'

'Of course.'

But he did not move. Sara in an accident—in hospital! He'd only had her letter a couple of days ago.

'I'll get the car,' Bill said. 'Anything you want to take?'

He shook his head.

'Don't worry about things here.'

'No—thanks, Bill.'

'Would you like one of us to go with you?'

Again he shook his head. 'Thanks, no. I'll be all right. Give me something to do.'

But it gave his hands something to do, not his mind. That was blank, recoiling from reality. Looking back on that trip, he felt nothing but a steering wheel, brakes and an accelerator. It was only when he found himself on the other side of the Royal's swing doors, with polished floors and an enquiry desk before him, the deathly hush of the sick and dying about him, and the sickly smell of flowers from the healthy world outside, that he realised he was afraid. Afraid to tell them who he was, afraid to hear them discuss in any way the slim little figure that was Sara—those beautiful legs, her deep quiet eyes.

'Can I help you?'

He turned and saw that a nurse was standing near him, her dress and cap immaculate, her cape resting on her shoulders with dignity. The expression on her face was calm and enquiring.

'Yes—my name is Hilyard. My wife—'

'Oh yes. Come with me, will you.'

He followed her across the echoing space of polished floor and into a lift. As the doors closed with a whoosh behind him and she pressed a button on the indicator panel, she said, with her back still turned to him: 'Mrs Hilyard is no worse, I believe, but I'll take you to the sister in charge.'

He thanked her inadequately and waited, his mind tormented by a hundred questions which he was quite incapable of asking. She left him in a waiting room somewhere along a quiet corridor, and presently the sister came silently through the doorway.

'Mr Hilyard?'

'Yes, Sister. My wife—'

'We have reason to believe she will recover, Mr Hilyard. She is, of course, in a serious condition and we are very sorry about the child.'

'The child—'

'The loss of an unborn child is always sad, Mr Hilyard, but with the mother's life saved there is at least a future. Now, I am going to send for something for you to eat and drink. I understand that you have come quite a distance.'

She saw that he was going to protest and smiled at him. 'It is better that you should have something while you wait. The surgeon is still with her. She hasn't regained consciousness yet.'

He could not argue with her. He suddenly felt very weary; he realised his hands were shaking. Sara unconscious—a child! He sat down in an upholstered chair and closed his eyes. He did not hear the sister go, and only realised she had returned when he heard the chink of china and, opening his eyes again, saw that she was directing a young girl to put a tray down on a table from which she was removing the magazines. The girl did not pay any particular attention to him, and it crossed his mind that a scene such as this must be very common to her. As she went quickly from the room, he sat up and ran his fingers through his hair as he watched the sister pick up the teapot.

'Do you take milk and sugar, Mr Hilyard?'

'Just milk,' he said and as he took the cup he asked: 'Could you tell me how it happened?'

'We have not much to go on as yet. The driver of the car is himself in a very shaken condition. Apparently she ran out in front of him, and in trying to avoid her he skidded and hit both her and a lamp-post.'

He shook his head. 'It doesn't sound like Sara at all. There must have been some reason.'

She smiled gently as she handed him a plate of sandwiches. 'Mr Hilyard, women often do things without reason when they are going to have a child. Apparently she was running across the road to help a lost child.'

'But she wasn't pregnant, you see. That was the trouble. She always wanted a child. We've been married four years, I—'

Once again the gentle but determined voice: 'But she *was* going to have a child, Mr Hilyard, there is no doubt of that. Of course she cannot have known for long. Perhaps she was waiting to make quite sure before telling you. That too is not unusual.'

He stared at her as though they were both going out of their senses. He had an insane desire to shake that calm, assured look from her unruffled face. She knew, and he knew nothing!

'Now, if you will excuse me, I will be back as soon as I have any news,' and she was gone before he could as much as begin to explain to her how wrong she was. He did not attempt to drink the tea or eat the sandwiches; the tray gradually acquired a forlorn and uncared for look, as a skin began to form on top of the tea and a small insect settled on the sandwiches.

He sat with hands thrust into his pockets and a frown masked the tired lines of his face as minutes slipped into hours. He didn't bother to look up even when anyone passed the door, as few did in those early hours of the morning. It seemed to him that the whole of their life together rushed through his mind in disconnected scenes, and he became aware of a great coldness that flowed over his body, in spite of the central heating around him.

Then he was aware that the sister was back and that a tall, dark middle-aged man was with her.

'Mr Hilyard this is Doctor West. He wants to have a talk to you about your wife.'

He got to his feet, and felt better for movement and standing upright again. They shook hands and looked briefly at each other.

'Mr Hilyard, your wife has regained consciousness, and I believe from now on we have more than a fighting chance of saving her. However I prefer not to commit myself until after we are able to X-ray more extensively.'

'You are telling the truth?'

'I believe so, but we may have to operate. I would like your permission for this at once, please.'

John went through the formalities, and handed back the slip of paper that gave this man the power to take and do as he wished with the one person who made life worth living, who in fact was the incentive for everything.

'May I see her?' he asked.

'For a moment, but you must realise she is under heavy sedation.'

Together he and the doctor went out into the passage, the sister following them. Suddenly he remembered Sara had been going to Launceston to see Lister. He must remember to contact him as soon as possible. Then a door was opened in front of him and he saw Sara lying in a hospital bed, a sheet drawn tightly up to her chin, her face outlined by a carefully shaded lamp. Her eyes were open but her whole expression was detached. He had a strange feeling that she had already left him, a helpless panic swept over him, halting him in the doorway. Then he felt the doctor's grip on his arm; his whisper: 'Remember what I told you. Nothing to excite her—and only a moment.'

As in a nightmare John walked across to the bed, and as he reached it her eyes moved and seemed to focus on his. He put his hand over hers lying so aimlessly on the sheet. For a moment he thought he saw a flicker in the depths of her eyes, but almost immediately she closed them, and once again he had that feeling that he was alone—quite alone. He stood there until he felt the doctor's pressure on his arm again, and knew that he must go.

Out in the passage he said: 'Are you trying to fool me? How could anyone look like that and live?'

'Of course she can. I have already told you she is under heavy sedation. You must trust us, we know more about how people look in these circumstances. Now, I am going to suggest you remain in the hospital tonight, and if we operate we shall let you know. In the meantime I am going to give you something to make you rest.'

In spite of himself John found that he not only rested but slept—the doctor saw to that—and when he wakened it was to be told that Sara had undergone a much less serious operation than had been expected, and was doing well. Once again he remembered Lister, and asked to put a call through to Launceston. Then, and only then, with a great sense of relief, could he turn his thoughts to the child that had lost its chance of living. Until now it had seemed so extraordinary as to be beyond belief, but now that normality had returned he found the child had become a very big factor.

He dreaded having to tell Sara that the only thing for which she had really longed, and which had at last been within her grasp, was lost. But why hadn't she told him? Had this weekend any significance? He believed suddenly that it had. It came back to him when, just now he had rung Lister, the agent had distinctly conveyed the impression that Sara had herself suggested their meeting, whereas in her letter she had stated that Lister had asked her to go. Why all the mystery?

Lying on the small hospital bed, his hands linked behind his head, he thought back over the last few months of their life together. Had the frustration, the inability of either to reach the other, been due to the biological change in Sara because of the child's presence, or was there some other reason? For the first time he realised that someone else could mean more to her than he! He had to accept the fact that he was not the father.

It was the worst hour he had ever spent. His feelings alternated between rage and wounded pride. His emotions were chaotic—for a while he thought he must be going mad. Then, extraordinary as it must be, he must have slept, or maybe it was just the after-effect of the sedative. In any case his feelings clarified. He forced himself to face facts, ugly as they seemed to him. She had lied to him about seeing Lister—had she been planning to see a lover? Or did she just want to be on her own? Forcing himself to be fair, he realised that it must be the latter. She was seeing Lister, that much was true; and for business reasons, that much was also true. Who then was her lover? Less than a second and he knew—Richard, of course, who else? Where then did Arna fit into it? And he knew the answer to that also—she was a cover, she provided the camouflage. For a while he was consumed by rage against her. They were probably all laughing at him—poor innocent John; it must be a joke for them all.

For several moments he calmed himself, then reason took over and real questions presented themselves. Was he in any way to blame? Had the road taken too much of his time and thoughts? He knew what she wanted above all else and it wasn't till recently that he had done anything about it. Then, inadvertently, a thing Hurst had said to him when they had been talking about his own career came into his mind: 'Let the end of the road give you its answer, and let your wife in on some of your thoughts on the way. Fifteen years ago I took your rough-shod solution, and I made a great mistake.'

Had he ever really "let her in" on his thoughts? Hadn't she been a necessary pawn he had placed for the success of his career? The comfort background to it? In honesty he faced the fact that he had never thought of her as a person. She was Sara, the quiet peaceful person to come home to; his possession. She had only ever expressed one wish and, in his egotism, he had believed it was her failing as a woman, and not his as a man, that had prevented her from fulfilling it. He had not even seen the importance of such a wish. You either had children or you hadn't; if you were one of those who hadn't—well, that was it; after all he had offered her adoption.

He kept remembering her last night, lying on the bed, completely lost to him. For the first time he had known the meaning of real loneliness; she was alive yet utterly gone from him. He knew then that he had failed her. He knew nothing about how a woman's mind worked. How much did a child really mean to her? So much that she found another man to father it? After all, if he wanted anything so much, would *he* allow loyalty to her to stand in the way?

He thought too how he had never consulted her about this move to Australia; she had taken it so well that even he had been surprised. Her submissiveness made him only too ready to leave her with cousin Judith because he hadn't wanted to be worried by her fears or loneliness. He hadn't wanted this new life of his interfered with in any way. Later he had been only too glad when she had suggested going to Hobart, setting up the boutique. Hadn't he, for a time, put her out of his existence, when he knew perfectly well she was in no way fitted to live her own life? Could he, with any honesty, blame her if someone else had offered her companionship; had wanted her presence—offered her the chance of a child?

It was some time before he reached the answer for them both; faced the simple fact that the question of the child must be ignored. In her own good time Sara would tell him how and why, and this he must accept. It was the future that mattered, their future together. Never again must she be made to feel she had been forced away from him. It was up to him—and in any case the specialist had given him a lot of hope. She must never know that he had been close to deserting her.

CHAPTER TWENTY

Richard whistled softly to himself as he held *Sunbolt* steady against a stiff off-shore breeze.

'I think we've got the right spinnaker at last,' he said to Michael up for'ard. 'Just the same, I'm not taking any chances. I've ordered a couple of spares to be flown over from Melbourne by the time we get back; we've had this trouble too long.'

'Nice to be some people,' Michael grinned. 'I wouldn't mind the few odd hundred you spend on spares.'

'You spend them on that old wreck of a sports car of yours; you can't have it all ways. Come and take her. I want to get the latest weather report; it's my guess it won't hold and we'll have some pretty dirty stuff between here and Maatsuyker.'

As Michael took his place at the wheel, Richard went below, still whistling, and just caught himself in time from landing on David at the stores cupboard as *Sunbolt* suddenly heeled over.

'Go and give Michael a hand; we've probably got our first sail change coming up.'

'Right. We're a bit light on the stuff that "tastes so good", I reckon. Thought we had ample. Everything else is jake.'

'You'll be popular. Get moving.'

After a quick glance at the rest of the crew off watch, sleeping in their bunks, Richard settled himself in front of the two-way radio and began to tune in. It was a routine that never failed to please him, the proof that water was under him and land only something to be got at by radio.

Signals began coming in, and after a moment of listening he knew his guess had been right: bad weather did indeed lie ahead. He grinned; nothing suited him better—the sound of wind in the sails and the slap of angry water on the bows were his world. He knew that some of the blokes suffered from a sense of frustration after about twenty-four hours, complained there was nothing but water and sky; it was only the thought of unseen racing opponents that kept them going. That, and plain hard work. Not so himself—sea, sky, the wind and a good yacht were just about all he asked of life; a few additions of course, the normal ones—women and good beer.

He folded his arms and sat on for a bit. Let them get on with the job on their own while the weather held. He was anxious to see how they shaped on this, their last real trial before Sydney. He'd know after this if he wanted to put the proposition to them to crew for him as far as America—it'd be easier after the race if things went well. It'd break up this thing between him and Sara too; it was going too far, getting out of hand for both of them—and he'd promised her to find a solution.

Yes, he'd spend a year or two drifting round the islands, the Queensland coast, and Asia. A job or two as it took their fancy and money lasted. After all, he'd done pretty well for the old man in the last two years, profits were high and that had been mainly due to him. He'd come back in the end, of course; a man had to have roots; but surely two years of sampling life wasn't too much to ask.

His ear caught the backlash of news from the radio '...*A young woman who was knocked down on Sandy Bay Road last night, and taken to the Royal Hobart Hospital, has been identified as Mrs Sara Hilyard. Her condition, though still serious, has improved considerably...*'

Richard brought his feet down with a thud. Sara! Knocked down! What the hell had the crazy idiot been doing? He started to his feet—then stood there. He had no right to go to her; John would have been notified. In fact it would only be an embarrassment if he did. But Sara, hurt! He suddenly found it hard to take, as he realised that even if she were dying he had no right to go to her; knew also that if he had that right he would turn *Sunbolt* about; for Sara he would put her out of her pre-race test round Maatsuyker. It shocked him just how much he would be prepared to do for Sara, and yet could do nothing.

He saw her as she had stood there in the bows, the first day she had ever set foot on *Sunbolt*—a quiet shiningly happy girl, knowing for the first time in her life what it was to respond to the leaning deck of a wilful yacht. There had been no need for words; he had known her immediate response to this yacht which was his life. He should have been warned, not flattered. Those feelings cannot be shared between three people, one of whom is married to the third who has no feeling at all for yachts and sails.

'I don't think you've cured that spinnaker, Rick,' Michael shouted down. 'Come up.'

He went up and saw that Michael was right; even with these first strong winds that were beginning to strike *Sunbolt*, she was fighting, wallowing. It would have to come in immediately.

'All right,' he called back, 'change all sail. We'll need heavy canvas from now on anyway.'

The hours of hard work ahead helped to put Sara in the back of his mind. In a way, the fact that he could not go to her drove him to take out his feelings on *Sunbolt*. He had the gear and the canvas; now or never could the yacht prove herself. The rest of the crew, who knew what the race meant to him, were nevertheless shattered by the way he drove her, sparing her or them nothing. He seemed one with the great combing rollers down whose sides *Sunbolt* slithered, to come springing up triumphantly to the crest of another giant ahead.

Even though he put her over the return line in the best time yet, he suddenly dreaded the reception committee awaiting him. His mind was back with Sara, not with the celebrations that were about to begin—the back-slapping; the unending discussions and race reminiscing; the drinking. Half of him was angry with Sara for having spoilt this moment for him, spoilt the supreme effort that he, the crew and *Sunbolt* had made for her; spoilt the moment when they all took the run to pieces in a spirit of get-together which only those who shared it knew and understood.

Sally was there at Constitution Dock, wildly excited by his success. Then, in the middle of her ecstatic congratulations, she stopped and stared at him. 'Rick, has anyone—did you hear about Sara, she's—'

'Yes,' he said roughly, 'we heard a bit about it on the radio. She all right now?'

'We've been ringing the hospital and they say so. No one's allowed to see her yet, though John of course—'

'Naturally. What exactly happened?'

'No one seems to know really. She was knocked down by a car.'

Her inadequacy annoyed him, and he was thankful that a crowd came up and carried him off to the bar.

It was not till late next morning that he could get to the hospital. There he was met with kindness and calmness. Yes, Mrs Hilyard was much improved, although she had undergone an operation for internal injuries. No, she had no facial injuries, but at present she was allowed no visitors other than her husband. Any message he cared to give?

He gave a suitable one in the name of her cousin, and went out and bought her flowers. He knew she couldn't live without flowers. But it wasn't until the following Thursday that he could persuade the sister to allow him to see her. In those lonely four days he had not been able to get her out of his mind, and when he was shown into her room he saw her as beautiful, though he never had before. She was a person who gained by the pallor of a sick bed. Her skin had a transparency that glowed, and her eyes a depth that made them suddenly excitingly noticeable.

'Well,' he said, to cover his increasing embarrassment—he and sick rooms were complete strangers—'you really do things in a big way when you start!'

'Did they tell you how silly I was—apparently I just walked out without looking. You see, there was a lost child crying on the other side of the road; I do remember that much.'

He shook his head at her as though she too were a child.

'Thank you for the flowers. They make all the difference.'

'I know.'

'Funny how you Australians do things like that, although you appear to live a life apart from your womenfolk.'

'No, we don't—we just believe in apportioning things; women and womanly things, hence the flowers; men and manly things.'

'It's fun mixing them?'

'Now, don't lets start arguing or that gorgon of a sister will turn me out. I've had a hell of a job getting in here.'

They both knew they were talking for the sake of talking, afraid to be silent.

'She's not a gorgon, she's a dear. But tell me, the run—how did it go? Was *Sunbolt* a good girl?'

'She managed to make the grade.'

'She brought down her time! That really makes things right.'

'In what way?'

'It solves problems for us both, don't you see? I—was going to have that child you promised, but of course I lost it in the accident. Sounds silly, but I didn't know—there have been so many false hopes.'

'I'm sorry.'

'Don't be. In some strange way I'm not upset. I know it's the beginning, not the end. Is that too womanish?'

'Not really.' He walked over to the window, knowing that as far as he and Sara were concerned it was the end, not the beginning. The only woman he had ever really wanted permanently—who had even been carrying his child—but the only one he had been denied.

'We weren't really any good for each other,' she said. 'You're a rover, a doer, like Arna. I've just come round to realising this. I'd never known anyone like you, Rick. Thank you for the fun—the mad moments. You've made me feel I missed all the things I should've had before I got married.'

'Thank you!' he said sarcastically.

'Don't, please, Rick.'

He turned angrily from the window. When he thought of that complacent young man uprooting trees in a stinking forest...

Then he met her eyes anxiously waiting for him to turn. Suddenly they both laughed until they were near to tears.

'Well,' he said at last, 'if I was a new experience to you, you're certainly a new one to me!'

When he had gone she lay without moving until they brought her her three o'clock cup of tea.

'Has your visitor gone?' the little probationer asked with surprise as she wheeled up the bed-table. 'I saw him come in with sister. He's *so* good-looking. Gee, he could have me any old time!'

'Yes,' Sara said, 'but he had to go.'

Then, as she was helped to sit up to have the pillows packed behind her, she caught sight of the journal where Arna had left it the previous evening, and remembered with excitement she still had Sarah's problems to discover. 'Could you hand me that journal?' she asked.

The probationer walked round the bed and picked up the leather-bound pages. 'That looks old,' she said.

'It is. It's the story of someone who lived here over 150 years ago.

'Really! Can I have a look?'

Sara nodded, and the girl turned back the binding, looking through the pages. 'They wrote very differently then, didn't they?'

'Not only wrote,' Sara smiled as she settled herself more comfortably on the pillows and took the journal to prop it against the bed-table. 'I wonder how Sarah would have felt if she'd known how much good she would do for me, all these years later,' she thought. 'Queer our names being the same!'

With a sigh of contentment she opened the book to the page she left it at.

CHAPTER TWENTY-ONE

'Ardrossan'
In the Colony of —
Van Diemen's Land,
In the year of our Lord, 1830

To:
    The Lady Anne,
    Milston Manor,
    Wiltshire,
    England.

My dear Sister,

    How can I thank you enough for your letter. My congratulations on your marriage. I hope only the best comes of it. I know you are interested in my life in Van Diemen's Land and I must send you some more information, but I very much fear that you still find it difficult to understand the way we live here.

    I won't go into details here for your latest news may change everything. I now live in hope. Eventually I suppose I will hear from Master Matthew. I can go on, for I now know that you are aware of the details, although not perhaps everything from my point of view.

After that scene in the kitchen I was exceedingly sick at heart. There seemed no one to whom I could turn. For the second time in my life, and I am not so very old, I have been made a plaything for others to dispose of as they wish.

I stood there alone in that kitchen, listening to Madam sobbing into her handkerchief, while the Master still held the shotgun belligerently in his hands, and the reverend gentleman gave his entire attention to the family Bible and prayer book. As for Master Matthew, when the formalities were at an end, he went to his mother and bid her cease crying. Then, with his hand on her arm, he turned and faced his father.

'Since, sir, my word is not good enough for you, as I have already said, I am leaving this place tonight. I shall not return until this absurd marriage has been put aside by law.'

At me he did not look at all, nor did I stir towards him. The next moment he strode the length of the kitchen, flung open its door, and we could hear him running up the stairs. In a short space of time he returned in his riding breeches and jacket, carrying saddle bags in his hand. Once again it was only his mother he made any show of noticing before he was gone through the yard door and across to the stables.

Minutes later we heard Oscar's galloping hooves and knew that they had left us. The only sound among us as we still stood there was Madam's endless weeping and the slight whisper of the reverend's lips as he quietly prayed.

I stole a look at the Master's face, and knew that he was oblivious to us all. No one would dare to offer him comfort, nor would he have received it; in that moment he looked a desperate and lonely old man. I wondered if standing in good stead with his conscience was worth breaking his heart.

'Sir,' I said, 'have I your leave to retire to my room?'

He put down the gun on the table and waved his hand at me. 'Go, girl, go.'

Oh, the misery of that night! My plans in ruins — how he must hate me! No foreseeable future, for of course he would find someone in Hobart Town to set aside such a marriage, and then clearly my position at Ardrossan would be impossible. I wondered if there were some way in which I could get my freedom from the Master in return for my assurance that I would go to seek my living in another part of the island. After what he had said, at least I need not fear that he would ever send me to the Cascades.

Yet, what freedom could I attain? Only another job such as I already had, with another family. Possibly the same kind of strife. I knew now that wherever I went in the presence of men there would be this kind of trouble. My looks were no asset, only a curse. Oh, the pity of it! Born in the right way in the right place, how well I would have enjoyed my life. But in a penal settlement such as this, what was there for such as I? A branded woman who had attained her freedom but had not even her virginity to offer.

Either I took menial jobs with hard-working settlers, or became a woman of the streets. An easy one that latter idea; women are at a premium in a place where there is such a shortage of them. For a few years in Hobart Town I could doubtless taste such comforts as there are to obtain. Or maybe, if I saw fit to work well and hard for the next few years, some male convict in circumstances similar to my own might suggest I marry him and help him to work equally hard on the grant he would undoubtedly obtain. Only in this way, Governor Arthur contended, could the island be financed, cultivated and populated — the free settlers not being in sufficient numbers to keep it from starvation. Also we understand there is a greatly increasing faction in England fighting the expense of maintaining Van Diemen's Land for the housing of England's overflow of felons. You doubtless will know more of this than we here.

However, in my heart I did not see fit to become involved in any of these schemes. Depressed as I was, I still had it in me to fight. But not that night! That night I was like a dog that had been severely whipped and deserted. Nor did I know what was expected of me.

But next morning the Master sent for me. He was waiting for me in the room that was his and his alone. No one dared enter without invitation; even Madam thought twice about interrupting him there. As I went inside I curtsied and stood awaiting his pleasure. I wondered greatly what he and I were about to say to each other.

When I went out of that room I would have a fair idea of what the future would hold for me.

I looked around the room, which was so much a man's room with its books, prints of his house and pictures of the hunt of which he had once been a Master in England. The oil painting of Madam when she was presented to his Majesty, hanging behind the massive desk where he was now seated, the account books of Ardrossan spread out before him.

The major difference was that he had abandoned the neat, laundered cravat he would have worn, had he sat behind that desk in a room such as this in England, for the loose-fitting smock-shirt adopted by most of the settlers for ease and comfort. But he lost none of the dignity that was his, independent of clothes or setting. I sensed too that as he sat there, silent and thoughtful, he was not paying attention to the books before him, but was as lost and shocked in his mind as was I, albeit he would neither give nor receive quarter. What he had done he had done and was prepared to stand by it, whatever the cost. Furthermore, all of his household would be expected to carry out whatever plan of campaign he had decided on.

At last he raised his eyes, set so deeply under overhanging brows, and looked at me.

'Come nearer to the desk, girl. That door was built without need of support.'

I did as he bid me, and stood directly in front of his desk. Dear God, how it reminded me of the day I stood in the dock at the Old Bailey. Everything in me resented this being made to stand before men who considered they were little gods, and made to answer for crimes I had not committed!

'Now, girl, no word of what passed last night shall leave your lips, to anyone, in any circumstances. You understand?'

'Yes, sir.'

'Should it come to my ears that you have in any way disobeyed this order you will receive punishment, in spite of the fact that before God you are my son's wife. I have never had recourse to my rights to have my convicts whipped before a magistrate, but as the good Lord is my witness, you shall receive chastisement should you forget what has passed between us this day.'

'Sir, I am well aware I stand before you branded as a felon, but I too have no fear in saying in God's name that I have not lied to you or any man. I am as innocent of what you accused me of last night as I was of the crime that brought me here. Have I not served you well these last months? Why should I now be so foolish as to disobey you?'

'You are not on trial here, Sarah,' he said more kindly. I could even trace weariness in his voice. 'It is because of your good service that I made the supreme sacrifice last night in the interest of justice. I am merely warning you that should you in any way prove unworthy you can expect no mercy.'

'Then, sir, you wish me to carry on with my usual duties?'

'Until such time as my son comes to his senses, when the matter will be further reviewed.'

And that, dear sister, was over twelve months ago!

Since then we have had no communication about my supposed husband until your letter. Yet, starting some weeks ago, I have noticed the mail-man on his fortnightly call slipping mysterious packages to Madam. She confides their possession to no member of the family. I can think of no reason for such secretive behaviour other than communication of some kind with Master Matthew whom she loves dearly, which I think must be ever so between mothers and their first born.

I am sure you are eager to know my true feelings about all these events, and I will as always be honest with you. What woman would not be hurt by such proceedings as the foregoing? At first I could think of nothing but my hurt; hence I did not write in this Journal — I was too sick at heart.

That night in the kitchen, when Master Matthew and I tried to save the life of a young animal, I glimpsed what it could mean to love such a man as he, and indeed the joy of being loved in return by him. For a few fleeting moments I dared to imagine that my ambition with regard to

Ardrossan could be fulfilled in a more ordinary, or should I say regular, manner. Imagine then how I felt when I suddenly found myself the means of dispensing justice in the cold sense of the word; and because of it I must watch this man, who, but a short time ago, I had felt could be a lover of the finest order, being turned into a cold, suspicious stranger. Think too what it was like, this time to preserve my own integrity, to announce publicly that I was not a virgin! Following this, to be forced through a ridiculous marriage and left without a word, branded as an immoral felon.

You will understand then that I was beyond taking up my pen. But now, with the passing of so many months and the receipt of your news, I should like once again to tell you what has gone on here, for there is no one else to whom I may open my heart.

It is truly amazing how this place has gone on for the last year. I was sorely afraid that the Master, without the assistance of his two eldest sons, would be hard put to it to carry on such an estate as this, even though he now has so many workers on the property. But Master Richard, though asking no questions — probably I think because he knew he would be given no answers — seemed to realise that now his father needed him more than at any time in his life. It was his opportunity, and he took it with both hands, and in doing so has grown great in stature both in mind and body. From early morning till late at night he has been behind his father in every task, so that the home fields are all cleared and fenced, and in them are a great number of the Master's stud — they make such a pretty picture round the big house and river.

Also, Oscar's foal has grown into a beautiful colt with gentle manners, and reminds me of his magnificent sire. No one is allowed to touch him save the Master, who trains him every spare minute he has. What a sight it is to see the big, ageing man and the frisking, gay colt. My gardening too has continued to prosper. In it I find my greatest joy.

How happy I could be in this simple, strange life if only I might be myself. Madam has made no reference to the night of my marriage to her son, and I have no means of knowing what she thinks about it. For an ambitious mother it must have been a sad, indeed shocking occurrence, but as her husband's word is law there is little she can do. As I have already said, I feel most definitely she is carrying on some kind of communication with Master Matthew, and at times my patience is sorely tried. Surely he could send me a few words. He must know the absurd situation between us is not of my making.

Strange rumours concerning him are brought to us by one means or another. Some say he has taken the King's shilling, others that he has become one of Governor Arthur's favourites, and there is talk of his becoming one of the Governor's six councillors who are periodically called to advise the Governor in matters of administration of the island. It would seem that these are matters for the Governor alone, for he rarely calls the council to assist. Repute has it that he is a man who brooks no advice and sees the whole island as an enlarged army camp, completely under his control.

Come the spring we had evidence of this, even in our lonely area. He decided that the blacks were becoming a nuisance to us all, that they must be rounded up and driven into one corner of the island, there to be collected and dealt with. It is true these coloured people are a great menace. There are more and more occasions of their robbing and spearing on the property of outlying settlers, and no community feels safe or free to move round the countryside after dark.

It seems there is no way in which to reach these poor souls. Undoubtedly the soldiery have grown rough beyond measure whenever they come up with them, delighting in teasing and torturing them so that they believe all white people are the same; therefore they show no discrimination, and if they can be revenged on any white person they have no hesitation in doing whatever harm they can.

To them the whole countryside is their home and they feel free to live and move in it as they wish. Their laws and their food belong to the wild, although they have the shape and habits of man. In their own way they happily combine the two, and there are many among the settlers who feel that if these people were ignored and allowed to live their lives unmolested, they would not harm us. Unfortunately there are other settlers who have undoubtedly been attacked and are afraid, and show their fear by as viciously returning the attack. So it becomes a sad impasse, which was brought to a head by the spearing of a woman and family — in broad daylight.

She had been so good to them, giving what she could ill afford from her own meagre rations of tea, sugar and flour. That morning Madam had sent me to take jellies and other conserves for herself and the children. I never wish to see a more dreadful sight than that which met our eyes as we drove into the small yard. Fortunately I had one of the Master's old grooms but lately arrived from England.

She was lying face down in the middle of the yard, a spear sticking up between her shoulder blades, her dress in shocking array revealing only too plainly what that poor woman must have suffered. While Davy, the groom, ran to her I rushed in the house to find the children who, I guessed, would be in a concealed room such as is built by many outlying settlers for their family.

I will not describe any more of the harrowing details, but I think you will realise that following other such shocking occurrences this was enough to cause a general demand that something be done. It was then that Governor Arthur sought to solve the problem by rounding up these unfortunate people like cattle. He tried to place a cordon of soldiers and settlers in a line across the country, like a fishing net. All settlers were asked to make safe their womenfolk and children and join the march.

The Master was too loyal to refuse his support, but was free with his opinions while he called in all the men off the property to drive as much stock as possible into the home fields, then batten up all shutters and doors. It took us three days of hard work to make Ardrossan secure, then finally the Master again sent for me in his study.

'Sarah, I do not suppose you have as much as seen a gun fired?'

'I have seen them fired in England, sir, but have never fired one myself.'

'If I showed you how to handle one, would you be afraid to fire if necessary? Say now if you would be, since I must leave you, old James and one other of the men to look after my family while we are gone.'

We faced each other eye to eye over the desk. Since six months had passed and I was obviously not with child, he and I had almost become friends, and at that moment I felt overwhelmingly proud that he would so entrust me.

'I am not afraid, sir,' I replied firmly.

'Good,' he said. 'Then should the occasion arise you are not to hesitate, be it bushranger or black. Weaken and you would be lost with both these people. This mission on which I am called, Sarah, will fail, but it is the Governor's command and he, poor man, is caught between Downing Street's ignorance of the problem and the settlers' demands that he deal with the situation. As yet there is so little real government on this island; if we fail to support the little there is, then lost we are indeed.'

'I understand, sir.'

'"Catch them like fish in a net" — I'll wager we'll not get one. These mountains and valleys are unexplored by us, but to these poor creatures with their animal cunning and movements, this place is their home and means of existence. They know it as well as I know my property. Well, come along and I will show you how to handle this gun.'

I enjoyed my lessons. He was a good teacher and had more patience than I should have imagined. That gun gave me a great feeling of power. It is hard to explain, but in my hands it became a friend; I could trust it. It was a source of strength; for the first time I really felt I had something on my side.

Just the same, as they all rode off down the track at five o'clock one warm spring morning, we watched them go in secret and silent apprehension. Enough stores, water and wood for at least a week had been brought into the house, and Mr and Mrs James had moved with the other families into a large barn built near to the back door.

But as it turned out we need not have feared. In the ten days the men were away we saw not a soul, and indeed the whole manoeuvre turned out poorly, just as the Master had prophesied, only one poor straggler being caught.

Miss Jessica and Miss Dorothy have grown up greatly in this last year. Since Mr Haynes's departure from the school room they have joined a small class of children who meet twice weekly in the parson's house for instruction by his wife, who, before she married, was a governess of excellent standing in several of the county homes in England. She is a far better influence for the young ladies than was Mr Haynes, and watches carefully their manners as well as their minds; and Madam allows me to instruct them in needlework. Even you, dear sister, used to praise me for my stitching.

So you see, though we live an isolated life, it is not without its gentility.

Miss Charlotte also has almost forgotten her first romantic love for Mr Haynes and, after a most lively winter season in Hobart Town, where she attended many well-conducted parties and social gatherings, she was still more pleased to return to the country social round and the daily happenings of Ardrossan — a circumstance not altogether to Madam's liking, as she had hoped so much for her daughter from this first mingling with the Government House society. However, I feel it is a state of affairs due to the firm friendship Miss Charlotte so quickly formed with the newly settled family I described to you a year ago.

Another thing I must tell you of: the little chapel designed by Mr Haynes is nearly finished. It is really beautiful. I find it hard to believe that such a man could have possessed so fine a talent. I wish, however, that his memory were not so forced upon me. Each morning when I go to open wide the big front door to let in the warm scent of eucalyptus and earth and the sharp tang of river water, I see in front of me, at the turn of the track, the little golden stone building, the first of its kind in this district to mark the faith of those around. So must I remember his name and what I did to him. I feel sometimes I should never enter its doors to kneel and pray. Yet it is so peaceful there, and sometimes I feel my mind is a raging torrent that must burst its banks and devour me.

At some perhaps not distant date my future must be decided. I cannot understand why it has taken Master Matthew so long to have our marriage put aside. I wish that he would have enough kindness in him to have done with this thing, so that I may know how to face the next step in my existence.

I must leave this now as the whole household is early to bed this night. At first light tomorrow Mr James leaves with the bullock drays for his annual trip to Hobart Town for stores and such commissions as Madam sees fit to give him. We have all been busy this last week checking the needs of this busy place, and making lists. I find it quite amazingly simple to forget the small needs, the everyday things that one takes for granted and can so easily obtain at home in the village shop. Here there is no village shop and whoever forgets must go without for another year...'

Sara woke suddenly as the journal slipped from her fingers and she realised that she had been reading automatically. In terror of damaging the precious book she put it in her locker and prepared for sleep. She consoled herself that she could go on with it tomorrow. She would also see John again and this time, tired as she was, she felt up to a serious talk with him. She wasn't looking forward to it, but knew it was inevitable.

CHAPTER TWENTY-TWO

After checking with Matron, John went home for a shower, a change of clothes and some breakfast. He tried to plan but could come to no conclusions. He drank black coffee at the window, watching the river.

Arna came in, looked at his back and turned to go, thinking he hadn't heard her, but he said suddenly without turning, 'What do you know of this?'

'Nothing. I went but they wouldn't let me see her.'

'I'm not referring to that. Did you know she was pregnant?'

She caught her breath and he heard, swung round and looked at her. Her face was genuinely shocked.

'She lost the child, of course,' he said.

'What happened? They said she had been hit by a car.'

'She had. Here, sit down. I'll get you a cup of coffee, I want one myself.'

When he came back she was still standing where he had left her. She made no attempt to take the cup he was holding out to her. He put it down and gently pushed her on to the sofa.

'They operated on her last night. Apparently things are not as bad as expected. I'm going back in a moment. Ring the Hydro, will you? They'll have to get someone to take my place.'

'John I—I didn't know...'

'No one does, it seems.'

'But you think I do—yes?' Ignoring the coffee she got to her feet and he was aware of her anger.

'I'm sorry. I had no right to say that. I've got to get back, make some sense of all this.'

He was out of the room before she could move.

She did sit down then; listened to the car being gunned up the road, went mechanically to the phone to ring the Hydro. Sara pregnant! Instinctively she thought of Rick, and heard the phone begin to ring; realised she hadn't told John the latest news about Rick. That his father had at last decided to take a hand in his playboy existence. Getting a bad report on his own health, he saw a way out by sending Rick to the American office of the business to be trained. After all, he would eventually take it all over. In fact, before all this Sydney-Hobart obsession Rick had shown a natural business sense. But a last fling with that yacht was only fair once he'd worked so hard at it.

At the hospital the sister on duty smiled at John. 'Matron said to tell you to go in; she's out of pain.'

He took her word and went through the door of Sara's room, knowing that she was expecting him. He drew up the only chair and sat down, reaching for her.

After a moment she whispered, 'We can't wait, we've got to settle this. The Sarah would, the one in that journal Aunt Judith left me.'

Holding her closely, realising how small she was, he said abstractedly, 'What's she got to do with this? Am I hurting you?'

'No. They've given me so many injections I can't feel much at all.'

'Then, my dear, if you're sure you're right, we've got to have this out once and for all.' Suddenly he knew it was as hard for him to find the words as for her, afraid too of what she was going to say.

'John, I'm sorry, sorry—'

In spite of himself he said, with the bitterness he couldn't keep back, 'Who for, the other man—Rick, I gather?'

'You knew about us? But what did you know?'

'It was a safe bet, wasn't it? He was the one who could give you what you wanted above everything, apparently what I can't—a child? The glamour boy who knew how to sympathise, who favoured you above all others, *for the moment.* Sara, I'm not a complete fool, but—no, wait...' as she struggled to turn to him.

'Please listen to me. Arna said—'

'I knew she was at the bottom of it!'

'Not the way you mean. She knew I'd lost myself. I needed someone like Rick to give me back my self-respect. He was a man of the world, had no intention of getting himself involved, women were his playthings, made him feel important—'

'I always knew she was no good for you—'

'Please, I'm—running out of breath. I've got to tell you this.'

'I don't want to listen.'

'You must, because I already suspected I was pregnant. Didn't want to tell anyone till I was sure—oh, John, don't you realise what I'm trying to tell you—that baby was *ours*, I'm sure of it. I was just so lonely, and without you from one weekend to the other. Rick gave me confidence in myself and I thought that if you and I had a baby to care for, we'd become a family again. Don't you realise I love you?'

Then it was too much for her, she broke into floods of gasping, hysterical tears which brought an enraged Matron on the scene.

'Really, Mr Hilyard. I can't imagine what you've been saying to your wife in these circumstances! I didn't realise you were such a foolish man. Please leave at once. You are doing her a great deal of harm; she is hardly over that operation.'

It was some time next day before Sara could completely calm herself, as Matron returned for yet another inspection. In spite of it, however, she was awake by 6am, rang her bell and asked for a cup of tea. Afterwards she lay for a long time before she rang it a second time. She felt it would be Matron who would come. If not, she would ask for her. It was!

'I must see my husband, Matron. I cannot rest, there are certain things I—I must discuss with him. Please.'

Matron looked at her flushed face, smoothed back the bed sheets she had thrown aside. 'It is wiser to discuss matters which are obviously worrying you, when you are recovered—'

'No, I can't rest until he knows certain things. Yes, you can give me injections to make me sleep, but in the midst of that sleep I will be aware of the problem.'

In her heart Matron knew the girl was right. After she had managed to put matters right was the time for healing. 'Very well,' she said, 'but you must realise I too have a problem, to return you to good health. I'll send for your husband again but I will *not* allow him to remain for long.'

She gave orders for John to return but to report to her before seeing his wife. When he entered her office she knew at once she had been right. She asked him to sit down and said, 'It appears it would have been better to let you remain yesterday. However she has had a bad time, for more than one reason, I gather. Let her do the talking. Listen, but do not argue; otherwise I shall have to take over again, causing a situation which could be serious.'

He stood up, thanked her and went to Sara's room, wishing he could talk to this understanding woman instead of Sara, tell her that his mind was more confused than his wife's. He had not slept well all night and could not relate to Sara's claim that the dead child had been his. What was she about to say now?

When he opened the door she was watching it, propped up on her pillows. The curtains were drawn back, letting the sun shine over the bed. He crossed the room to take her hands, realised she was smiling. Said, 'I'm told you are to do the talking or I'll be booted out again.' He found himself kissing her as they hadn't kissed for a long time.

At last she said, 'I'll try to be quick. I've been thinking about it all.'

'Thank God!'

'I'll have to go back a long time—two years. Whatever you say about Arna, she was right. At twenty-two, having our marriage as it was, everything we had wanted and done, together as we had planned. It was perfect...'

'Remember Matron.'

'Yes, but then without telling me anything, you came home and swept everything away, the whole world, your job, your career—everything. We were to go to another world about which I knew nothing, among people about whom I knew nothing; even the dog and precious possessions had to go, and you had discussed nothing with me! There wasn't time, just those twenty-four hours—all the arrangements, selling the house, the plane tickets and the rest had to be finished in six months, but you forced me to make my decision in just twenty-four hours.'

'I tell you there wasn't time; I could and did explain to you on the aircraft. There were plenty of people on the spot ready to take the job and the opportunity. I took it for granted you would trust me.' He had bowed his head but still gripped her hands.

'But you took too much for granted.'

'Let's leave it there, it has nothing to do with the present.'

'Everything to do with the present. You're doing it again. You left me to Aunt Judith, sweet as she was. Arna and Rick saved my life. All *you* could talk of was the future. After I met Arna and we decided on a boutique, you were only too pleased to leave Rick to arrange the finance. I felt brushed to one side. There was only one subject you discussed—the bush. I even went up to the camps to see if I could live there, knew I couldn't, even though I tried. Yes, Arna was right, I had lost myself, I didn't know myself any longer. Was it any wonder that I found myself gaining an interest in Rick! He made me feel a woman again.'

'There is such a thing as loyalty!'

'Yes, and it needs proof. I've given you that proof. Now it is you who don't trust me. Even if that child had been Rick's, it was ours to bring up, not his. I was practically certain before you went back to camp last time that I was pregnant but I wanted to be sure before I told you, give you your own way of doing things. Do you really think in these circumstances I would have betrayed your trust had I not been pushed to the very limits of my endurance?'

He did not answer for a time, still holding her hands. Then, 'I have a surprise for you. I finally swallowed my pride and came to realise that the cause of the infertility could have been mine. I saw a leading specialist for male infertility and from the tests he has already done he does not think I am completely infertile. The final result will be ready this week.'

In spite of herself Sara began to shake with laughter. 'What are you going to tell him? Perhaps we've already seen the result!' she stuttered.

'Very awkward!' he smiled as he drew her into his arms.

Hearing nothing from Sara's room for some time, Matron, went down the passage and knocked quietly on the door. Still hearing nothing, she opened it to find them asleep.

After a moment she withdrew with a smile and, seeing a probationer coming towards her, stopped her and told her to put a notice on Sara's door, "Do Not Disturb".

Walking back to her office Matron thanked God that it was many years since she had been their age.

Later, much later, Sara settled down to read the last entry of the journal.

CHAPTER TWENTY-THREE

Three weeks later:—

Now, dear sister, after such a period of peaceful hard work came great excitement and apprehension all in one for me. I feel certain you can guess what I am about to write, but I shall not anticipate.

Mr James returned from his trip to Hobart Town in just one week and six days after setting out, which was exceeding quick when one thinks he must take some days executing his many orders. Also, on this particular trip there were unexpected heavy rains so that the track was very bad in places, particularly in the area of the ferry, where the Derwent had overflowed its banks. However, he reported that a gang of convicts was hard at work on a causeway just up the river from the ferry, at what is to be called Bridgewater. This will be of great value to all of us who live on the northern side of that beautiful river.

On the day he returned to us and was unloading the drays, while everyone stood round looking to see if he had forgotten their special requests, a man on horseback came galloping down the track.

We all turned aside from the dray for a moment to look at him. You must know that the arrival of a stranger is of such interest as to be the topic of conversation for weeks. To begin, a stranger though he be, he must return, for the hospitality extended to him, the news, gossip and happenings of all those through whose properties he has passed. We may not know these people personally, but the stories of their lives we do know, and it is only right that we be acquainted with the latest developments, if any.

This particular messenger, however, had little to relate. He had left Hobart Town at dawn that morning and ridden fast, so fast indeed that his horse, though a good one, was showing signs of exhaustion, so that when his rider dismounted he stood with trembling legs and drooping head. The Master, I could see, viewed such a sight with distaste.

'Young man,' he said, 'you need a lesson in the care of your animal. James, leave your unloading and take the poor creature and give it the attention it needs.'

Whereupon the young man looked most uncomfortable.

'I regret his sorry plight, sir, but it was your son who bid me ride him hard, if necessary until he dropped!'

He could not have startled us more, one and all. The Master's order to Mr James to cease his unloading and attend to the exhausted horse had drawn disgruntled pouts from the girls, but now they rushed up to the young man and grabbed his arm. 'Matthew! Do you mean Matthew sent you?'

My own heart jumped, and I saw that Madam's colour changed violently as she hurried forward to restrain the girls.

'Jessica, Dorothy, Patricia, where are your manners?'

Only the Master remained unchanged. He did not lift his eyes from the messenger as he said in exactly the same tone of voice he had used to bid Mr James remove the exhausted horse: 'That remark is singularly unlike my son. Let us hope the reason that brings you here explains it.'

'It was to hand you this letter, sir.'

There was a complete silence among us as he handed a long, buff envelope to the Master. As I watched it change hands, my heart lost its excited beat. Such an envelope had the look, the colour and the shape of one that would contain official papers, and official papers could mean only one thing for me. Well, at least my period of waiting had come to an end. It would certainly be better to know. Only by knowing could I begin to plan my life afresh.

Just the same, I found it hard to contain myself while I listened to Mr and Mrs James talking in front of the kitchen fire that night. At least, it was as usual Mr James who talked and she who listened as she sat looking into the fire, her hands folded on her round stomach.

Hobart Town, it seemed, was full of crews from a whaling fleet that had put in for shelter and repairs. They were of all nationalities, and there was much drunkenness and brawling in the taverns. There were also two naval ships in, and apparently a party had been given by their officers for the Government House officials and their ladies such as had never been seen in Hobart Town before. The ships were dressed out in flags from stem to stern, and there had been music and dancing into the small hours. Indeed there were apparently many breakfast parties in the pretty cottages of Hobart Town, with people parading the streets still in fashionable evening dress.

'You'd never think this 'ere was a penal settlement,' Mr James said, and I could more sense than see Mrs James looking in my direction. She and I had never become friends, nor ever would.

Then came the summons for which I was waiting. Miss Patricia brought it on her way to bed. She poked her elfin face round the kitchen door and said: 'Mamma and Papa want you, Sarah. They are in the study.'

I followed her from the kitchen and she waved a hand to me as she skipped up the staircase. I knocked at the study door and went inside, determined they should have from me no sign of weak emotion.

The Master turned from the window where he must have been standing looking into the blackness of the night.

'Come in, Sarah. As you were present this afternoon you know that my son saw fit to communicate with us by means of a fast messenger. The message he brought concerned you.'

I waited. It did not seem to me there was anything I was expected to say, but I wished he would not be so deliberate in his speech.

'He requires that we allow you to leave as soon as possible for Hobart Town. You are to go before the Governor!'

'Could it not have been done by means of legal documents?' I asked slowly.

'So I should have thought,' he replied heavily, 'but he says you must go before the Governor. Maybe he has obtained your freedom in payment for what he terms "a great injustice". He has not seen fit to acquaint us with the details.'

'Matthew! He has written you a very pretty apology for all the trouble and inconvenience he has caused you, and for which in due course he hopes to re-imburse you,' Madam broke in impulsively.

'I brought Sarah to this room to acquaint her with what concerned her in this dispatch,' her husband reminded her coldly. 'Now, young woman, you must be prepared to accompany the messenger to Hobart Town on the morrow. You may have the gig, but tell my son to make certain it is returned in better condition than was his messenger's horse this afternoon.'

I curtsied and left the room. Tomorrow to go before the Governor at such short notice! No time to bid goodbye to all that I had come to love so dearly in this place. I walked toward the kitchen in a daze, but almost at once I heard Madam's footsteps behind me.

'Sarah!'

I turned. 'Yes, Madam.'

'Come to my room. I wish to talk to you.'

I followed her up the stairs and noticed that even with the gentle grade she was more out of breath than I had ever seen her. It didn't seem possible that one as active as she could put on weight, but I realised as I went behind her that this was so.

Once inside her room she closed the door and faced me, still out of breath.

'Now, Sarah, soon you go before the Governor as my son's wife. I know we have not discussed this — I could not. But whatever comes of this summons, you must at least attend it dressed as my son's wife should be—'

'Madam—' I tried to stop her, but I might as well have tried to stop the river outside.

'I have a blue travelling dress. Before you go to bed tonight you must alter it. It has a bonnet and muff to match. Come, get me down that box.'

Following the direction of her pointing finger I climbed upon the wash-hand-stand, and dragged down the big box. She threw aside the lid and littered the floor with sheets of paper, from the depths of which she drew a velvet gown of deep sapphire blue. Not since the days when your wardrobe was my care, dear sister, had I seen anything so beautiful in its simplicity.

'Madam, you must not!'

'I — Sarah — must not! Come, put it on and let me see how much alteration will be needed.'

Like one in a dream I slipped the soft caressing velvet over my head and felt as one transformed. She was right; for just this once why shouldn't I go before the Governor as I would wish to go? It was they who had put me in this position. Even though I was her son's wife in name only, and shortly would be bereft of that too, at least to wear this dress would give me a moment of triumph.

So, without further arguing I set about altering it, which was not a great task. Madam and I were about the same height and obviously she had bought the dress before she had married. A few tucks here and there soon made it a fashionable garment. As for the bonnet, it too was easily changed and given a fashionable tilt. The muff? Muffs are muffs, and Van Diemen's Land was no Bond Street.

On the morrow, when I was dressed ready to go, I knew the children's cries of excitement at my changed appearance were not empty ones. I would have been a fool not to accept their unstinting praise, and even noticed an unguarded look of astonishment in the Master's face as he stood waiting patiently for us to be off.

'Young man,' he said to the messenger sitting beside me, already taking up the reins, 'your horse will be well rested by your return. Never let me see you on my property again with an animal in such a condition.'

With that we were on our way, and my thoughts were so confused between sadness and exultation that I knew not how to compose myself. In one way the journey irked me: I wanted to get this interview over and done with, the whole thing finalised. In another I dreaded the moment, perhaps this was it, I had no way of knowing, when I would have to finally part with the children and the beautiful home which, in my overweening conceit, I had been certain I could win.

Underneath too I disliked as always, this high-handed manner in which my life was being settled for me. But common sense warned me that this time I was in no position to fight. Quite apart from my mock marriage being set aside, there was still the question of Mr Haynes's death. Even though I was still not positive of my actions, it was obvious that Master Matthew had witnessed much of the scene in the river, and had been at pains to tell me so. But how much? And seeing it, what interpretation had he put on what he saw? If he believed the worst, then it would be the simplest thing in the world to hand me over to the law, and this time there would be no mercy.

'Upon my word, I had not realised you would prove such a remote companion,' the young man beside me said, and I saw with a shock I had forgotten his presence entirely.

'I am sorry. My mind is full of so many things that I quite forgot I was not alone.'

'Horses can't drive themselves,' he pointed out.

'I apologise. Where do you come from?'

'Kent. I've been in this .... begging your pardon, hole for six months. Anyway, you look wonderful in that dress. He said you were beautiful — and now what was the other thing — oh yes, self-willed. That's it. I wasn't to take any notice of what you said in the way of wanting to go off round Hobart Town on your own. I was to drive you straight to Government House.'

I did not ask who gave such a description of me. There was only one "he". I did not know whether I was incensed or flattered. I was too tired of everything and everyone, even this poor young man who was obviously sent to keep me in close custody. Therefore I was more than glad to break our journey at Clegysons' farm. The Master had given me a letter asking their kindness in putting us up for the night.

The next day, the grey pony pulled us smartly along by the Derwent sparkling in the morning sunshine. In other circumstances I could so have enjoyed that drive. The magpies were warbling in the bush, and the bees were humming lazily in the cottage gardens as we neared Hobart Town itself, lying below its blue mountain ranges.

The streets were very busy and, judging by the cattle and dogs with flocks of sheep which were getting mixed up with carriages and gentlemen on horseback, it would appear to be some kind of market day. There was a stiff breeze blowing from the harbour, and dust was rising in clouds from the animals' feet.

I asked my young escort if we could stop at one of the shops where I had once before looked for commissions for Madam, on the only other time I had been in Hobart Town since being put ashore from the Elderburn, two or more years ago. I felt I must repair my appearance before presenting myself to Governor Arthur. Seeing the look on his face, I smiled: 'I will not run away,' I told him, 'but I cannot appear before the Governor without making my toilet after such a long drive.'

'You look all right to me,' he said, remembering his orders, whereupon I snapped back at him: 'It does not happen to matter how I look to you!' And with one move I had jerked back the pony's reins and sprung down to the road. 'Kindly wait,' I continued, looking up into his startled face, 'and I will not keep you long.'

I turned and, sweeping up my velvet skirts, went into the shop.

When I returned it was a chastened young man who drove me slowly through the bustling street to Government House, shaded by its colonial verandahs.

As we approached I saw a man's tall figure standing by the steps and recognised, with a shock, Master Matthew. Somehow I had not expected to see him here, but common sense should have told me that he too must be present at this interview.

He met me as calmly as though he had not stormed out of the kitchen twelve months ago. He then smiled in his old sarcastic way as he gave me his arm from the gig. For my part I was having great difficulty with my breathing.

'You look well, Sarah, but then, you always do! Thank you, Tom. Take the grey to the Ship Tavern and have her looked after. I shall see you there later. Come, Sarah, we must not keep the Governor waiting.'

There were so many angry things I would have liked to say to him. In fact the words tumbled over themselves in my mind, so that my tongue could not utter one of them. Instead I found myself walking by his side out of the sunshine into the dim, quiet atmosphere of Government House with its unhurried officials; men who had important expressions on their faces, though maybe the papers in their hands were not quite so important.

In spite of myself too, the light, firm touch of his fingers on my arm (as he steered me through a labyrinth of passages to a small ante-room where we obviously were to await the Governor's pleasure) gave me an indescribable feeling of joy that would not be stilled, even though it must be short-lived.

I was so grateful to Madam that she had made it possible for me to look as his wife should look, for this brief period of time, that I was to appear beside him as such.

It was very quiet in the ante-room. Through the latticed window with its dimity curtains, I could see the warm sunshine on the verandah and the garden filled with English flowers amidst the gum trees of Van Diemen's Land, and felt sure it warmed the bones of the old gardener working in his faded blue smock. Down the harbour were a number of three-masters, their spars silhouetted against the dancing water. I kept on noticing everything. I wanted this scene to remain for ever in my mind. I even saw that the carpet was becoming threadbare in places and that the cushions could have done with new tapestry.

Then the waiting was over and we were called to the inner room. I had a quick glimpse of a sombrely dressed man in military attire as he greeted Master Matthew by his Christian name, and Master Matthew's courteous reply before he turned and took one of my hands firmly from its muff.

'Sir, I have the honour to present my wife.'

It was now my turn to sink into a curtsey with, I regret to say, an uncomfortably beating heart.

The Governor himself raised me from it and led me to a comfortable chair by the window.

'We are delighted to see you here today, Mrs Roland. I trust you have not had too tiring a journey. I regret we called you at such short notice, but the papers for which we have been waiting have only just arrived from England.'

He returned behind his desk and sat down precisely in its chair.

All I could think of was those papers, and how quickly this business could be got through; he did not look a man who would waste time needlessly.

'Mrs Roland, you are — er — connected with the Countess of Deen in a —somewhat unusual way?'

'I —yes, sir.'

'I am happy to say that I know the Lady Anne is in very good health. Her husband is of great assistance to me with the British parliament. Therefore, when two years ago she wrote to me, asking me to use my influence in tracing your whereabouts, and to see if there were any way in which your — er — unfortunate predicament could be ameliorated, I was only too happy to do what I could. Of course you will understand I needed proof: details of your trial, etc. These things take time, as I explained to your husband twelve months ago when he also was anxious for this matter to be expedited. Communication between this island and England is also slow. However, the coincidence of his coming to see me enabled me to assure Lady Anne of your excellent circumstances. It will be my pleasant duty in a moment to hand your mail from her—'

I gasped in spite of myself.

'Yes, Mrs Roland, you wish to say something?'

'Nothing — nothing, sir. I am so — so exceeding grateful.'

A smile hovered for a moment round his straight-cut lips.

'And if I may say so, so you should be, Mrs Roland, so you should be. It is Lady Anne's wish that I hand you this package and that you open it in my presence. Will you do so now, please.'

With shaking knees I rose from my chair and went forward to his desk. He handed me a square package and a sharp paper knife, and himself helped me to cut through the strong binding with its heavy seals. Then, as I undid the many wrappings, there lay before us the magnificent winking tiara, necklace and ring of blood-red rubies which had once caused me such anguish!

I saw a small piece of paper with your coronet embossed on it, dear sister. My heart was too full to speak. There the words danced before my eyes. Dearest Sarah, may these stones bring you greater happiness than they ever took from you. At the urging of your husband, Matthew, I gave Mrs Maitland no peace and we re-opened your case until the truth was revealed. She finally made a full confession of her scurrilous lies and jealousy concerning you. That, together with all legal proceedings against you, have been sent to Lieutenant Governor Arthur. He is a just and fine man, and I am sure will see that justice is done...'

'Mrs Roland,' the Governor said, 'I trust you and your husband will take a glass of wine with me before I attend a Council meeting.'

I raised my eyes and saw that a servant was standing by me with a silver salver on which were glasses of wine as red and clear as the rubies lying on the desk.

As I took my glass the Governor lifted his and, holding it to the light of the window, looked carefully into its glowing depth before he turned back to us.

'Young woman, I am greatly honoured to give you a personal toast and a more general one. Firstly a legal document, already signed by the Colonial Secretary in London and now counter-signed by me, granting you a full pardon for any crimes committed by you. Of course you realise this is only a legal formality — it really means that officially and personally we know you never committed them. Then there is a more general one — to this little island of strife, which will one day be a great addition to that other and larger one across the world. Here too, to you both, as I believe you will help this same little island to take its place in the world of achievement.'

As we drank in silence I became aware for the first time that Master Matthew had rested his hand on my arm. I realised there were no papers of annulment; the only papers were those which had come from England! I was Mrs Matthew Roland!

'I must go now,' the Governor said, 'but take your time in leaving.'

As we made our obeisances he stopped once more by the door. 'I would suggest, Mrs Roland, you leave that singularly fine set of jewels in safe custody here. Matthew, arrange with my secretary. Bushrangers unfortunately still plague us, but we shall look forward, Madam, to seeing you wearing them at our New Year Ball.'

When the door finally closed, Master Matthew drew me across to the window.

'We shall have a town house, Sarah. I have become very interested in matters of government.'

'What are you doing to my bonnet?' I whispered. Somehow I seemed to have lost my voice.

'Taking it off, attractive though it is. Mother did well by you, followed my instructions implicitly in fact, but I want to see and feel that glorious hair, and know that it belongs to me!'

'Your mother! You mean — Master Matthew —'

'Master?'

'Matthew,' I said and stumbled over the word, whereupon he held me tightly against him.

From the middle of his linen ruffle I said: 'She knew? You told her and not me?'

'I decided the Governor had better tell you. You never did take much notice of me! Which reminds me, Oscar is waiting down there.'

CHAPTER TWENTY-FOUR

Sara turned over the last page only to be faced by blanks. Sarah *had* decided to end it there. She swore under her breath with frustration—was she never to find out more about what had happened to this couple?

Sarah in particular she had come to know. She admired her courage and single-mindedness—the way she faced every challenge, even the threat of death, to save others, and against all odds succeeding in her battle for respect. Even the forces of nature; bushfires, floods—nothing could stop her.

The next question was almost inevitable. Would she, Sara, have the courage to do the same? She didn't know and thought over her life since the great change—the move to Tasmania. And suddenly the answer was there. Yes, she would be able to face it. She would be up to the challenges. She had arrived as a girl without any real experience of life. She had grown up since then, she had almost single-handed created a prosperous business, and reached the position where it would remain so. More importantly she had found herself able to save her marriage on the edge of collapse. It came to her then that she had forgiven John and he her. They knew what to do for the future. One dark patch remained and she could not avoid the state of sorrow—but, yes, she would overcome this too. It was up to her and this too would be overcome. It did appear that she may be able to have a child after all—with John.

Idly turning the journal, as she deliberated, she vaguely realised that the back cover was thicker than the front. But it was only later, when in a half-doze, that the idea came to her—Arna! Full consciousness returned suddenly and she pressed the button for the nurse. The woman was mystified but she did as she was asked. When Arna eventually arrived she expressed a little annoyance at being called from work, but she collected the journal and took it with her. Within an hour she returned with the back cover open and a tightly compressed package revealed. Sara could hardly conceal her impatience for her to go.

At last the clock blessedly showed eight o'clock and as the door closed, she greedily reached for the packet. She took a few deep breaths and with her scissors carefully cut the tightly bound and stuck leather.

Then there was the difficulty with the pages. Over the hundred or so years since they were put together they had adhered in a number of places. There were in fact two separate packets of records. For that was what they were. They were dated separately.

The first was not in Sarah's writing and it took some time to sort it out, but eventually it became clear. It was dated April 1875 and was brief and to the point.

To whoever may read this document, my name is Thomas Roland, the grandson of Sarah Roland, whose journal is left as I found it some weeks ago. For the sake of continuity I am adding some brief notes of her life, and her husband, my grandfather Matthew.

In spite of her expressed wish for a quiet life (although I doubt her sincerity) it was not to be. Matthew, as he wished, became one of Governor Arthur's advisors, and a very important one too. If the reader is interested he will find this summed up in any history of the period. It was largely due to these two that transportation was eventually abolished and the treatment of those already here greatly improved. My great-grandfather, also named Matthew, who pioneered the family settlement in Tasmania, died when he was seventy and his wife followed shortly after. Matthew and Sarah moved back to Ardrossan about 1860, although Matthew remained for many years a senior advisor to whichever Governor was in power. Incidently, their dream came true—Ardrossan became one of the most prosperous in the colony...

November 1910.

My name is James Roland, the son of Thomas Roland, the writer before me, and the great-grandson of Matthew and Sarah. I was born in 1890 and a great deal has happened to the family since then....

Here, Sara, reading the entry, realised why the writing appeared so familiar. She had seen it somewhere before. She puzzled over it for some time and suddenly she remembered—it was the strange, almost gothic script of her grandfather! She had seen it often in the letters her mother had shown her—sent from France to her grandmother in England during the First World War.

....I am writing this in 1915 on the eve of sailing for France—a Lieutenant in the 12th Battalion.

There was much more about the members of the family, their increase and dispersion throughout the world, but mainly Australia, especially Tasmania. He was especially full of plans for Ardrossan when he came back.

He did not, of course, know when he wrote, only twenty-four years old, that he was to die a year later in the process of winning a VC. She felt the tears come to her eyes, but more memories came back. The family was always proud of her grandfather especially as he had married an English girl before his death and she had produced a child posthumously—Sara's own mother. Other things came to mind also, vague memories of what she had heard about her grandfather. The family had always been tremendously proud of him and his decoration—the highest which can be awarded—but she remembered there was always a mystery about him. Perhaps after all he and his 'wife' were not, in fact, married. For herself she could not care less, but she could understand the older generation keeping quiet about it.

She was filled with enormous pride and realised why—not only was she the direct descendant of a hero, but she was also *directly* descended from Sarah—a heroine if ever there was one, and the very person whose words had given her such inspiration over the past months and who she felt had been writing to her personally.

She put the journal aside. She would read the details later; it was simply too much to absorb all at once.

The next morning she felt much better but was sure the nurses thought she was having a relapse. And, in a way, she was—the magnitude of the discovery was impossible to absorb immediately. First was the shock of discovering an important historical document, and she had no doubt that the State Library and the Archives would be falling over each other to get it. Second, and more importantly for her, was the discovery that she was a direct descendant of "her" Sarah. She found it almost impossible to believe that a mere five generations existed between herself and this incredible woman—could it be possible that some of her qualities, her genes, had been passed down to her, and perhaps could even be passed to her own children? She prayed that, should she ever have children, they would be worthy of such qualities.

And there was one last surprise to come before her new life began. Two weeks later she was discharged from hospital as John had got four weeks' leave to look after her; they enjoyed it as if they had just been married. They saw little of others. Arna ran the business with a little help from Sara with the books and Rick simply kept out of the way.

They were a little startled one night when a knock on the door heralded his appearance. Both he and John were embarrassed but Sara made little of it, especially when he offered more flowers in his usual way—as if it were the most natural thing in the world.

'Well,' he said, 'I've come to say goodbye. We're sailing *Sunbolt* to Sydney on Saturday for final preparation for the big race; I would imagine you'll wish us luck.'

'Not only that, Rick, but we'll be there to see you off,' said John, and Rick, seeing that he was being forgiven, replied immediately, 'Well, we're having a few beers on board before we sail so come and do the thing properly.'

So, on a day when the roses were blooming in all the gardens, and the Mountain stood massively blue against the white cloud banks, when girls hurried through the streets in sleeveless cotton frocks, and a slight wind, just enough, ruffled the waters of the Derwent, *Sunbolt* slipped her mooring, slid out to mid-channel, leaning a little to land, and cut away to South Arm.

With her went the thoughts and hearts of many who never had, and never would, set foot on a racing yacht. But to all Tasmanians on that day she became theirs, the representative of their way of life. She carried the name of Tasmania to the forefront of this classic world race, a reminder that out of conflict had grown love and respect. From bitterness, tragedy, poverty and hard endeavour had grown an island of achievement—touched by all nations, but still holding its own stubborn individuality before all men.

Eleanor Graeme-Evans was born in Melbourne in 1913, and was always keen to write. Her first book, *Virgin Soil*, was published in 1938, followed by *Mistrel* in 1941 and *I Lived with Greek Guerrillas* in 1943.

When her fiancé, Frank, a Royal Airforce Officer (and a Tasmanian) returned from the Second World War, Eleanor's activities became focused on family and service life. They raised two children, Alexander and Rosemary. In the fast moving pace that was service life at that time, they lived in countries such as Cyprus, Egypt and Great Britain, before returning to Tasmania on Frank's retirement from service life.

It was in 1964, that the ground work for this novel was completed. However, the draft novel was put away, as the family moved to Adelaide shortly afterwards at the commencement of Frank's second career as an Administrative Officer with CSIRO.

On his second retirement and their return to Tasmania, the novel was finished, and it received the prestigious Alan Marshall Award in 1983 for the best unpublished novel of that year.

It is appropriate that the novel should be published in 1999, the International Year of Older Persons, with Eleanor now aged eighty-six.